THE
COMPANION

THE
COMPANION

KATIE ALENDER

putnam

G. P. PUTNAM'S SONS

G. P. Putnam's Sons
An imprint of Penguin Random House LLC, New York

First published in the United States of America by G. P. Putnam's Sons,
an imprint of Penguin Random House LLC, 2020
First paperback edition published 2021

Visit us online at penguinrandomhouse.com

LIBRARY OF CONGRESS CONTROL NUMBER: 2020941339

Printed in the United States of America

ISBN 9780399545924

1 3 5 7 9 10 8 6 4 2

Design by Suki Boynton
Text set in Agfa Wile Roman Std

For Chris, Gwendolyn, and Ginger

MARCH
~30~

MY SISTER DINA'S last words were "I'm telling you, that hamburger tasted like it had boogers on it."

My sister Siena's last words were "Are you saying . . . it was a hambooger?"

My mother's last words were "Tony, do you see that—"

My father's last words were "Oh God—hold on, girls. *Hold on!*"

Then the car plunged off the side of the road and sank darkly into a drainage canal full of icy slush. And *poof!* the Radegan family was finished.

Well, except for me.

Apparently I didn't get the memo.

I remember thinking, *Mom, I can't breathe.* And then somehow I found myself gasping in the frigid air, dog-paddling, too dazed to know which way was up, fading in and out of consciousness, and then, at last, facedown and elbow-deep in a patch of frost-crunchy mud.

I turned to look for the others. The water was horribly still and silent, except for the occasional gurgle of air escaping from the car below like the belch of a beast that had eaten its fill.

The scene remained mostly quiet until emergency vehicles arrived. There were bystanders up on the road, people milling about at the top of the steep hill, pondering the horror of what they'd seen. Snippets of their shocked reactions reached my ears, oddly clear in the damp air—all those *oh no*s and *I can't believe it*s and one particularly heart-wrenching *Merciful Mary, Mother of God*. They didn't come looking for me because it was unthinkable that anyone could have survived.

So I lay in the dark without making a sound, waiting and wanting to die.

Three months later, I was still waiting.

CHAPTER
~1~

MY TOOTHBRUSH WAS slime green, and the bristles, after only six weeks of use, were beginning to fray and spread outward. They also came unattached and got stuck between my teeth when I brushed, which I did, twice a day, for the full two minutes that my mother would have insisted upon had she been around to do so. The end of the toothbrush's handle tapered to a sporty point, and the gold-embossed brand name, WALLYTEETH, was chipping quietly away. It was as if someone at the Wallyteeth factory had said, *We want it to* look *like a toothbrush, but basically it should suck.*

And it did. But what *really* bothered me was that someone else's hair was taped to it.

The day I'd arrived at Palmer House, a woman named Ms. O'Neil, who had long, curly auburn hair (as I was later reminded twice a day for two minutes at a time), gave me a short welcome speech, followed by a tour. She had a stack of supplies waiting for me on her beat-up wooden desk, including a pair of pajamas still on their plastic hanger, a thin graying bath towel and washcloth, the green toothbrush, and a small blue stuffed bunny.

"The pajamas and the rabbit are donations," she said, almost an apology. "You don't have to keep them if you don't want them. I'm sure once your things arrive, you'll want to wear your own clothes, but that may be a few days—"

"No, I don't have anything," I said.

"Like I said, it may be a few days before it gets here," she said, with the unpleasant smile of someone who was being very patient in the face of stupidity. "But your caseworker will arrange to ship everything—"

"No," I said. "There's nothing to ship. They thought I was going to die, so they donated everything."

Blink. Blink-blink. The smile never left her face. Her silence seemed like a call for more information.

"They thought they were being nice," I said, feeling like I had to cover for them. "My dad's law firm handled the estate pro bono because there was a lot of debt from my mom setting up her dental practice. And . . . mistakes were made."

"I see," Ms. O'Neil said.

"There are a few boxes," I admitted, not wanting

to seem melodramatic. "Mostly paperwork. It can stay in storage."

I turned away to inspect the pajamas, noting that the print on the polyester fabric was hot-pink lipstick kisses and that the front read #TOTESFAB. I handed them back to her and was on the verge of passing the bunny back, too, when I decided to stuff it into my backpack instead.

Ms. O'Neil tossed the pajamas onto the table in the corner and held the door open for me.

I hadn't known until a few days before my arrival that there still *were* places like Palmer House: technically an orphanage (which made me technically an orphan?), officially a home for kids who needed somewhere to stay but hadn't yet found their way into the foster care system, or had been slightly chewed up and then spit out by it. Palmer House certainly didn't look like the prison-style brick structures of my childhood nightmares (*oh, you naive little nightmares*); it was just a dated beige stucco house with a treeless yard, designed maybe twenty years ago by someone who wasn't particularly good at designing houses, with five bedrooms and a kitchen and some bathrooms and all the other things you might expect to find in a house. It had been donated to the Children's Relief Society by the Palmer family—hence the name. My caseworker, an obviously overworked woman named Frankie, told me I was supremely fortunate to get a spot here. It was "one of the nicest in the system."

And I was its newest resident.

Efforts had been made to find me an actual home, but I had no living relatives, and staying with my best friend Becca's family had ended badly—probably because of my nightmares, nosebleeds, and middle-of-the-night screaming episodes that kept the family awake and sent her younger siblings to therapy. Becca and I discovered that we hadn't been very good friends after all. In fact, that had happened with all the people I'd thought were my friends. While finishing out the school year, I realized that what had bound us to each other was just that we were all kind of . . . mean. Mean to other people and mean to each other.

I guess I didn't have the energy to be mean anymore. I didn't have the energy to be anything at all.

Palmer House's administrative offices were in a converted space that had once been the garage, so we emerged into the kitchen and went from there to the living room, where some of the other girls were lounging, watching TV, or absently scrolling on their phones.

"Hey, everyone," Ms. O'Neil said. "This is Margaret."

Actually, I go by Margot, I didn't bother to say. In my

old life, no one had called me Margaret except substitute teachers, but I let it go for the moment. Margaret was an old family name, and Mom had agreed to the name only if she could shorten it.

A vague chorus of *hello*s answered her, and a few of the girls glanced up, but they all quickly turned away again.

Except one girl with dirty-blond hair and a scowl.

"Hey!" she snarled. "That's *my* toothbrush!"

Ms. O'Neil blinked, looking down at the toothbrush sitting atop the graying towels, and then sighed. "Tam, this is not yours. It's a new one from the supply closet."

Tam sat up. Her too-big T-shirt read #GIRLSQUAD. Her eyes were watery blue and her face seemed weirdly flat, like everything except her nose and eyes were on the same level. "Well, it *looks* like mine," she said. "And that means at some point she's going to mess up and use mine. Which is disgusting."

Ms. O'Neil turned away with an eye roll. Tam saw it, too, and her lip curled as she prepared to say more.

Then Ms. O'Neil held up her hand, warding off the attack. "Okay, okay, don't worry, I'll take care of it."

"*Disgusting,*" Tam repeated.

"Come on, Margaret," Ms. O'Neil murmured, and we retreated to the garage. She grabbed a roll of duct tape out of her desk drawer and started to write on it with a black marker.

Since it seemed like I might be here for a while, I decided to take a chance. "You can just write *Margot*," I said.

"Oh, is that what people call you?" she asked. "Okay."

She wrote *Margo*, ripped the tape off the roll, and wrapped it—along with a wayward strand of her own long, curly hair—around the handle of the toothbrush.

"Ta-da," she said. "Now it is clearly your toothbrush."

In my old life, I would have said, *Oh, excuse me, there's a t at the end of my name.*

Maybe even, *Oh, excuse me, you've attached a piece of your hair to this device I'm supposed to insert into my mouth.*

But now? Nah.

She carried it out and held it up to Tam, like a flag waved in a parade, as we passed the TV room. Tam didn't quite seem to process what she was seeing, but she didn't get up and follow to air further grievances, so I figured it was fine.

And it was. It worked out well enough, in the sense that I never used any toothbrush but my own for the entirety of the six weeks I spent at Palmer House. Tam found several other reasons to despise me, but Tam despised everyone, so I didn't dwell on it.

ON THE MORNING of the third day of the seventh week, I was in the bathroom, brushing, when Tam came in, grabbed a random towel off the rack, and began using it to dry her hair. She glared at me in the mirror.

"Hah," I said, with the toothbrush between my teeth.

"Don't *hi* me," she said. "I'm exhausted, and it's your fault."

"Uh-kah," I said.

"Can I just tell you how miserable it is to have you here?"

I spat into the sink. "Sure."

Tam stepped closer. Not threateningly, but close enough to speak quietly so no one else could hear. "Everyone else here feels bad for you, but I don't. I'm the only one who'll tell you the truth, which is that we're all sick and tired of you waking us up every night, shrieking like a maniac."

I wobbled as though a pebble caught in my bloodstream had forced its way through the valves of my heart.

"You were in an accident," she said. "So what? Get over it and let the rest of us sleep."

"All right," I said. "Great advice, Tam, thanks for the words of wisdom."

She leaned against the wall. "I'm serious. Things were peaceful until you came. Now every night's a horror movie."

"Okay," I said, rinsing out my toothbrush.

"Look at me, Margot," she said.

I looked at her. Her eyes were flat and dull, but they weren't stupid. And there was a glint of self-satisfaction in them that told me she was carrying out a rather pleasant errand. Had the others nominated her to tell me all this?

Probably.

"You should go," she said.

"Cool," I said, letting my attention drift away.

It was the first hit I'd scored on her. She tried again, less certain. "I mean it. You should go somewhere else."

"*Tam,*" I said sharply, turning on her. "I'd love to. But where would I go?"

I heard something in my voice then—something dangerous and biting, like the strike of a snake.

Again, she wavered. "I don't care," she said. "Talk to Ms. O'Neil. She'll figure something out. I'm sure you'll be fine. You're the luckiest person I know."

Then she stormed away before I could reply.

I went back to my room at the far end of the hall. One thing that made them all angry was that I was the only girl with my own room. My roommate went to live with her grandmother two days after I arrived, and by then everybody knew I screamed all night, so they didn't want to share with me. In that regard, Tam was right. I was lucky. She'd lived here for going on two years, and by all rights the single should have been hers. But Ms. O'Neil refused to switch us, because no one who roomed with me would get any sleep.

I lay on the bed with Blue Bunny sitting on my chest, wondering in what other way I could possibly be considered lucky. The lawyers at Dad's firm had held a fundraiser for me, so I had a little money waiting for me when I was an adult—not a ton, because my parents had cashed in their life insurance policies to build Mom's practice. But it would be enough to get me through college, if I chose a cheapish school and lived on a strict budget, working weekends and summers to make up the difference. I was pretty sure none of the other girls could say that—but Tam couldn't have known about the money, so that wasn't it.

Did she think I was lucky because I had made it out of the water when my parents and sisters hadn't?

That was lucky? Really? Surviving to see my family home emptied and sold? Surviving so I could wake every night in a cold sweat after some horrific nightmare? Be rejected and unwanted by all the people I'd thought were my friends? Surviving to end up *here*?

Lucky?

I turned to my side, feeling exhaustion coming for me, not wanting to let my eyes slip shut but knowing that it was inevitable. Last night, I'd probably managed four hours of sleep, and that wasn't enough to get me through the day. Still, I fought the nap as long as I could. At least when I was awake I could stop myself from focusing on the accident. If I fell asleep, all my protections and distractions melted away.

Lucky.

I tucked Blue Bunny into my armpit and tapped his nose three times, hoping it would wake up whatever magic bunny energy he possessed and help him guard me from the shadows.

Then my eyes closed.

The shadows descended almost immediately—gray, black, and a sick mildew green, and behind them all was Tam. But not normal Tam—Tam's dead body bloated with canal water, floating out of her bedroom and down the hall into my room. I dreamed that she came hovering through the door and then slowly, like a seesaw, her feet lowered and touched the ground, and she came closer and stood over me and looked down with her cold, wet dead-fish eyes. I waited for her to speak, but she didn't say anything.

She just reached down and put her hand over my mouth, and it felt like a giant slug. A scream began to grow in my lungs like a train approaching from far down the tracks.

Then, suddenly, I was awake.

Someone had knocked on the door. When I opened my eyes, Ms. O'Neil's head was poked into the room. Her eyes were agleam with something like confusion, or maybe excitement.

I'm leaving, I thought.

Ms. O'Neil, like the rest of them, basically hated me. I don't think she wanted to, but all I did was make her job harder, and not in an interesting way like Tam did. With Tam, she could spar, and roll her eyes, and complain—but with me, what could she do? You can't roll your eyes at the sole survivor of a tragic car accident.

I mean, I guess you could roll your eyes at anything if it got aggravating enough.

I'll bet I'm aggravating enough, I thought.

The shiny-eyed moment hung in the air half a beat too long, and I had to break the silence.

"Hi," I said.

Her left eyebrow went up. "You," she said to me, "are a lucky girl."

CHAPTER

~2~

MY ROOM LOOKED out over the driveway, which meant that as I shoved my few possessions into my backpack and a plastic grocery bag, I could look down and see the massive black SUV idling there, waiting for me. The business-suit-clad man who'd arrived in it, Mr. Albright, had told me to take my time, but I didn't have enough stuff to take my time with.

The door pushed open, and I expected to see Ms. O'Neil. But it was Tam who came in, looking around in a curious, wide-eyed way. She had a duffel with her, and she heaved it onto the bed.

"My room now," she said, as smug as a house cat.

"Good for you."

She sighed and sat down on the mattress, arms folded. Then she leaned forward to peer down at the car in the driveway.

"So you're just getting, like, adopted?"

"No," I said. "I don't want to be adopted. I'll be a ward."

"They're probably going to make you their servant or something." She didn't sound entirely disappointed by this idea. "Lock you in the cellar and all that. I'm sure you'll be miserable."

"You never know."

She sat back and shook her head. "Ridiculous."

"Yep." I finished folding my third and final T-shirt and stacked it in the bag on top of the other clothes.

"If you're rich now, will you send me stuff?"

"I'm not rich," I said.

She pointed out the window. "That's a hundred-thousand-dollar car. You're rich."

"It's not my money," I said. "I'm the servant, remember?"

She snorted. "Fingers crossed."

"Make yourself useful," I said. "Take the sheets off the bed."

She obeyed without complaint, reaching across to pull the fitted sheet out from under the mattress.

Then, driven by curiosity, I asked, "What kind of stuff would you want me to send?"

"Hmm," she said. "A pair of sunglasses. Like, really nice ones. And a crossword-puzzle book. And—"

I reached into my backpack, pulled out a crossword-puzzle book, and lobbed it at the bed. She picked it up, studied the cover, quirked her mouth into a smile, and went on.

"—a better phone?" She watched expectantly to see if I was going to give her mine.

I was not.

She shrugged. "So your whole family is dead, right? No grandparents or aunts or anybody?"

"Nope," I said. "My parents were only children and my grandparents are all dead."

"Hmm," she said. "I have aunts, but it doesn't do me any good. My mom's sisters. They won't take me because they think I'm too much like my mother. I don't care, though. I turn eighteen in seven months, and then I'll go do my own thing."

"Where will you go?"

"New York," she said. "I'm going to be a model."

I looked at her in disbelief, but even as I prepared to mentally dismiss the idea, I suddenly felt as if I was seeing her clearly for the first time—that simple, odd face. The impossibly tall, slender frame. I could totally see her slinking down a runway in some outlandish outfit. Her scowl was perfect for it, too.

"Good luck," I said. "I think you *could* be a model, actually."

She rolled her eyes. "I wasn't asking for your opinion."

Never change, Tam.

"Anyway, you're the lucky one." She dumped the bundle of sheets on the floor.

"You keep saying that," I said. "I don't know if you realize how much my life has sucked over the past three months."

She stretched out on the bare mattress, relishing it. "I never said your life didn't suck. Only that you're lucky. Those are two totally different things."

Huh. Were they?

"For instance," she said. "My mom is a homeless meth head who stole my grandma's life savings and her pills, which is probably why Grandma died. Be careful who you let handle your meds, by the way."

I was about to reply, but she silenced me with a finger.

"My last foster family fed me exactly one bowl of generic-brand Cheerios per day. I had a kitten there, but Palmer House made me give it away before I could come. I haven't seen my brother in seven years. My life sucks. And yet—no rich people have *ever*, even once, swooped in to adopt me. Hence, unlucky."

I looked down at the SUV waiting to cart me off to an enormous estate in the country, owned by millionaires who (I assumed) would not actually make me live in the cellar and carry trays of food around.

Then I looked at Tam, whose left hand was curled around a small stuffed kitten wearing an Easter hat.

Well, maybe I am lucky, I thought. *But my life still sucks.*

"So then—" I said, and I wouldn't have gone on except she took the trouble to open her eyes and look at me. "If things are so terrible, what's the point?"

"The point of what? Of life?" she asked.

"Yeah, I mean . . . it's so hard." I felt myself blush. "I can't believe I used to think there was anything wrong with my life. I was so ignorant."

She shrugged. "Nobody has a perfect life. My cousins are rich, but they hate themselves."

"Doesn't everybody hate themselves?" I asked.

Tam's eyes narrowed contemptuously. "No. I don't. I've never done anything bad enough to hate myself. Have you?"

I felt as if our eyes were locked together. She was waiting for an answer, but I didn't have one. Or maybe I did, but I didn't want to say it.

"You're overthinking this," she said finally. "You're alive, so you might as well go along with it. There's no big secret. You live, and then you die, and that's it."

"That's it?" I half laughed.

"*That,*" she said, closing her eyes, "is plenty."

I carried my bags and the bundle of bedsheets to the door. "Tam, we could have been friends if you weren't such a jerk."

"I don't want to be your friend," she said, not even bothering to open her eyes. "I don't like you."

I closed the door and went downstairs.

I didn't bring the toothbrush.

CHAPTER
∽3∽

I'D NEVER BEEN to a country estate before. I didn't actually know what a country estate *was*, but I had a vague idea that it was where a duke or an earl would live if we had dukes and earls in America. I figured Mr. Albright was being melodramatic about what would end up being a big house in a nice suburban neighborhood.

I was wrong.

I mean, it *was* a big house, yes. It was enormous. But it wasn't in a nice neighborhood—it wasn't in a neighborhood at all. It was (as one might have guessed) out in the country. About ten minutes before coming into view of the stone pillars at the entrance to the property, we'd passed through a minuscule town with one traffic light, a small row of stores, a used-car lot, a doctor's office, and a single-story building with a sign reading COPELAND COUNTY SCHOOL. And that was it, as far as the local society went.

I watched helplessly as the signal on my phone weakened, like blood draining from a body, and then disappeared altogether, replaced by two small words: NO SERVICE. It wasn't that I had any friends to call, but it still felt strangely and almost spookily like being cut off from the world, or going back in time.

The SUV slowed as we approached an elaborately scrolled iron gate centered in a brick wall that went on forever on both sides of us, and Mr. Albright looked over at me from his spot in the driver's seat. He was in his forties, balding, and judging by the puffiness around his eyes, could have used a good night's sleep. His gray suit jacket was draped over the seat between us, and his sleeves were rolled up.

"Are you ready?" he asked. "It's a new beginning for you."

What was I supposed to say, that I *wasn't* ready? I nodded and tried to smile and went back to looking out the window.

Mr. Albright was the Sutton family's business manager, which meant (he'd told me) that he handled just about everything for them, because when you had that much money, everything was business. He described them as if they were dolls in a collection, with an odd, patronizing note in his voice. But at the same time, he never missed a chance to say that looking out for their family was basically the purpose of his life.

To his credit, despite this great sense of combined ownership and deference he felt toward the Suttons, my going there didn't seem to worry him. In fact, he acted like it was natural, even charming, that they should take me in.

To me, it seemed kind of random and strange, but what do I know about how super-rich people think?

Here's what I did know: John Sutton, the patriarch of the family, had gone to law school at Northwestern with my father twenty years ago. One day, they both happened to be swimming laps in the college pool, and John, who hadn't been feeling well, slipped into unconsciousness in the water. My dad crossed the two lanes between them, pulled him out of the pool, and performed CPR.

"Thus saving his life," Mr. Albright had said in the garage office at Palmer House, interlacing his fingers as if he were offering a silent prayer of thanks. "And so, when the news reached Mr. Sutton that your family had encountered this great tragedy, he felt compelled to reciprocate in any way he could."

Your family had encountered this great tragedy. He said the words so impersonally, as if the deaths of my parents and sisters were footnotes in a legal document.

Then again, what were his alternatives? What did I want him to do, break down and cry about it?

The iron gates began to open for us. Not wanting to seem overly awestruck, I tried not to crane my neck to see the house. I may have spent six weeks brushing my teeth with someone else's hair, but I had a smidgen of pride left.

As it turned out, I didn't need to crane my neck. Copeland Hall, as Mr. Albright called the house, was too big to miss. It was a huge gray building, both long and tall, with boxy outcroppings and peaked roofs and windows, and towerlike projections poking out from various places. Ivy clung to the stone walls, and gnarled trees threw patches of dappled shade against the facade.

When the SUV rounded a corner, I spotted a pair of huge wooden double doors on the side of one of the stone rectangles that bulged off the main structure. The doors faced the side of the property, not the front, as if the house was turning away, hiding its face from visitors.

A two-story garage with spaces for six cars hulked behind the building, and we pulled all the way into one of the bays before the SUV came to a stop.

"Leave your things," Mr. Albright said, as if my luggage had consisted of five trunks, eight suitcases, three hatboxes, and a birdcage. "I'll bring them later."

I looked helplessly at my backpack, not wanting to be parted from it. After only six weeks at Palmer House, I'd begun to develop the anxiety that all the girls shared—the nagging feeling that someone wanted to steal from me. But seeing the lumpy, over-stuffed canvas and the broken zipper that only closed halfway, I decided to leave it behind.

"We'll go in the side entrance," he said, leading the way toward a single door near the corner of the building.

I scanned the grounds as we approached the house. The lawns were immense and lushly green in the summer sun. It was a pleasant day, not too hot, with a light breeze. Birds twittered lazily from their shaded hiding places and a squirrel hunched under a bush, working hard to tear apart some small fruit or nut.

I live here now, I thought, trying the thought on like a dress.

Shouldn't a person feel a rush of emotion at the thought of being part of such a grand place? Shouldn't I feel happy? Or intimidated? Or . . . lucky?

I felt . . . nothing.

Until, that is, I stepped through the door behind Mr. Albright and saw the Suttons standing right there, waiting for us.

Then I felt something: completely embarrassed.

I'd assumed I'd have the chance to wash my face, brush my hair, psych myself up.

But instead, I found myself being inspected by a man and woman standing about ten feet away—a perfectly matched set of well-bred, meticulously presented rich people.

Mrs. Sutton, who was as sleek and slim as a greyhound, wore an ivory sweater and a pair of pale beige pants, with pointed-toe copper-colored flats. Her hair fell in a glossy light brown sheet, just skimming her shoulders. Her watch and earrings were simple gold. Her makeup was subtle and flawless, setting off the glittering brown of her eyes and the pearly white of her teeth. Her smile was warm and welcoming. She was, in a word, tasteful.

Mr. Sutton looked a little less comfortable in his own skin but no less refined. His long-sleeved shirt was blue and crisp, and the hem of his gray trousers broke in just the right spot over his shining loafers. His hair was silvery brown, cropped close to his head, and he wore a smile that had a touch too much tension behind it to be perfectly sincere.

They were elegant in a casual, uncomplicated way—not like showy rich people from the city but like people so rich they don't have to live in the city. Their money lived there, and they hired Mr. Albright to carry it back and forth for them.

"I'm sorry to surprise you," Mrs. Sutton said, seeing what must have been a mortified expression on my face. Her voice was as smooth and polished as the rest of her. "We've been so looking forward to your arrival that we couldn't bear to wait in the sitting room like a couple of posed dolls. We wanted to meet you right away . . . but now I can see that wasn't very thoughtful of us."

"Nonsense, Laura, she's fine," Mr. Albright said cheerily. Then, turning to me, he said, "Margaret, allow me to introduce you to John and Laura Sutton."

"At your service," Mrs. Sutton said, her smile more subdued.

There was silence as everyone waited for me to speak. I didn't think I was going to be able to come up with anything, but when I opened my mouth, a few words tumbled out. "Thank you so much for having me," I said. "It means a lot."

To my horror, Mr. Sutton stepped closer and put a hand on my shoulder. "For a very long time, I've wanted to repay the debt I owed your father. I'm glad to have a chance, and I'm sorry that it's under these circumstances."

I tried to think of a suitable response.

"Oh, John, now's not the time for speechmaking," Mrs. Sutton said, swooping over and swatting him away. "I'm sure Margaret wants a few minutes by herself before we descend on her."

I did, desperately. But maybe their classiness was rubbing off on me, because it seemed impolite to go off alone so soon. "I'm okay," I said. "Could I please maybe have a glass of water?"

They leaped into action, thrilled to have a task. Mr. Sutton rushed away to fetch the water, while Laura ushered me down the hall to a room where the blessed rehydration could take place.

"The west parlor," she said, with a subtle flourish of her slim hand. "Please make yourself comfortable."

I looked around as she steered me toward a small sofa. The room was like something from a museum— every detail looked as if it had been left untouched for a hundred years. The walls were polished wood, adorned with large paintings of horses and hunting dogs. The furniture was ornate and old-fashioned. The love seat I found myself on was upholstered in a satiny fabric of blue and white stripes, with tufted green velvet pillows nestled in the corners.

Mr. Albright waited off to the side while Mrs. Sutton perched on a leather armchair and looked at me like I was the dessert cart at a fancy restaurant.

"Was the drive all right?" she asked.

"Yes," I said. "Thank you."

"Long, though, wasn't it?" She glanced almost accusingly at Mr. Albright, as if the distance were somehow his fault. "Did you get lunch?"

"A long ride, but very pretty," I said. "And yes, we did have lunch."

"We stopped in Hopkins," Mr. Albright said in his own defense. "We had sandwiches."

"Oh, Hopkins, that's good," she said, relaxing and sitting back. Then she sat up again. "You have to tell me if there's anything we can get for you. We aren't in town every day, but we can send out if there's something you require."

I was about to deflect the question, but then I realized I had a real need. "I could use a toothbrush, I guess," I said. "I left mine at Palmer House."

"Palmer House," she repeated. "Is that where you were staying?"

I nodded.

"Was it nice? Did you have friends?"

I stared straight into her eyes, which were nearly the same brown as the wood paneling on the walls behind her. Despite her kindness, their undeniable generosity toward me, I couldn't help feeling that this was all some kind of assessment. A test.

Better pass it.

"Oh, yes," I said. "It was very nice. I had a lot of friends."

I could feel Mr. Albright's eyes on me. "Excellent facility," he agreed. "Bright, a lot of natural light."

"That's good," she said, compassion in her voice.

"I imagine the girls there have all had a hard time. It's nice to think they have a comfortable place to live. I—I guess I just don't feel that girls belong in 'facilities.' But of course that's not a problem for you any longer. You live here, Margaret, with us. And you absolutely must let us know what we can do to make you feel at home."

Let's see. If I were at home, I would be in my room, on my bed, listening to music and browsing my friends' social media accounts to see what everybody was up to. And my parents and sisters would be alive. So good luck trying, Laura, but I can't see that happening.

"We only have one rule here, really," she said. "To respect one another—and the house, of course. I find that if respect is in place, everything else falls into line."

Doable. "Of course," I said.

The sides of her eyes crinkled in approval as Mr. Sutton came through the door with a glass of water— not a normal glass, but one made of intricately cut crystal that weighed about three pounds. I thanked him and took it with both hands, sipping as carefully as I could and then resting it on a coaster that Mrs. Sutton slid across the enormous wooden coffee table.

She fidgeted and looked up at her husband, who was still standing off to the side. "I was telling Margaret that I don't think girls belong in facilities."

He gave her an impatient look and spoke with an edge to his voice. "There's time to discuss that later."

I grabbed for my water like it was a life preserver. The room was totally silent as I drank, and at one point my teeth clanked against the crystal. The sound seemed to echo off the walls.

Finally, when the glass was empty, I set it down for good and looked up at them.

"Thank you, Mrs. Sutton," I said. "And Mr. Sutton. I hope this doesn't sound rude, but could I please see my room?"

They exchanged a glance.

"Call me Laura," Mrs. Sutton said. "And *Mr. Sutton* is John. We can't be formal. We're all going to be good friends. We're like . . . a team. Working together toward a common goal."

A goal? Okay, was this the part where they sent me to the maid's quarters to fetch the broom so I could sweep the house before they tossed me a crust of bread?

The air dripped with unspoken words. I thought I was imagining it until I glanced over at Mr. Albright, whose cheeks seemed slightly flushed. Then, after a peculiarly weighted look from Laura, he lurched into action, walking to the fireplace mantel and picking up a crystal picture frame. He carried it over and handed it to me. It was so heavy I nearly dropped it. Why did everything rich people owned weigh twice as much as normal stuff?

It was a family portrait, taken on a wildflower-covered hill on a beautiful cloudy day. Mr. and Mrs. Sutton—or should I say John and Laura—stood in the background. In front of them were two young teens: a boy with neatly cut dark brown hair and brown eyes like Laura's, and a teenage girl who was beautiful enough to be a movie star. She had long waves of golden hair, perfectly chiseled cheekbones, and glinting, intelligent blue eyes.

"That's our family," Laura said. Her voice was strained, like she was worried I wouldn't approve. "Barrett—he's sixteen. He goes away to school, to St. Paul's in Thurmond, about a three-hour drive from here. He's been in Italy with one of his friends, but he flies back in a few weeks."

"Oh," I said. "Nice."

She drew a deep breath. "And that's Agatha."

"Does she go away to school, too?"

For a moment, no one answered, but when I looked up at Laura, she smiled almost painfully. "No."

Oh no. Oh God. She was dead.

Why did *everyone* have to be dead?

The silence that followed was agonizing. Finally, it was broken by Laura's shaky inhalation.

"Agatha is upstairs," she said. "Would you like to meet her?"

CHAPTER

~4~

I FOLLOWED JOHN and Laura down the long wall-papered corridor and into the grand main hall, with its two-story ceiling of ornamental plaster. I was vaguely aware of faces staring at me from paintings, of glass-doored cabinets packed with figurines—a flock of delicate birds, a squadron of tiny ballerinas, collections of vases and teacups and tiny bowls—but they passed into my head and then out, like snapshots of things I'd seen long ago.

Why couldn't Agatha just come downstairs to say hi? I tried not to dwell on the question, just as I tried not to dwell on the fact that I was pretty sure I'd asked Mr. Albright if the Suttons had children and he hadn't said yes.

I don't know . . . maybe he hadn't said no, either. But he *definitely* hadn't said yes.

Two separate sets of stairs wound dramatically up

opposite walls and met on a shared landing. Laura paused at the base of one set of the stairs. "To the right, here, is our bedroom. Our offices, as well— and straight ahead you can see the library. The door behind the stairs leads to the service hall, which you won't be needing to visit."

Shows what you know, Tam, I thought.

She looked over her shoulder. "And obviously, back the way we came, you saw the kitchens, the dining room, and the breakfast room. Plus the drawing room, the music room, and the sitting room."

Did I see those things? It was all a blur.

When the four of us reached the top of the stairs, I could see that the landing branched off into three halls: left, right, and center.

"This way," Laura said, starting straight ahead. "You won't need to use the green wing or the west wing. I keep the doors closed, to save energy. As you can imagine, it's quite a feat to heat or cool a house this size."

I nodded, as if I had spent time imagining such a thing. "Are they all bedrooms?"

"Oh no," she said. "There are anterooms, dressing rooms, bathrooms, the old sauna, a gymnasium, linen storage . . . And several guest rooms, as well."

My head felt like it was spinning. Was this supposed to make sense to me?

"Actually, Margaret, I think I'll go see about your belongings," Mr. Albright said suddenly, reversing course and heading back downstairs.

Coward. I helplessly watched him go.

I tried to ignore the prickling sensation on my skin as we walked farther down the hall, stopping outside the second-to-last door on the left.

John put his hand on the knob, but Laura lightly touched his shoulder. "I like to knock," she said softly. "Even if—well, we should get into the habit anyway."

So he knocked. Then he opened the door.

Laura paused in the doorway and turned to me. "She hasn't always lived in here. We just felt it was . . . simpler."

And then, leaving me to cope with that extremely mysterious pronouncement, she went inside.

I had nowhere to go but after her.

It took me a moment to figure out where I was, but after taking everything in, it hit me: This was a nursery, a room for small children. The wallpaper was an old-fashioned pattern of fruits and flowers arranged in rings around little scenes of woodland creatures hanging out together—bunnies, squirrels, birds, and turtles, all with the creepy wild-eyed expressions people somehow used to think were normal and cute.

There were no cribs or bassinets, but there was a white wooden toy chest carved with stars and moons against one wall, and a few feet away, a small desk had the same pattern carved in its legs.

I looked around the room. Two beds, decorated with the same celestial motif, were pushed up into the corners against the far wall.

"Agatha," Laura said softly, "there's someone we'd like you to meet."

And then I saw her—sitting in a high-backed wooden chair by the window, her body angled so she could look outside.

My throat went dry. A very bad feeling began to tap-dance in my mind.

She didn't turn to look at us, but Laura went on walking toward her, talking as she went. "Her name is Margaret," she said, in a voice as thin and clear as a rod of glass. "She'd like to say hello to you."

My heart and stomach felt like they were in a wrestling match. I told myself, *Calm down, you're making assumptions, you're being ungrateful* . . .

Laura waved me forward, and I followed a few steps in her wake, because what else was I going to do? Run hyperventilating out of the room?

I was only there to meet Agatha, who was apparently not a very social person.

"Margaret has come to live with us," Laura said. She put a hand on Agatha's shoulder.

Up close, I could see that she was as beautiful in

person as in the photo—maybe even more so. Wavy hair, pulled back with a white ribbon, reached almost to her waist, and her face, though clear of makeup, was lovely because of her luminous skin and those killer cheekbones. Her eyebrows were slightly furled, coral lips gently pursed.

I saw all this in profile. She never so much as turned to look at me.

Her clothes were like younger interpretations of her mother's style: a cornflower-blue sweater and a knee-length plaid skirt. Her ears were pierced and she wore small silver hoops. Her shoes were simple penny loafers of smooth gray leather.

Laura gave me a questioning smile, perhaps checking to see if I *was* planning to run hyperventilating out of the room, and I had no choice but to give her a small smile in return. This was a delicate moment and I needed to play it cool. There would be plenty of time later for freaking out.

"This is our sweet Agatha," she said to me, letting her fingers trail slowly down a lock of the wavy hair. Then she reached over to a side table for a brush, and smoothed the hair back into place.

Agatha didn't react. She might as well have been in another dimension.

"Nice to meet you," I said to Agatha, fighting the urge to back away.

This delighted Laura. "How *lovely*, Margaret," she said. "You know, that's a very empathetic instinct, to speak directly to her. You'd be shocked by how many people treat her like she's not even here."

"Yes, very good," John said, startling me. I'd forgotten he was in the room with us. "Perhaps it's time for us to have a little talk."

WE DIDN'T RETURN to the west parlor. Instead, Laura stopped short at the base of the stairs and said, "Oh, let's talk in the library; the view of the grounds is so nice this time of day."

So we went into the library, which was a large room almost entirely walled in by overflowing bookshelves. In the center, four olive-green leather chairs faced one another, each with its own little wooden table and an antique reading lamp dipping its nose over the chair's shoulder. On the far wall of the room, an expanse of windows looked out over a breathtaking vista of velvety green hills backed by silver-pink late-afternoon clouds.

I had the distinct feeling they were trying to distract me with how lovely the property was.

"Please, Margaret, sit," John said, and I sat in one of the chairs and then tried to make myself appear fascinated by the walls of books. Whatever they were about to say loomed over us like smog, and I didn't want to look up into their eyes and see that they knew it, too.

Laura began to speak, then stopped herself and coughed a little, as if the words had choked her. There was a long silence. It was so painful that I was compelled to speak.

"So . . . Agatha," I said. "How old is she?"

They both answered at once. "Sixteen," John said, while Laura said, "Seventeen."

They exchanged a tense look, and then Laura sat down in the chair across from mine. "Seventeen," she said again.

"And what's . . . wrong with her?" I cringed inwardly when I heard myself ask the question, but neither Laura nor John seemed bothered.

"Agatha is sick," Laura said. "Up until eight and a half months ago, she was your typical happy teenager. She went out with her friends, went to parties, loved shopping . . . you know."

I nodded as if I could relate. I had no memories of being a happy teenager. Everything in my life before the accident had been wiped into a smeary haze. Maybe I'd been happy. I guess so. But I didn't remember much about it.

"And then, one day . . . everything changed. *She*

changed. It was as if she became a different person. Angry. Disturbed, almost. We were baffled and help-less—we had no idea what could have caused it. And then just as we were getting help, she . . ." Laura's voice trailed off.

I looked at John.

He swallowed hard. "She . . . shut down. Like someone had flipped a switch. And she became what she is now. She's very cooperative and doesn't cause any trouble. She can feed herself, dress herself . . . shower with a bit of help. She can walk. And we *think* she can read, though we're not entirely sure."

"She's not interested in reading," Laura said.

"What is she interested in?" I asked.

They glanced at each other.

"Nothing, as far as we can tell," Laura said, her voice straining to sound casual. "Whatever you feed her, she'll eat. Wherever you take her, she'll go. Doc-tors' appointments, needles, examinations—nothing bothers her. The doctors think it may have been some kind of aggressive bacterial infection that affected her frontal cortex . . . Do you know much about the brain?"

I shook my head and sat back in the chair. *Well, no big deal,* I told myself. *So they have a catatonic daughter. Agatha's a person with a medical condition. You can live with a person who has a medical condition.*

I had nothing against sick people. When you thought about it, it really had nothing to do with me.

"You're probably wondering," Laura said slowly, "what this has to do with you."

Oh.

"I'm afraid," John said, looking down at his hands, "that our motives for bringing you here weren't *entirely* as Mr. Albright explained. The fact remains, obviously, that we want to provide you with a comfortable home, with people who care about you. We are committed to giving you the same life we are giving our own children—spending money, clothes, even paying for your college education. The debt of gratitude I owe your father is in no way diminished by the fact that this situation is slightly more complex than it seems at first glance."

There had been a little tower of feelings inside me. Something small and fragile, a house of cards made of hope. I'd thought I might be okay for a while—

"But—" he said.

—*but.*

"But we *are* going to ask you for something in return," he said.

The tower imploded. I stopped pretending not to look at them and faced Laura head-on. I could see, suddenly, every flaw in her impeccable facade: wispy hairs rebelling against her sleek mane, fine lines at the corners of her lips and eyes. The way she held her shoulders so primly square, so purposefully rigid.

"We'd like for you to be Agatha's . . . companion," Laura said. She bit her lip. "The doctors have said that, while she can't be out in public, it's not good for her to live in total isolation. She needs people around, and not just her parents, or even a nurse. She needs . . . a friend."

"A friend?" I asked. "How can we be friends? She didn't even notice I was in the room."

Laura leaned forward. "Of *course* she noticed. I could tell how happy she was to meet you. She was thrilled to have a visitor her own age."

"We don't mean you have to spend *all* of your time with her," John said. "We have other help, and Laura manages most of it on her own. But a fair amount of time, every day—when you're studying, perhaps. Just for her to have the sense of not being without friends. That's all we want." His voice tightened, like there was a fist around it. "If you had known her before—if you had met her before she got sick, you'd understand. She could light up a room. She was so vivacious and charismatic."

"She was very popular," Laura added, sounding proud. "She had so many friends. Unfortunately, when she fell ill, her friends abandoned her. It only took a few weeks for them to stop calling, stop offering to visit."

"To be fair," John said slowly, "the calls and visits may not mean anything to her."

"They tell us she's still in there," Laura said. "Trapped in her own mind. But for whatever reason, she can't get out. And we can't let her think we've given up on her."

But this was all wrong. Couldn't they see? Agatha, when she was awake, charming, full of zest and fun and sprinkled with popularity like some magical teenage cupcake, wouldn't have wanted me as her friend. I had nothing to offer. Maybe once upon a time we would have gotten along. But now? I was a hollowed-out shell. In some ways I was basically a version of Agatha who could talk.

Laura dug her manicured fingernails into her palm. "They told us to send her away. To a—a facility. They call it a home, but how can a place like that be a home?"

John reached over and patted her knee, and she dialed back her emotion.

"This is her home," she said. "And we'd like for it to be yours, as well. It's not perfect, but life never is."

Now wasn't *that* the truth.

John leaned forward. He was trying to look relaxed, but I could see his forehead twitch. "What do you think, Margaret? Do you want to try?"

The Suttons didn't come right out and say that if I refused to be Agatha's companion, they'd ship me back to Palmer House. In fact, I was pretty sure they didn't think they would. But I knew it would come to that, in time. If I said no, the mere sight of me would be an ever-present reminder of my selfish choice to neglect their darling Agatha, and what was I doing with my time otherwise? Reading? Surfing the internet? Couldn't I do those things with her in the room? It wouldn't take long for them to see me as a greedy person who was taking advantage of their kindness.

It wasn't a yes or no question. It was a stay or go question.

I didn't really want to stay.

But I *really* didn't want to go back to Palmer House.

So I reached up, scratched the back of my neck, and said, "Okay."

And their expressions, like banners advertising joy and relief, actually warmed my heart and made me glad I'd said yes. Maybe I couldn't help them, but it was nice that they thought I could.

There was silence for a little while, during which Laura made a show of looking out the window and smiling.

"It's a beautiful evening," she said. "Should we have dinner on the terrace?"

John jumped slightly, as if he'd forgotten we were there. "No, I can't," he said. "I'm sorry. I have a call at seven. I'll eat in my study."

"Very well," Laura said. "Then Margaret, Agatha, and I will eat in the breakfast room."

"Actually," I said, "people call me Margot."

"Margot," Laura repeated carefully. "Spelled with a *t*?"

I nodded.

"How sweet," she said. "Agatha will love it."

I was saved from having to reply by a soft knock on the door signifying Mr. Albright's return. He was carrying my backpack and the plastic bag.

"I can take these upstairs," he said. "Which room?"

"Oh, the nursery, Tom, of course," Laura said. "She'll be staying with Agatha."

CHAPTER
~5~

AS LAURA AND I walked back up to the nursery, a lump rose in my throat. This was not what I'd signed up for. No, no, no. Not this. Being friendly was one thing. Being *roommates* was different.

What would happen when I screamed at night?

Laura, ahead of me, knocked on the door and pushed it open.

"Agatha, we're back," she said.

The figure at the window didn't move.

"This bed is Agatha's," Laura said.

Trying to conceal my dismay, I looked at the other bed, not six feet from Agatha's. Like hers, it was perfectly made with a quilted white bedspread and a pale yellow throw pillow.

"I was thinking . . . if you'd like a *little* more space of your own, you could take the nanny's bedroom," Laura said haltingly, gesturing toward a door in the wall to our right. I walked over and peered inside. It was a tiny space, painted pale gray, and the furniture looked like it was a hundred years old. The bed had a chipped white metal frame, and the dresser was ancient and sturdy with two missing drawer pulls. "I hate to even suggest it, because it's so small and plain."

"Oh. Yes," I said immediately. "This will be great."

"Okay," Laura said, fighting to keep the disappointment from turning down the corners of her lips. "The doctor thought it would be good for you girls to be near one another . . . but this is close enough." Her tone veered toward doubt as she finished the sentence.

"We'll be close," I said quickly. "I'll hardly spend any time in here. Only when I'm asleep. Mostly I'll be . . . out there, right? With Agatha."

This appeased her. "The light's so pleasant in the main room, don't you think?"

"Definitely," I said, as if I'd taken any time to notice the quality of the light.

"All right," she said. "There's the bathroom, that door right there, and then if you want to unpack, you can put your things in the dresser and closet . . . goodness, is that all you've brought?"

She was staring at my two meager bags.

If she thought the bags were unimpressive, wait until she saw the clothes inside them. My shirts had come from the charity rack at Palmer House— misprints from a souvenir T-shirt factory, shirts whose decals had peeled off unevenly, leaving incomplete phrases like MIAM IS HOTTER THAN HO and I LFFT MY HEAPT IN FLORID.

The only halfway decent outfit I had was the one I was wearing: a ruffled blue blouse one of the nurses at the hospital had given me as a gift, a pair of old jeans from another nurse, and a pair of flip-flops one of the volunteers bought me at the drugstore down the street when she learned I didn't have any shoes.

What I wore hadn't mattered at Palmer House. Once school started in the fall, it might have been an issue, but even then I couldn't imagine caring.

"It's all I have," I said.

"Well," she said, "we'll need to get you some things, won't we?"

I can't afford things, I thought, and then I remembered what John had said. Were they really going to buy me clothes? Give me money to spend on whatever I wanted?

Maybe I could save up for a laptop, to replace the one I'd lost.

"Wear whatever's comfortable for tonight," she said. "Tomorrow, we'll take care of the rest."

I nodded. I didn't want to unpack with her standing there, though I could sense her curiosity about my belongings.

"Do you think I might be able to have that toothbrush?" I said.

Laura stepped back. "Oh, yes. Give me two minutes. Will you be all right in here with Agatha?"

"Sure," I said, and she scurried away.

While she was gone, I hurriedly dumped the contents of my bags into the top two drawers of the dresser. After that, which had taken maybe fourteen seconds, I wandered back out into the main part of the room and stopped short.

Agatha's chair was empty.

The whispery silence of the room turned to a roar in my ears.

I looked around but didn't see her anywhere. And there was nowhere for her to hide.

She was gone.

The door to the hall was closed—I would have heard it open, right? And the bathroom door was wide open, the light on. There was no one in there.

Oh, God, I'd lost her already. They were going to kick me out.

Deep breath. First of all, *I* didn't lose her. She lost herself. Second of all, it wasn't my job to keep her in one place, was it? What should I have done, commanded her to stay still? Wrestled her to the ground? This wasn't my fault. Of course it wasn't.

But I knew I needed to find her before Laura came back.

Could she be hiding under one of the beds?

I stared at the nearest one warily, half expecting Agatha to be hiding underneath, waiting to jump out at me when I leaned close. I crossed the room, steeled myself, and knelt down to push away the white bed-skirt and look under the bed frame.

Empty. Not so much as a single dust bunny.

I went to the second bed, knelt, and lifted the bed-spread. This time, I had no doubt that when I bent down and got my face near the floor, Agatha would come flying at me like a bat out of a cave.

Nope.

Some companion I turned out to be. I surveyed the room, wondering if Laura and John would simply send for the car and load me right back up.

I walked over to the open bathroom door and looked inside. The walls were tiled with shining squares of pale blue, the floor a spotless retro checkerboard of white and black. The toilet squatted in the corner by the bathtub—

And as I looked at it, the shower curtain rustled.

Okay, I told myself. This is good. She's in the tub. She's waiting there for you to find her. This might even be her idea of a joke—like she's hazing you. If she was capable of playing a joke, maybe we could communicate. Maybe it wouldn't be a creepy one-way friendship. It could be a creepy *two*-way friendship.

I walked over to the tub, paused, and said, "Agatha?"

I gently pulled the curtain back, trying to figure out what I was going to say to convince her to return to the chair.

But the bathtub was empty.

Then I heard a low *bump*, the sound of an elbow or knee thudding against something solid.

I waited.

Bump.

It was coming from the nanny's room. *My* room. My stomach clenched and I felt an indignant flare of temper. Was this how it was going to be? Would I not be entitled to even a little bit of privacy?

I expected to find her in there, but still somehow the sight of her startled me—her slender form, held stiffly with mannequin-precise posture, standing in front of my small dresser.

As I watched, she removed the last of my clothes and dropped them carelessly to the floor.

"What are you doing?" I asked.

She looked over at me silently through owlish, indifferent eyes. I felt almost as if we were in a staring contest, but apparently that was just me, because a few seconds later she shifted her blank contemplation to the door of the small cabinet behind me.

"What are you doing?" I asked again. But even then, so early in our acquaintance, I knew better than to expect an answer. "Why don't you go sit down?"

Without so much as the involuntary twitch of a muscle in her jaw, she wandered out of the room. I followed her as far as the doorway and watched her return to her chair.

"Are you trying to make me feel like I don't belong here?" I asked her. "Because if that's it, you don't need to waste your energy. I could never belong in a place like this."

I know she heard me—she must have. But she didn't react.

"I probably shouldn't be here at all," I said, more to myself than to her.

It was the strangest thing. There was no one else in the room with us, and obviously Agatha hadn't spoken—I was looking right at her, so I would have known. She didn't even open her mouth.

But I had the distinct impression that I heard someone say, *You're right.*

AFTER PUTTING MY things back in the drawers, I sat at the top of the stairs, waiting and watching the front hall below me. Finally, I heard Mr. Albright's voice—that blend of hearty good humor and polite obedience. He made some kind of goodbye to Laura and then came shuffling closer, humming quietly.

As soon as he came into view, I practically tumbled down the stairs. He looked up, alarmed, clearly thinking I was about to bowl him over.

"Margot," he said, smiling. "Are you settling in?"

I had to say it quickly, or I'd lose my nerve. "I can't stay here. I'd like to go back to Palmer House, please."

His eyes widened in surprise.

"I just don't think I can be a companion." The whole idea was ridiculous. Me, keep Agatha company? How, by screaming at her? "I'm not good at things like this. And I don't think Agatha wants me here."

Mr. Albright raised his eyebrows. He took a deep, relaxed breath. "I see," he said quietly.

"Can you please tell Mrs.—I mean Laura?—that I'm grateful, but I think I would be better off at Palmer House."

"But surely you understand," he said slowly. "You *can't* go back to Palmer House. As your caseworker must have told you, spaces there are in high demand.

I recall Ms. O'Neil saying that a new girl was coming to occupy the vacancy this afternoon."

I froze.

"I apologize," he said, bowing his head slightly. "I assumed you would have known that."

"No," I said. I grabbed the banister to keep from wilting to the ground. "I had no idea."

He cleared his throat. "I don't know your exact history, but from what I've gathered, you are a . . . difficult placement in terms of foster families. I could take you away from Copeland Hall, but your only alternative at this point is the state institution."

The institution? "But . . . I don't need to be in an institution."

"Of course not." He patted my shoulder, two brief thumps of support. "Margot, you're tired, you're overwhelmed, and you're in a strange new place. You haven't even had the chance to take your shoes off."

We both looked down at my feet, in their cheap rubber flip-flops.

I lowered my voice. My body was still thrumming with adrenaline. "Agatha doesn't like me."

Mr. Albright cast a glance down the hall—I presumed he was looking for Laura. Seeing that the coast was clear, he lowered his voice, too. "Agatha doesn't like or dislike anything, I'm afraid. Her reactions are reflexive. The doctors know this. Laura knows it, too.

Only . . . she hasn't been able to admit it to herself quite yet."

Now he seemed sad. I wondered what it was like to be expected to show up happy every day to a place like this, a house with so much sadness hanging over it.

And if it was hard for him, what must it be like for Laura?

A daily grind of misery. I certainly knew how *that* felt.

Maybe I did belong here.

"Why don't you give it a chance?" he said. "A couple of days. In the meantime, I'll speak with your caseworker about finding you a place to go if you still want to leave."

Of course I would still want to leave. But for the moment, what else could I do? "Okay."

"You'll do great," he said. "Wait and see."

"I'd better get back up to Agatha," I said. I was already feeling bad about leaving her, and worried about what Laura would say if she found me out here.

I had no idea what to expect when I returned to the nursery. Would Agatha have done something to my clothes?

No. She sat at the window, meek as a kitten.

"I'm sorry," I said to her back. "I tried to go away, but there's nowhere for me to go *to*."

No answer. Of course not. She didn't care either way.

I just had to keep telling myself that until I believed it.

CHAPTER
~6~

"DOES THE FOOD taste all right?" Laura asked, her eyes roving over my plate.

"It's great," I said. It wasn't a lie—our dinner was simple but delicious, a Caesar salad topped with grilled salmon, a side of garlic bread, and a glass of some kind of fancy sparkling water, which I'd never really liked before but went well with the meal.

We were eating in what Laura called the breakfast room, a narrow space off the side of the kitchen with blue floral wallpaper, blue floral curtains on the bay window, and matching cushions on the chairs around the eight-person table. A vase of fresh daisies sat in the center of the table, which Laura apologized for—adding that daisies weren't "dinner" flowers.

"Okay, I won't eat them," I said, and for a moment, she looked mystified.

Then she brightened. "A *joke*," she said, laughing approvingly, as if the idea of a joke was the funny part.

Laura sat at the head of the table, and I sat to her left. Across from me was Agatha, who took small bites of her salad with the tranquility of a horse at its trough. Laura had chopped it into toddler-sized bites for her, explaining, "We always make sure that her food is cut into small pieces. She seems to prefer it that way. You'll get used to it."

I tried to imagine what Tam would say if she knew I was sleeping in the nanny's room and charged not only with babysitting a beautiful heiress who hated me, but also with cutting up her food. I had a feeling she'd laugh her head off and say it served me right.

It was still better than the state institution.

My main concern, looming larger as night approached, was the fear that I'd wake up screaming—not that the screaming itself would be so bad, because who knows? It might get me an actual room of my own. But what if Agatha freaked out and wouldn't calm down? What if the Suttons decided I was more trouble than I was worth?

I considered mentioning my nightmares to Laura, but decided not to do it in front of Agatha. Instead, we filled the time with small talk, Laura describing the layout of the kitchen and pantry and telling me to make myself at home. She explained that there were no full-time staff at Copeland Hall, but a cook came in the late morning, and cleaners came twice a week.

"I'm happy to help clean up," I said. "I can cook a little, too." (Not technically a lie; I could scramble eggs and cook spaghetti, if there was a jar of sauce on hand.)

"No, that won't be necessary." Laura looked vaguely alarmed. "Please don't worry about it. They— they prefer to be left alone and uninterrupted. That's how we've always done things here."

In other words, *Back off with your peasant ideas, Margot.*

As we spoke, Agatha sat with her hands resting on the tablecloth in front of her. Every few seconds, the fingers of her right hand would gently flutter up, move in a small, quick spiral, and then sink back down, like she was conducting the world's tiniest orchestra.

Laura didn't seem to notice, so I figured it was just one of Agatha's usual quirks.

"What kind of things did you do for fun at the group home?" Laura asked.

"Mostly we watched TV or spent time on our phones. We had board games, but they were all missing pieces. You'd get halfway through a game and realize you couldn't finish."

"Oh, how awful," she said with a concerned head tilt. "Maybe we should send them some new games."

Awful, yes. And yet at that moment, I would have given almost anything to be back there, wallowing in the comforting communal bleakness, instead of being here in this terrifying castle. "I'm sure they'd appreciate it."

"I'll speak to John. We're always looking for ways to help the underprivileged."

I could hardly summon more than a weak smile. It was exhausting to be continuously grateful and impressed.

Laura carefully balanced her fork on the edge of her salad bowl. "You know . . . this may be as good a time to speak to you about this as any."

Oh, God, there was *more*? I braced myself.

"John, as you know, is a lawyer."

"Right," I said. "He knew my dad in law school."

She smiled gently. "Yes. I met your father as well—only in passing, but I recall him seeming very gentlemanly. John and I married quite young, so I vividly remember the late nights and early mornings he spent in study groups—they were all so busy with their courses. And John's been practicing law ever since. He's very gifted. He takes excellent care of his clients—he represents several very high-profile companies between here and Chicago. And because of that, he takes his reputation in the community very seriously. We all do."

I blinked. I felt like I should understand what she meant, but I didn't.

"The Copelands have lived here for almost a hundred and fifty years," she said, a note of reverence in her voice. "This family has been a pillar of the state—the entire country, some would say—for generations. My own great-grandmother was presented at court to the Queen of England. Everyone in the county looks up to us."

Did they? I guessed I'd find out. I'd never lived anywhere but the suburbs, and I'd never even heard of someone being famous on a countywide level. The only thing people in our neighborhood looked up to was the Homeowners' Association Board. But maybe things were different out here. Maybe it was a slower, more genteel lifestyle, and when people saw Laura and John coming, it was like the arrival of a minor celebrity.

Yeah . . . maybe?

I didn't dwell on the *maybe not*. I was too worn out from the day. Besides, what did I care if the Suttons had delusions of grandeur? It wasn't hurting me. And maybe Laura seeing herself as a great lady was what had led them to pluck me from the orphanage. Kind of a PR stunt, but for their own egos.

She leaned forward. "It means that you represent this family wherever you go, and whatever you do. We all do. So we must take care, in public, to comport ourselves in a way that upholds our legacy."

I must have looked either confused or idiotic, or both, because she went on.

"Just yesterday, for example," she said. "I was driving in town, and I pulled out of the parking lot at the pharmacy, and the car that was approaching in the lane had to slow down. He honked at me, and I almost honked back. But then I thought, *I'd better not.* We can't have word getting around that the Suttons are bullies." She gave me a conspiratorial little smile.

"Well," I said, "I can't honk at people if I don't have a car."

I guess I was hoping for some acknowledgment that I might like to drive somewhere at some point. I loved driving. Dad had taken me for the driver's test on my sixteenth birthday, and I passed on the first try.

"Yes, perfect! So that won't be a problem."

Well, that backfired.

"Does that sound reasonable to you?" she asked. "Do you think you can help carry on our position in the community?"

No, I'd prefer to bring shame and scorn to your family. I nodded. "Yes, I think so."

"Of course we can count on you," she said, relaxing

a little. "I can tell that you're a thoughtful, caring person. And look at how much Agatha likes you already!"

Uh-huh. I looked at Agatha, who raised her fingers and dropped them. Her eyes were locked on a spot somewhere out in the yard behind me.

"Funny, too," Laura said. "Making jokes."

I tried to smile.

Agatha sighed, which caused her mother to check her watch and rise from the table as if we'd been ordered to leave immediately.

"Agatha," Laura said in a clear, firm voice, "let's go upstairs and get ready for bed."

Agatha pushed her chair back and stood up, without turning her gaze from the window. Then we headed back to the stairs in a line, Laura first, then Agatha, then me.

"Do you happen to know the Wi-Fi password?" I asked. I'd rehearsed the question in my head fifty times. I don't know why it seemed like such an intrusive thing to ask.

"I'm afraid John handles all of the technology," Laura said. "We'll have to check with him tomorrow. I hope that's all right."

"Sure," I said. I could fend for myself for one night. "I'd use my data, but there's no signal."

"Oh, no," Laura said. "You won't get cell service out here. It's a nightmare. I don't even carry my phone unless I'm going into town. We do have a landline if you need to make a call."

Is that what she thought people used phones for? "Maybe tomorrow I can help you get your phone on Wi-Fi," I said. "I set up all my family's phones. I was like tech support."

"Perhaps," she said pleasantly. "Like I said, John makes all of those decisions."

She said it so naturally that I was halfway into another thought before I realized what she had said. Decisions? What kind of "decisions" needed to be made about Wi-Fi?

Well, sometimes technophobes didn't know what they didn't know. Olivia, one of the girls at Palmer House, was like that. We all spent a surprisingly enjoyable evening investigating exactly how she thought the internet worked—something to do with your phone loading up data when you plugged it in. Tam actually convinced her that she could wirelessly charge her phone by setting it on top of a package of AA batteries from the supply closet.

"If you like, the bathroom in the nursery can be your own," Laura said to me. "We've had a larger one modified for Agatha, with a walk-in shower and safety rails."

We reached an open door and Laura beckoned me in. It was a huge bathroom, exactly as she'd described, the walls lined with handles and the shower wide open so you didn't have to step over the side of a tub. There was a chair in there, and a row of bath products—expensive-looking shampoos and conditioners, a comb, a loofah. On the wall hung a plush pink bathrobe. Beneath it, waiting neatly on a bench, was a pair of folded pink pajamas, a little square of undies, and a pair of pink ballet-style slippers.

"We'll be finished in about twenty minutes," Laura said. "Why don't you shower? It always feels good to get cleaned up after a day of traveling. Maybe after I put Agatha to bed, we can talk for a few minutes and get to know each other."

"Okay," I said, but to be honest, I wasn't sure I needed another round of awkward conversation to cap off this endless day.

"I've stocked the bathroom with towels and a few bath products for you," she said. "Some of my favorites. If you don't like them, we can get whatever you prefer. And I also left you a pair of pajamas—I didn't know if you brought any."

"Wow, thank you," I said, feeling genuinely touched by her thoughtfulness.

"Agatha, let's go," she said.

But Agatha seemed not to have heard her. She stared at the wall.

"Your ears must be painted on today," Laura said, gently guiding her into the bathroom and then closing the door.

I stood in the hallway, rooted in place.

When she thought I was ignoring her, Mom used to ask me, *Are your ears painted on?*

A little tornado of longing and grief seemed to move through my body. And when it was gone, I felt emptier than ever.

But I was also . . . intrigued. And as I listened through the door to the sound of water running, of footsteps, of a quiet, instructive voice, the curiosity sharpened into a feeling that could almost be described as *hunger.*

What else might Laura say that would bring up, so viscerally, the memory of my own mom?

THE PAJAMAS SHE'D left on the bed for me were made from dove-gray cotton so smooth it almost felt like silk, with lacy white ribbon sewn around the neckline and sleeves. The buttons were white with small flowers carved on them. Guaranteed, these pajamas cost more than the rest of my clothes put together.

In the bathroom, draped artfully on the small

counter next to the sink, were a fluffy white towel and washcloth. And on the shelf in the shower was a neat row of brand-new bottles of shampoo, conditioner, and body wash, all with the same fancy floral labels as the ones in Agatha's bathroom. I opened one and sniffed it. The fragrance was as far from my style as you could get—the heavy, perfumed smell of roses and jasmine—but I would never tell Laura I didn't like them. I'd just go around smelling like an old lady for the foreseeable future.

I'd forgotten how nice it was to take a shower with plenty of hot water and no one banging on the door shouting that your time was almost up. I stood with my eyes closed, enjoying the excellent water pressure and the solitude and the admittedly first-rate lather of Laura's bath products. The fragrance was already growing on me.

Finally, not wanting to give the impression that I was wasteful, I turned off the water and climbed out, wrapping myself in the fluffy towel and puttering over to the sink. A fancy new hairbrush was on the counter, along with the toothbrush Laura had given me—a fancy electric one, brand-new in its box. And a tube of organic cinnamon-flavored toothpaste.

I hung the towel on the bar, changed into the pajamas, and brushed my hair and teeth. By the time I finished, I felt warm, relaxed, and sleepily optimistic in spite of Agatha's rejection. There was more to life here than Agatha.

I opened the door that led back to the nursery. The ceiling lights were off; just a single dim lamp was lit in the far corner. Laura was perched on the side of Agatha's bed, reading to her from a small book she held in her hands. Her voice was low and steady, like the drone of a prayer.

"—be banished from this realm. And may virtue stand as a wall before you and leave you cast into the dark night, apart from innocent souls and the homes of righteous men—"

Suddenly she froze and half turned toward me. The curves of her face were outlined by the warm lamplight, but I could see a bright, surprised look in her eyes.

"I'm—I'm sorry," I stammered.

"I didn't see you there," she said. She deftly closed the book and slid it out of sight. "No need to apologize. I was just finishing up Agatha's nightly reading."

"Sounds heavy," I said without thinking.

"We try to read widely," she said, and I caught a hint of offense in her tone.

I nodded, knowing I'd done something wrong but not sure how to fix it.

"Go ahead," she said gently. "I'll be in shortly."

Then she leaned over Agatha's motionless form and kissed her forehead.

A searing sensation tore through my heart, and I closed my eyes and turned away.

My mother used to kiss my head like that.

I tried not to stumble as I made my way to my little room and put my dirty clothes in a tight bundle on the plain wooden chair in the corner. Then I sank onto the bed, facing away from the door, desperately trying to keep the tears out of my eyes. I felt myself on the edge of something huge and dark and yawning, some deep hole of loneliness I might never climb out of.

I'd been on this edge before and had always managed to back away from it—usually with the help of the arrival of a bossy nurse or a conveniently petty squabble with one of the Palmer House girls. But there was nothing like that here. No distractions. Nothing to shove me back from the edge.

There was nothing at *all* here.

Still, I shook myself—literally shook myself—and forced the darkness back.

I couldn't fall apart on my first day.

Laura's voice came from the doorway a few minutes later. "Margot? May I come in?"

I nodded and managed a yes that didn't sound like it was being forced out of my mouth by a waterfall of impending tears.

The door opened, and Laura stepped halfway in. I

could see that she wore a long, high-necked nightgown under a satiny floral robe cinched tightly around her tiny waist. "I brought you some tea. It's chamomile and lavender—caffeine free. Tea always helps me relax."

She set a cup of pale yellow liquid on the nightstand. "Thank you," I whispered, desperate not to make eye contact.

"I wanted to mention . . ." she began. "I read through the medical information your caseworker sent. I hope you don't mind—I just thought it was best for us to know what the doctors were thinking about the course of your recovery."

This was a little confusing. "I'm—recovered," I said. I'd broken a clavicle and bruised my sternum, but the rest of my trauma was your basic girl-escapes-from-sinking-car stuff: cuts, bumps, bruises, a little hypothermia. All in the past.

"Yes, although—" She stopped and scratched the corner of her eye. It was so unlike her that I knew she was profoundly uncomfortable with whatever she was about to say. "There's more to recovery than just physical healing."

Well, obviously. I wished I could reassure her that my emotional defects wouldn't be a hindrance to her well-ordered life, but in truth I had no idea.

Should I come clean? Tell her about the nightmares? Or did she, perhaps, already know—was there some reference to them in the files she had snooped into?

I surprised myself with that word—*snooped*. That wasn't fair.

"I wanted you to know that if you need to talk about anything, you can come to me. It's quite common for there to be lingering effects after the kind of trauma you've been through. They can surface at unexpected times."

Such as, for instance, a generalized sense of having no idea why you were still on the planet, maybe? I wouldn't say it came at unexpected times. It was like a winter coat someone had superglued to my skin.

I gave her a tight-lipped smile and a stiff shrug.

"But please," she said. "If you see anything, or—"

"See anything?" I asked. "What do you mean?"

She blushed, looking like she wished she could vanish into thin air like a genie. "I mean—the reports mentioned—I'm only quoting the doctors, you understand . . . but the hallucinations?"

"What?" I asked. "Hallucinations? No, no, I haven't had those."

"And memory loss?" she asked. "Time sort of . . . slipping away?"

"No," I said, and as soon as I said it, I wondered if not remembering anything about the actual accident counted.

"Oh, well, *good*," she said quickly, too brightly. "I'm so glad. That means your recovery is going smoothly."

Yeah, you think that now, I thought. *But wait until the screaming starts.*

"I'm sorry to burden you with this," she said. "Today wasn't the right day. You're already processing so much, coming here and adjusting to the way we do things. I wanted to make sure you felt that we were looking out for you . . . the way your parents might."

Her words sliced like a knife right into my soft parts. I looked up at the ceiling, trying not to show how deeply they wounded me.

"I'm sorry, Margot," Laura said. "I'm so sorry."

Oh no. Come on. I didn't need anyone's understanding or compassion. I *knew* how terrible it was—why did people think I needed reminding? Why did they think I needed to rehash the accident all the time?

But that wasn't what she meant.

"It was unfair of us not to tell you about Agatha before you came," she said in a rush. "I think . . . we were so happy at the idea that someone might come and . . . and like her. I know that sounds ludicrous, because to someone who never knew her before, it probably doesn't seem as if there's anything there to like. But beneath it all, she's still a person. And she still gets lonely, I'm sure of it. But that's selfish, and it wasn't fair not to give you a choice—a real choice."

So great was my surprise at the conversation going in this direction that I forgot all about hiding my face. I looked straight at her, at her sad, sheepish expression.

"No, it's all right," I said. "I swear. It's fine. I mean, it's not what I expected . . . but when do you ever really get what you expect?"

A tiny light seemed to flicker behind her eyes. "That's very generous. But I don't want you to suffer in silence. We want you to *want* to be here."

"I do want to be here," I said. Did I? Whoops, too late to take it back.

She smiled. "Are you going to sleep now?"

I reached over and tapped my phone to see the clock. It was barely past eight. But what else was I going to do? It seemed too soon to start roaming the house, even just to go down and find a book in the library. I wondered what Laura did at night. Did she watch TV? If so, she would invite me to watch with her, right? I tried to imagine her kicking back on a comfy sofa and putting her feet up—her feet in their silky white slippers. Or in an overstuffed reclining armchair, like Mom used to do, snoring in her reading glasses and fuzzy socks. But I could only picture Laura sitting straight up, perched on the front edge of a sofa, sipping tea.

"Probably," I said. "I'm pretty tired."

"I understand. I've gotten into the habit of going

to bed when Agatha does. Isn't that awful? It makes me sound about a hundred years old." She smiled ruefully. "Sometimes I *feel* a hundred years old."

"Is it just you with Agatha?" I asked, trying to recall what John had said. "Don't you have a nurse or anyone else to help you?"

Laura tucked her hair behind her ear. "We tried nurses in the past, but—this sounds silly—they did their jobs too well. They would get into a schedule, and then I found myself avoiding them so I didn't disrupt their routine. I could go a whole day without seeing Agatha. And . . . even though it made my life easier, I missed her. She's my child, and I think . . . I think she needs me. Children, especially girls, need their mothers."

I must have reared back. I felt like I'd been punched.

"Oh, no—what have I said?" she gasped, stepping fully into the room, her hands on her cheeks. "Margot, I'm so sorry. I'm an idiot. I'm worse than that, I'm—"

I held up my hand. "No," I said hoarsely. "No."

I meant, *No. Please stop talking. You're making it so much worse.*

But she seemed to think I was saying she wasn't an idiot, or that there was nothing to be sorry for.

"I am, I am. I'm sorry, I'm sorry." Her voice melted

into tears as she sank onto the bed and wrapped her arms around me.

I resisted, inwardly and outwardly, for a fraction of a second . . .

And then something inside me snapped. I closed my eyes and went limp. I let the weight of my cheek press against her thin, warm shoulder and let her arms curl tightly around my ribs.

"Oh, sweet Margot," she breathed. "Oh, sweet, sad Margot."

Stop talking, please. Stop talking now so I can pretend you're my mother.

I didn't want to cry, but I ended up crying anyway. And I felt her body shake with quiet sobs. The room was nearly silent, but the air was thick with our grief. I could smell it. I could feel it coming out of her skin.

"The real truth is," she whispered, her voice jagged around the edges, "I know you want to leave, but you *must* stay. So much depends on you."

She was quiet then, and the silence was as tight as a stretched-out rubber band.

I breathed in her scent, pretending that my mom had decided to try a new perfume and laundry detergent. That she'd gone on a diet and lost twenty pounds. And I bet Laura was doing her own version of the same thing: pretending she was hugging Agatha with a haircut.

CHAPTER
7

A LOW RUMBLE of thunder shook the house.

We leaned apart. The moment had passed.

"Tomorrow, we'll see about your clothes," she said kindly but a little stiffly. "And anything else you want."

"Okay." She clearly meant it as a gift, but in the moment it felt oddly like a bribe. Like she was buying her way out of the situation. Her earlier words were just now beginning to seep in. I *must* stay? Why?

I couldn't bear to ask, though. I was way past my maximum allowed number of emotionally draining conversations for the day.

"Did you like the soaps?" she asked. "I make them myself."

"Wow," I said. "That's amazing. They smell so good. How do you do it?"

"A little bit of this, a little bit of that." She tried to

look modest, but I could tell she was pleased. "Drink your tea. I find chamomile so relaxing, don't you? Oh, I make a chamomile lotion you should try. I'll bring you some tomorrow."

A huge yawn rolled through my body. I was already tired, but I reached for the teacup and took a sip of the warm, mildly sweet liquid.

"Good girl," Laura said. "Now, don't worry about Agatha in the morning. I'm sure we'll be downstairs before you're awake."

I took another long drink. "If you need help, I can get up early."

Her smile was kindly approving. "That's very thoughtful, but no need. We'll figure out the routine later. Tonight, rest."

She stood up and started to leave, then turned back around . . . and gently kissed my forehead.

After she left, I finished the tea, turned off the light, and burrowed under the covers. Her kiss still burned on my skin, and I let memories of my old life coalesce around me.

Mom came in to say good night after stopping in for one last peek at my little sisters, who'd been asleep for an hour. Next, she would head downstairs and prep the coffee maker for the morning, then surf the internet on the kitchen computer until Dad's show (anything about military crime solvers would do) was over. They'd go upstairs together, holding hands. I would hear their whispers and soft footfalls pass my room, a distant echo at the back of my dreams. They were especially animated because they were planning a surprise for us—a road trip to New York City for spring break.

And then, like in every dream, the images began to melt into blackness, and I sensed myself sinking, frigid water drenching me as it poured into the car. I felt a shock of panic—water filling my mouth and nose—

Breathlessly, I opened my eyes into the utter darkness of reality.

We never made it to New York, I reminded myself as I rose into consciousness. *We died halfway there.*

I always thought of it that way. *We died.* We. All of us.

By then, I was wide awake, but I didn't bother to correct myself. I checked my phone—1:15 a.m. I set it down and closed my eyes, waiting to fall back to sleep.

But as I lay in the dark, trying to force the dream into a secret closet in my head, I realized that I could *still* feel the water in my nose.

Oh, not this. Please not this.

I sat up and switched the lamp on, looking at the pillow in horror.

It was smeared with bright red blood. And so were the sleeves of my fancy new pajamas.

I hadn't had a nosebleed since leaving Becca's house—the day I ruined her great-grandmother's heirloom quilt. My heart beat fast in my chest as I tried to assess the damage and watched another drop of blood hit the pillow, spreading in slow motion through the fine weave of the fabric.

No, no, no. I looked for a box of tissues—why weren't there tissues in here? I found myself irrationally annoyed at Laura's lack of forethought. Shouldn't they have assumed I was going to cry all the time?

I pinched my nose shut and tipped my head back, hurrying to the bathroom and then leaning my head over the sink, where more blood fell in lazy drops and mixed with the water from the faucet. I managed to grab a wad of toilet paper and press it to my face, finding that it was the supersoft kind that left lint everywhere and made me sneeze, which was gross.

Finally, the bleeding stalled, and I went to my room to survey the damage.

It was worse than I'd thought. The pillow looked like a murder scene, and there was blood smeared on the sheets from my hands and sleeves.

For a while I stood there, feeling hopeless and lost. I couldn't let Laura see any of this. It felt like a personal insult. It felt . . . disrespectful.

When the bleeding finally seemed to have stopped,

I removed the pajama top and slipped on one of my T-shirts. Then I pulled the sheets off the bed and the case off the pillow and balled them up.

I'd been operating on pure adrenaline, but now that I was slowing down, I felt fuzzy and drained. Part of me was tempted to just spread one of my other T-shirts over the pillow and climb into bed. Deal with it in the morning.

But I couldn't do that, not on my first night. What, then? Should I wake Laura? No, terrible idea. The mere thought of tracking down their bedroom in this sea of closed doors, then knocking loudly enough to get her attention, then dragging her out of bed to see the chaos I'd brought into her perfectly controlled home was enough to make me need to sit down and catch my breath.

I had to clean up my own mess, and I had to do it before anybody saw.

Agatha was still and silent as I crept through the nursery and tried to silently open the hall door. The old knob made a distressing series of clanks and whines, but she showed no sign of waking.

Now to find the laundry room.

I stood in the dark hall, looking around at the somber, melancholy paintings that lined the spaces between doorways. Serious women and sad farmers with droopy-eared dogs . . . No happy summer scenes, no portraits of smiling children. Copeland Hall, for all its beauty, was not a cheerful place.

First, I tried to open the doors of the other upstairs wings, but they were locked. Then I remembered the service hallway Laura had pointed out as a place I'd never need to go.

I hurried downstairs and tried the door, which thankfully opened, and flipped a light switch to reveal a hall much plainer than the one upstairs; there were paintings on the wall, but they were simpler— landscapes of empty fields and moonlit lakes.

Next to the first door, a small metal plaque read HOUSEKEEPER, and under it was a neatly typed label in a tiny frame: MRS. BYERSMITH. The paper was yellowed with age, and I guessed that Mrs. Byersmith was long gone. *Dead,* I thought, and a cold tingle went up my spine.

Curious, I pressed on the door, and it quietly opened. The room was spacious and austere, with a tiny kitchen area, a fireplace, a wooden table with two chairs, and a neatly made bed. Under the small window, with its short, ruffled white curtain, was a bookcase that was nearly empty, except for a paperbound telephone directory with yellowing pages.

My curiosity sated, I carried my bundle of sheets and pajamas into the corridor beyond.

Here, safely out of view of the family, function ruled over form. The floor was tiled with linoleum and the walls were bare of decorations. There were clocks, schedules, a wall calendar from 1964, and numerous faded posters reminding passersby to *Serve with a Cheerful Heart* and *Take Care in All Tasks, Great and Small*.

Now I looked in earnest for the laundry room. At the end of the hall—miracle of miracles—I found it. With a sigh of relief, I opened the washing machine and stuck the soiled items inside. Then I found a box of powdered laundry soap and sprinkled in what I hoped was a reasonable amount.

The machine looked ancient, but sturdy and clean and with mercifully few options to choose from. I turned the dial to REGULAR, pressed START, and prayed for the best. Water began to spray onto the sheets and pajamas, and soon they were being tossed in a sudsy bath.

It was out of my hands now.

All I had to do was fill the time until the clothes were ready for the dryer. Because this machine was about fifty years old and there was no digital display, I had no idea how long that would take. Thirty minutes? An hour?

I went back and began exploring the hall. There was a massive storeroom with mostly empty shelves and a mop leaning in the corner with its ropy head turning to dust on the floor.

The next couple of doors revealed small bedrooms

very much like my own little room. They'd been abandoned in a pristine state, beds made, hangers left on their hooks. Even now, the only thing unkempt about them was the fuzzy coating of dust on every surface, including the Bibles centered neatly on each nightstand. At one point I found myself gazing at one of the beds, entertaining a mini-fantasy of lying down just for a moment and sleeping until the washing cycle finished. But no, it was too risky. What if I slept the whole night? What if Laura found me in here in the morning?

After a while, I heard the washing machine's distant whir die, and I went back, pulled out the ball of wet things, and turned on the light to inspect them.

The blood was mostly gone, the stains now so faint that they might not be noticed until my standing with the Suttons was more secure. If I folded the pajamas carefully and turned the pillow to face the wall, Laura probably wouldn't know anything was wrong. With a sigh of relief, I stuck it all in the dryer and turned it on.

I went back out into the hallway, continuing my exploration. When I opened the last door and found a stairway winding up, I felt a twinge of uncertainty. But Laura hadn't said I couldn't look around, had she? I wasn't going to hurt anything.

I flipped a switch on the wall, and about half of the lights came to life, filling the air with a grumpy buzz. Then I climbed the stairs.

On the next landing was a door with a label next to it: ACCESS TO GREEN WING.

Should I enter? Well, the alternative was to sit around downstairs, possibly fall asleep in one of the maid's rooms, and wake to find Laura and John standing over me, scandalized. So . . . onward.

The green wing was, as one might have guessed, green. The carpet was a dull hunter-green shade and the walls were papered in olive-toned stripes. In general, it was much messier than the main hall. The sconces on the walls were tarnished brass, and the frames of the pictures—not to mention the pictures themselves—were coated in dust.

I walked silently past the closed doors. Anterooms? Dressing rooms? What else had Laura said was in here?

I paced the length of it and then back. And just as I was about to go downstairs again, something caught my eye.

One of the doors wasn't like the others.

Specifically, the knob was different. Instead of being antique brass and smudgy like all the rest, it looked newer. If it hadn't been covered in a quarter inch of dust, it would have been the bright, showy gold of the 1980s. And above it was a dead bolt—the kind you needed a key to open.

Except when I pushed on the door, it was unlocked.

I opened it and looked around, turning on the light. An ornate fixture hung in the center of the room, but only one of its six bulbs was still working.

The room itself was nothing special, really—there was a bed with a dark green bedspread centered on a dull-colored rug. A dresser on one side, a small desk on the other, with a heavy-looking leather-upholstered chair and a lamp with a green glass shade.

As I looked around, I became conscious of a low, repetitive sound:

Thunk. Thunk. Thunk.

It wasn't loud. It was just slowly insistent.

Then a small movement caught my eye—across the room, at one of the two windows, the shade was gently moving back and forth as though it was caught in a breeze. Every time the bottom hit the window frame, it made the sound: *Thunk. Thunk.*

At that point, I would have happily left and gone back to the laundry room. But it seemed rude to leave the window open—what if it rained and water got inside? So I crossed the room, lifted the shade, closed the window, and then turned to go.

With a small *pop!*, the last light bulb went out.

In the sudden darkness, I tripped on something hard and heavy. It crashed to the ground with a bang that seemed to reverberate through the night. I bent down and saw a metal trash can on its side. As I stood it up, I saw something caught in the bottom, in the corner where the metal pieces were joined together.

I pulled it out and stared at it in the faint moonlight. It was a single small sheet of paper—thick, expensive stationery. There was a name at the top, in fancy raised letters: LILY COPELAND. And it was completely covered in messily scrawled sentences that were so chaotically arranged I couldn't even read what they said.

Lily? Who was Lily? Laura hadn't mentioned her . . . She was probably someone who had lived here sixty or seventy years ago. Maybe even Laura's grandmother or something.

I picked up the trash can and carried it over to the desk, where it seemed to belong. But I didn't put the paper back inside—I thought Laura might find it interesting, this little message from the past. I pulled the chain on the desk lamp and set the paper down in the light to see if I could make out what it said. I lowered myself onto the leather chair and felt a flutter of excitement, thinking it might be something cool and fun.

But it wasn't cool and fun at all.

It was kind of disturbing.

The first line of text was, *The moral sense of the world is reflected in the individual soul, and only with the greatest care can we avoid the descent into the darkest and most vile tendencies of human nature.*

It went on to ramble about the struggle between our divine natures and our animal selves and then turned into a rant about the iniquity of the modern age.

I only made it through a few lines before the harsh, unforgiving tone made me too uneasy, and I pushed the page away. These weren't the words of a well-balanced mind. And sitting in a small pool of light in a strange, dark room only made me feel that more deeply. I stood up and stretched my stiff legs, then folded the piece of paper and stuck it in the pocket of my pajama pants. Because I was creeped out, I didn't turn off the desk lamp until after I had opened the door to the hall, letting light spill in through the doorway.

Then I made my way back downstairs to check on the sheets and clothes.

In the laundry room, the dryer was silent—so soon? Was it broken? I opened the door, dreading the sight of wet sheets. But to my surprise, it was all totally dry. And not just dry, but not even hot as you'd expect from a just-finished cycle; it was all only slightly warm.

There would be time to figure that out later. I grabbed the clean linens and my pajama top and headed back up to the nursery. I opened the door quietly, keeping a careful eye on Agatha to make sure she hadn't woken. Soon, I was safely in the small bedroom.

I made the bed and changed back into my fancy pajama top, then climbed under the covers.

As I prepared to let my eyes fall shut, I reached over and checked the time on my phone.

Suddenly I was wide awake.

It was 5:14 a.m.?

That was impossible. If it was past five o'clock, that would mean I had spent four hours in that hallway, when I was positive I'd only been there for . . . I tried to piece together the time in my head. Less than an hour for the washing machine, and how long for the dryer? Fifteen minutes?

No. Clothes don't dry in fifteen minutes.

They certainly don't dry *and* cool to room temperature in fifteen minutes.

I remembered how tempting the beds had looked. Had I napped without remembering?

Then an image came into my head—well, not a single image as much as a collection of sense memories:

The way the scrawled text seemed to swim in front of my eyes. The stiff soreness of my legs and back when I stood up to leave the bedroom . . . How long had I sat there? It felt like minutes, but if the time on my phone was correct, it had been much, much longer.

I closed my eyes, not wanting to think about it. Not wanting to dwell on how close I may have come to being discovered out of bed, exploring rooms I had no right to explore, bleeding my gross orphan nose-blood on their fancy bedsheets.

And dark, spidery suspicions crept around the edges of my thoughts—Laura's questions about my health, about lingering effects of the accident.

I fell asleep, that's all, I insisted to myself. And if I was smart, I'd get some *more* sleep so I wasn't a zombie all day.

I crushed my eyelids shut.

Then I heard a sound from the nursery.

Had I woken Agatha? I held my breath and listened, hearing nothing else, but still feeling a tingle of suspicion that someone was moving around out there.

Finally, I swung my feet to the floor and got up, opening the door and peeking out.

Agatha stood in the center of the room. The faint light from the lamp behind her turned her silhouette into a glowing halo.

Somehow, though I'd expected to see something, I hadn't expected to see her, standing there, in that peculiarly intense posture. I clutched my chest and let out a gasping "God, you scared me!"

She didn't move. Had she forgotten who I was? Had I scared *her*?

I held my breath for a moment, then said, "It's okay, it's just me. Margot."

She seemed to sway slightly, but didn't speak.

"Go back to bed," I said firmly. "It's not morning yet."

She turned and walked away, and I shut the door and returned to bed. I would have locked myself in my room, but the door didn't have a lock, so I had to settle for shifting the small nightstand over a few inches to block the doorway. Then I kept my eyes on the knob, waiting for any sign that she was trying to enter.

The thought of Agatha scurrying soundlessly and maliciously around the nursery while I was trapped in here made me feel shaky and restless.

Laura and John clearly believed Agatha was a silent, well-behaved angel.

But I wasn't quite so sure.

CHAPTER
~8~

I FINALLY MANAGED to go back to sleep. Later (maybe after an hour? two? four?), there was a soft knock on my door, and I got up and opened it before I remembered that I was a little afraid of Agatha.

But it was Laura who stood outside, wearing a baby-blue silk blouse and a pair of white pants, with a small blue-and-white scarf knotted neatly around her neck. Her hair was in a low, tidy bun, and her makeup was perfect. I wondered how long it took her to get ready in the morning. You got the feeling she had it down to a ruthless science, without a single second wasted.

Her smile was slightly shy, which reminded me instantly of our mutual meltdown the previous night. If she brought it up, I might die of embarrassment. Fortunately, she seemed eager to leave it in the past.

"How are you feeling?" she asked.

I paused. Was this a trap? Did she know about the nosebleed?

"Was the mattress comfortable?" she asked, a little more gently.

"Oh," I said. "Yes. Yes, it was very nice. Thank you. Nice. Yes. Thanks." *Babble some more, Margot, it makes you sound incredibly sane.*

"We're heading down to breakfast," she said, indicating Agatha, fully dressed and seated in the chair by the window. "No need to rush. But I wanted to let you know that I've brought you some clothes, in case you need anything to tide you over before we have a chance to go shopping."

She motioned to the far bed, which was strewn with small stacks of clothing.

"Take your time, look it over. Anything you like, keep. They're extras of Agatha's."

"Wow," I said. "Are you sure she doesn't need them?"

"She has plenty of clothes," Laura said. "And it's important to us that you feel comfortable here. I don't want you to be worried about how you look. Just let me know if you want me to get rid of your old things for you."

I nodded and stared wide-eyed at the bed, suddenly feeling the worry she suggested. Just how bad did she think my "old things" were?

Too late, I noticed that she and Agatha had left before I could thank her. I imagined a scorecard somewhere, and a check mark appearing in the BAD ORPHAN column.

I walked over to the clothes, leaning down to inspect them. To say they weren't my style would be the understatement of the year. There was an assortment of cashmere sweaters and silky blouses in pale, chalky tones, and several pairs of pants in muted neutrals—gray, beige, ivory, darker gray. Under the pants were skirts in dusty tones of plum and peach. There were shoes lined neatly on the floor, loafers and sandals in various shades of brown, ranging from caramel to chocolate. On one corner of the bed, segregated from the other things, was a pile of brand-new bras and underwear, and pairs of socks still tethered together at the toes.

These were the clothes of a person who emerges from the shower smelling like roses. They were, without a doubt, Agatha's clothes. If I wore them, I would look like a shorter version of her with a bad haircut. Also less pretty. And poor. And friendless. (Actually, friendlessness was the one thing we seemed to have in common.)

I tried on one of the loafers and was surprised to find that it not only fit but also seemed like it had been made for my foot. The leather was supple and soft, and it felt more like wearing a sock than a shoe.

I examined the clothes one piece at a time, and decided in a rush that felt like an impulsive, dangerous choice that I would keep and wear it all. Who cared if it wasn't my style? No one was around to judge me. And how could I possibly reject such a generous gift?

Still, it was with great relief that I found a small pile of jeans folded under the sweaters. They were made of stretchy denim, and the cuts were slim, but not tight—far from trendy, but they would do. I pulled on a pair and chose a light pink sweater. I'd noticed that Laura kept the house cool, the air conditioners running almost constantly—an extravagance that would have scandalized my own mother.

I didn't own any makeup besides a single tinted lip balm and a tube of mascara I'd impulse-bought on a trip to the grocery store. There didn't seem to be much use for eye makeup here—I didn't want Laura to think I was trying to look glamorous or anything—but I brushed my hair and balmed my lips and put on a pair of white socks. I carefully made my bed, sitting Blue Bunny up against the pillow. Then I took a deep breath and headed out into the hall.

Feeling less overwhelmed than I had the previous day, I went slowly toward the stairs. I studied everything from the burgundy wallpaper, with its design of delicate flowers in faded tints of orange and gold, their long stems intertwined, to the opulent brass light fixtures hanging from the ceiling, with frosted glass bowls hiding the bulbs.

Hung on the walls between the doors were a number of oil paintings. They depicted people and life from at least a hundred years ago, including a portrait of a woman in a lace-collared black dress with a tiny black cap and a sheer black veil trailing down from the back of her head. Her eyes were large and soft and hazy with sorrow.

A small brass plate was affixed to the wall under the bottom left side of the frame.

THE WIDOW COPELAND—CIRCA 1884, it read.

I gazed around the somber corridor. How spooky and strange to be a child in this house.

As I reached the top of the stairs, a cheery voice shocked me out of my reverie.

"Hey! She's awake!"

John stood at the foot of the stairs, dressed in tan slacks and a green sweater. He looked better today than the day before—happier. Maybe the stress of having lured me here had worn on him, and now that the hard part was done, he'd managed to sleep it off.

"I'm sorry I missed dinner last night," he said, pausing to wait for me as I came down the steps. "Was the food all right? You don't have any allergies, do you?"

"It was great," I said. "Um . . . I'm allergic to eggplant, but that's it."

"Really? Eggplant? I've never heard of that." He smiled. "I mean, I've heard of eggplant, but not of being allergic to it."

"It helps that I hate it," I said.

"I hate it, too. Spongy, you know?" He was downright jolly. "Are you headed to breakfast? You look nice. Did you bring those clothes with you?"

"Yes—to breakfast," I said. "And no, I didn't bring them. Laura gave them to me."

"Good, good. Like I said, we're happy to provide whatever you need. Talk to Laura about it and she'll arrange everything. She's a world champion in arranging things."

"She's been very helpful," I said.

He was quiet for a moment, and when he spoke again, the carefree happiness had drained from his voice, leaving in its place a bleakness that made me realize it was all an act. All the hey-ho and good-humored compliments and small talk were part of a mask that hid something else. Something darker.

"She's a very caring woman," he said. "And her heart has been broken—more than once, I'm afraid."

And that's when I realized that my happy face had been a mask, too.

"But I don't have to lecture you about that," John said quietly. "I imagine you know all about it."

"I'LL BE RIGHT downstairs if you need me," Laura said for the eighth time. "Just open the door and— actually, I'll leave the door open. Give a yell and I'll come right up."

"I'm sure we'll be fine," I said. In spite of the dread I felt at being left alone with Agatha (John's idea, and apparently when John had an idea, we all went along with it), Laura's nervous energy was on the verge of making me laugh. What exactly did she think was going to happen? Agatha, the cause of all this anxiety, was currently sitting in her chair and staring placidly out the window. Today she wore a sage-green dress with softly ruffled cap sleeves. Her hair, so perfect it could have been a wig, fell over her shoulders in bouncing layers.

Finally, Laura had no choice but to retreat down to her office ("the morning room") and leave Agatha and me to deal with each other.

Which we did, by Agatha remaining in the chair by the window while I carefully hung and folded my new clothes in my tiny bedroom.

As I worked, I tried to reconcile Laura and John's image of Agatha with the impression she'd made on me. Was I misinterpreting the things she'd done? After all, how bad was any of it, really? Hiding from me and putting my things on the floor? Those were just little pranks. Or it was entirely possible she'd just been confused. Maybe Agatha didn't like change. Maybe she didn't even understand what was going on.

After a few minutes, I started to feel genuinely guilty for my negative assumptions. I also worried that maybe I was missing the point of this exercise, which was for us to spend time together. So I walked over to the window—slowly, so as not to startle her—and said, "Agatha, would you like to come sit with me while I put away my new clothes?"

I figured I'd let her ignore me for a respectable amount of time and then get back to work. But just as I was about to give up, she stood.

"Oh," I said. "I didn't think you were actually going to come. .Okay, hang on. I'll clear you a spot."

I hurriedly pushed some of the clothes out of the way to make room for her.

She sank onto the bed without comment, then proceeded to stare at the door.

"It was nice of your mom to give me these clothes," I said. "I guess they're yours, so . . . thank you."

No answer, obviously.

"They're not really my style, but they're, um, high quality. I mean, I don't have a style anymore. I used to—I used to be, like—well, not trendy, I just wore what I liked. I was cool, though, I had cool friends. I can say that now because I'm not cool anymore." As if *that* needed to be pointed out.

My voice trailed off as I realized that nothing I was saying seemed to be making any sort of impression, positive or negative.

I looked at her for a second and sighed. How could I have thought she was plotting against me?

Whether she answered or not, it felt wrong to be in such close quarters with someone without talking. So I babbled on.

"I can't imagine growing up in a house like this," I said. "It seems like there's so much history. My family's house was built in like 2008. It was two stories, and halfway up the stairs was a window seat with built-in bookshelves around it. I used to sit there and read. Rainy days were the best. There was a little lamp on the wall with a ceramic goose head for a shade. My mom got it at a flea market in California. She was obsessed with flea markets. There were cute things like that all over the house."

I noticed that Blue Bunny, who'd been leaning on the pillow next to her, had tumbled over and landed on his face, so I sat him up before returning to my work, folding sweaters and hanging pants.

The minutes ticked by, and Agatha's silent presence started to feel less intimidating once I came to the conclusion that she really, truly didn't care whether I was a human or a feather duster, whether I hung up clothes or danced the cha-cha, spoke to her or recited epic poetry aloud.

Blue Bunny had fallen over again, so I set him back up.

Without moving her gaze from the closet door, Agatha reached over and swatted him down.

"Hey," I said, grabbing him and holding him to my chest, my heart pounding. "Why'd you do that?"

She didn't answer.

"Because I hate bunnies, Margot," I said in a high-pitched voice. *"Bunnies are the worst."*

"Well," I said to Agatha, setting Blue Bunny up on the dresser, "he's my only friend. So you'll have to learn to like him."

She slapped him down again.

"Agatha," I snapped. "Quit it!"

Her shoulders stiffened.

"Why did you do that?" I demanded.

No answer.

"Also, why were you out of bed last night?" I asked, keeping my voice low.

Agatha's eyes meandered up to mine, and deep behind their glassy surface, I imagined that she was thinking: Why were *you*?

I felt slightly ashamed for losing my patience. I left the bunny as he was and got back to work.

After a while, Laura came in, her mood much improved now that the trial hour was over. When she asked how it had gone, I was able to give her a favorable update (not mentioning the stuffed bunny shenanigans), and she smiled approvingly. Checkmark, GOOD ORPHAN.

After she led Agatha out of the room, I sat down on the edge of the mattress, feeling suddenly exhausted, like I'd passed a huge, important exam by two measly points.

Now what? I could go down to the library. Or take a nap. It was only 10:30, which meant there were two hours until lunch. And after lunch, a whole long afternoon before dinner.

I flopped back against the pillow with Blue Bunny on my chest.

Could I really spend the next two years in this suffocating, isolated house? Trying to live up to Laura's expectations, trying not to overstep in any way that might be annoying to her or John—or, God forbid, damaging to their family's vaunted legacy?

So much of me was already numb. If I closed the curtain on the rest, what would be left? But maybe that didn't even matter. Misery was misery, right? So what if I was miserable here versus being miserable

somewhere else? At least here I could take long show-
ers. And the food was good.

Enjoy it, purred the cynical voice inside me. The
air was still and quiet, and I began to coast downhill
toward sleep. *Give up and enjoy it* . . .

"Go!" said a voice.

My eyes flicked open.

"Agatha?" I asked, my voice groggy with sleep.

Slowly, I sat up and looked around, but I knew
even before my eyes made it all the way around the
room that I was alone. That I'd been alone the whole
time. No one could have come in here, could have
opened that creaky door while I was—

I froze.

On the wall behind the door in streaky, handwritten black letters was a single word:

GO

I climbed off the bed and approached the wall,
thinking that I must be seeing things, that this
was a trick of light and shadow and my exhausted
imagination.

But no. When I touched it, my fingertip came
away black. I stared, dumbfounded, wondering who
could have done such a thing.

I mean, there was only one explanation, right?

Agatha must have sneaked in here after I'd fallen asleep.

The weird thing was . . . I didn't really think I *had* fallen asleep.

It didn't make sense. Just say she did get through the loud door and move in utter silence across the squawking floorboards while I dozed. There would still have been *some* noise. The sound of a bottle opening? The swish of a brush?

One thing was clear, at least: the meaning of the word *GO*. I didn't need that spelled out for me.

There was a knock at the door, and without stopping to think, I leaned against it with all my weight, holding it shut.

"Yes?" I said, trying to disguise the tension in my voice.

"Hello, Margot." Laura's voice was softly insistent. "Could you please open the door for me?"

I froze. *Why, no, in fact, I cannot.*

"Margot?" she repeated.

I opened the door. What would she say? Would I have a chance to explain, or would the sight so enrage her that she would immediately send me away? Would she think I had done it?

Laura stepped into the room. She turned to the right. A half step more and she would see the word. But then her eyes flashed back to mine.

"Looks nice," she said. "You're very tidy."

I froze, too distracted to form a sensible sentence.

Laura seemed almost embarrassed. "I was wondering . . . would you like to see the garden?"

"Okay," I said hurriedly. Anything to get her to leave.

"Great," she said. "Come on down. Agatha's downstairs in my office. John will keep an eye on her."

But—if Agatha was downstairs, how had she managed to write on my wall?

Laura ducked out for a moment and returned with a bundle of clothing in her hand. "I brought you some things to wear. Gardening clothes. I hope that's not presumptuous."

She could have reached over and pinched my cheeks and I would have been too surprised to consider it presumptuous. I accepted the stack of clothes and agreed to meet Laura downstairs in ten minutes.

After she left, I closed the door and slowly turned back to the mess on the wall. The mess that Agatha hadn't made.

But if it hadn't been her, then who . . . ?

GO

My chest felt tight, on the verge of panic. I had to clean the wall before anyone saw, but what could I use? When I tried some toilet paper, it came away in sticky shreds. Finally, I opened the top dresser drawer and stared down at my HOTTER THAN HO shirt. In spite of how much I hated it, I was still reluctant to ruin it. But I had no other options, so I wet it in the bathroom sink and then scrubbed away at the writing.

It took a couple of minutes, but it worked.

When I went to rinse the black substance off the shirt, it stayed put. So after a few seconds of trying to make sense of the simmering swamp of emotions it conjured, I balled up the shirt and threw it away.

Not like I had any use for it here, anyway, right?

CHAPTER
～9～

I PUT ON Laura's gardening "things," which consisted of army-green pants made out of some parachute-like material, a tan T-shirt, and a white apron with approximately four hundred pockets. In the hallway downstairs, she met me with a pair of rubber clogs and a straw hat that made me feel like someone's grandmother.

I was kind of excited to see the garden, though I'd never gardened in my life—we always had a yard service that came once a week to mow, rake, and weed. Maybe it was just the idea of getting out of the house.

From the back door, we went through a gate in a high stone wall and followed a narrow path between two colossal rows of shrubbery. Where the shrubs ended, a pair of wrought-iron benches faced each other, with a mirrored sphere the size of a bowling ball on a stand in the center of the path.

"Here we are," Laura said, stopping just past the benches.

Like I said, gardening was never my thing. If I spent time outside, it was playing tennis or lounging in the sun, blithely ignoring my mother's dire warnings about skin cancer. I had no interest in getting my hands dirty and no use for a place that required so much labor to make it beautiful or interesting. I'd never seen a garden that intrigued me in any way.

But this . . . this was different.

It was huge, explosive with color and the scent of fragrant flowers, and the path wound away through a cluster of topiaries in the shapes of animals, like a secret walkway into another world. I wandered through arbors draped with delicate vines and down short straightaways lined with grasses that bent over into my path and brushed against my green pants. Every so often, a rosebush was placed like an elegant chaperone to the rest of the sprawling madness, and the roses were in full bloom, in shades ranging from pearlescent white to a red so velvety and deep it didn't seem like my eyes were processing the whole color.

"Do you like it?" Laura asked, a few feet behind me.

I nodded, still looking ahead. A sprawling plant with enormous leaves draped over a huge area of ground, and under the leaves I saw the pale green baby pumpkins, each one tiny and perfect. Beyond those were three long rows of pepper plants in flawlessly straight lines.

"The women in my family have always cared for the garden," she said. "Every fall, we carry what we can into the greenhouse, and every spring we bring it all back out—well, most of it. Sometimes I don't get to everything. You wouldn't believe my collection of old bulbs! Of course, some species can't be transplanted, but most of it will survive. And some of them are tough enough to face the winter without help."

"It must cost a fortune," I said, and then I blushed and looked away, hoping she hadn't heard.

"Oh, it does, I suppose." She didn't sound bothered—by either my question or the idea of spending tons of money. "But it's tradition."

I walked past a small colony of tomato plants in their little round cages and reached an empty area, two long planters' worth of plain dirt. At the end of the rows was a stock of pots, empty buckets, stacks of bricks, and bags of soil and fertilizer.

"Oh, that's just storage," Laura said.

But beyond those, where the walkway curved, there was a gate made of ironwork in the shape of a man and woman, fig leaves tastefully placed, an apple in the woman's hand and a snake wrapped around her ankle.

I walked closer, inspecting the craftsmanship. It was handmade, and you could still see the marks of hammers on the iron pieces.

"My great-grandmother designed that herself," Laura said, unable to hide a note of pride in her voice.

"It's amazing," I said, because there never was a safer adjective than *amazing*.

"She was intensely preoccupied with the fall of man," Laura said, as if that were a normal hobby, like, *She loved to knit.*

"What's behind it?" I asked. All I could see through the small holes in the gate was a wall of leaves, some kind of overgrown bush.

"Oh, nothing," Laura said. "The edge of the property."

I stared at it for a while. What a shame that something as incredible as that gate should be surrounded by bare dirt and chipped flowerpots.

"Nothing grows back here," Laura said, as if anticipating my question.

"That's too bad," I said.

She shrugged. "Well, they *were* expelled from the garden."

I looked over at her, impressed that she had made a little joke, expecting to see a wry smile on her face. But she looked serious and—maybe I was imagining it—a little contemptuous.

Sensing my eyes on her, she snapped back to serenity. "If you turn left, you'll find the exotic tropical flowers . . . the showgirls of the place."

I did turn left, and was happy to find a jungle of vividly colored flowers in all shapes and sizes.

Laura eventually left me to explore on my own, and when I found her again, she was kneeling on a foam pad in front of a bed of fluffy yellow-orange flowers on short stems, surrounded by delicate leaves.

"I'm weeding the marigolds." She held up a scraggly plant with its roots exposed, like a hunter showing off a dead animal. "Would you like to help?"

She produced a second foam pad and a pair of purple gloves, and I knelt next to her.

"Marigolds are hardy little helpers," she said. "They're not flashy, but they deter bugs. That's why we plant them around the tomatoes. I'm rather fond of them—they don't ask anything of you, they just bloom and stand guard. Anything else you find here is a weed."

"Like this?" I pointed to a flat plant that was a spreading web of oval leaves.

"Yes. That's purslane. Grab it around the stem, right next to the ground, and pull."

I did, but instead of pulling the roots out, I only managed to rip off the leafy top.

Laura handed me a small shovel. "If that happens, you dig out the roots."

After the whole weed had been removed, Laura and I worked in silence, moving in opposite directions. I lost myself in the work—so simple, so methodical. It was a relief to do something that made sense, for a change. Something that wasn't colored with eight kinds of nuance and ways I could mess up or say the wrong thing. *Kill bad plant.* Easy enough, right?

And it was nice to be out in the light of day, where things were open and uncomplicated. The strange events of the past twenty-four hours were beginning to form a heavy ball of worry in my chest. The shock of Agatha's existence, her immediate dislike of me (and of poor Blue Bunny), the technological isolation, Laura's breakdown, my nosebleed, the mystery of Lily's strange notations (whoever Lily was), the missing hours of my life, the wardrobe that made me feel like I was pretending to be somebody I'd never met before, the writing on my wall . . .

Alone, any one of these things might have seemed like a little blip, a minor hiccup in my quest for peace and happiness.

But together? One after another? It was kind of a lot.

It just made me feel, in the pit of my stomach, that there was something about this place that was unwelcoming. That didn't want me here. (Gee, Margot, was it the word *GO* graffitied on your wall, maybe? No, not just that. And not even as small as that.)

This isn't right, I thought. *I shouldn't be here.*

This time, no disembodied voice answered me. But that didn't make me feel any better.

For the moment, out in the fresh air with the sun warming my back, I could still kill bad plants.

After a while, Laura wiped her brow with her sweaty arm, leaving a streak of dirt across her face. Her cheeks were pink, and her eyes were serene. Somehow her whole energy was calm, and it made me realize how tense she had been at every other point since my arrival.

"We should get inside," she said. "You can shower off before lunch and spend the afternoon relaxing instead of working. John will be appalled that I have you out here doing manual labor."

The idea of being cooped up again sounded horrible, but it wasn't like I could insist on staying outside by myself.

I helped Laura pack up the gardening tools and carry them over to a little shed tucked under the branches of two huge, gnarled trees. Sharing the shade with the workbench were a pair of small wicker chairs and a little side table.

"Does Agatha come out here with you?" I asked.

Laura shook her head. "I tried for a while, but she got too restless. It might be sensory overload, you know—the scents and colors, the way the light's always changing. She does much better inside. It works out fine, since it gives her a chance to do her schoolwork."

Ah, yes. Agatha's "schoolwork." A misleading term for Agatha sitting at the small writing desk in the nursery, a blank notebook in front of her and the audio version of a textbook droning on as she ignored it and looked out her favorite window.

"Barrett helps me, sometimes—when he's home. But he's no good with the details; he's more of a pack mule. Once I asked him to weed the herbs, and he killed every last one of my chives." She shook her head. "He's all boy . . . you'll see when he gets back from Europe."

I was intrigued by the mention of Barrett. Aside from his photo and the fact that his bedroom was the door past the nursery, I knew nothing about him. Weirdly, as Laura talked about him, I felt a pinch of envy. And I found myself pondering his homecoming and hoping that, when he finally got here, he'd stay out of the garden.

This can be our thing, I thought. *Mine and Laura's.*

"Well, I love it out here," I said. "It's beautiful."

My reward was a genuine smile. "I come out here every day," Laura said. "It's so grounding to connect with the earth."

"Literally," I said.

"Oh, another joke!" Laura said, beaming. Then her expression turned shy and searching. "Margot, you're welcome to join me anytime."

I knew I should play it cool—thank her and then make some excuse to decline the offer. Nobody likes a needy orphan.

But then she rested her hand so gently on my arm. "Don't say no," she said. "I don't need an answer—it's an open invitation."

CHAPTER
~10~

MOM ALWAYS SAID a person can get used to anything, and I never thought about whether that was true until the days at Copeland Hall began to grind by. Time seemed to slow inside the great gray house. The hours between meals were long, barren stretches with little to do. The Suttons had no televisions—at least none purchased during the current century—and the Wi-Fi password was lost somewhere in John's home office, which (from what I could see as I passed by the open door) was an endless sea of papers. Laura promised to call "the internet people" and get it for me, but I didn't have a lot of hope that would happen anytime soon.

As much as my brain itched to log on and scroll through the perfect lives of strangers, I had to admit that it was, in a way, a relief not to. Since the accident, I'd learned that the number of posts where

people casually mentioned families/sisters/mothers/
fathers was high enough to make me feel like I was
having holes poked in me constantly. Going a couple
of weeks without having to read about how someone's
dad is the BEST DAD EVER because he had fixed their
sagging bookshelves would probably be good for me.

So instead, I braved the library, and found that it
was pretty easy to tell which books were the priceless
first editions (steer clear) and which ones could be
held and read without fear. There were novels, cook-
books, gardening books . . . nothing remotely current,
but they passed the time.

After a week, I felt almost at home. Agatha and
I had achieved a wordless truce—at least, I assumed
we had, since she hadn't messed with me since that
second day. Instead, she seemed to think of me as
another piece of furniture that had, for some reason
she didn't care about, been dragged into the nursery.

At first, I'd thought she was basically a zombie.
But it didn't take long to figure out that Agatha, while
being completely different from whoever her old self
had been, still had a shadow of a personality. She had
likes—the window, orange juice, listening to music on
my phone, even though the tiny speaker was terrible.
She also had dislikes—blueberries, stuffed animals,
and the way her mother clapped to get her attention.
She was calm in the mornings and anxious at night.

She always looked up when her father came into the room, and she enjoyed shoving things off the table near her chair by the window (as I learned when I set a completely full glass of water there for her on the third day and spent the next hour sweeping up shards).

Was this a glimpse of her old personality or something completely new? I had no clue. But she definitely wasn't the ghostly blank slate I had initially taken her for.

One day, while Agatha sat in her chair and I read on the extra bed—"quality time"—I happened to glance up and see a bird land on the windowsill.

"Look," I said, setting my book down. "A bird."

The bird was scratching in the accumulated dust, and it didn't notice as I came over and stood next to Agatha.

Maybe this was what she was waiting for, every day, for hours on end. A little peek at wildlife.

"See the bird?" I asked, bending down next to her. "Is that what you do when you're sitting here, Agatha? Look at the birds?" Ideas began forming: maybe I could talk to Laura about installing a bird feeder, or one of those birdhouses that has a suction cup so it sticks directly onto the window.

Then I looked at her eyes, and saw that the bird hadn't even drawn her notice.

"So what is it, then?" I asked. "What's out there that you like so much?"

Her eyes didn't move, but to my infinite surprise, her lips did. They parted, and she made a soft sound—"*Kah.*"

"What?" I asked, trying to stay calm. I didn't want to spook her, but I was desperately eager to know what she was trying to say. This could be huge.

"*Kah,*" she said, in one short puff. And then, apparently exhausted by the effort, she closed her eyes.

I was thrilled by this development, but when I mentioned it to Laura that afternoon, she waved it off. After seeing my disappointed reaction, she softened.

"I'm sorry," she said. "I can see that it means a lot to you, and that says a lot about who you are as a person, Margot. But the truth is that Agatha's random utterances mean no more than a baby's babbling."

"But it seemed like she was really trying to make this specific sound," I said. "Maybe she was trying to speak."

And then there was the faintest change in Laura's energy. "I doubt it," she said flatly.

That was my signal to drop the subject, so I did. Later, turning it over in my mind, I wondered if I had somehow offended Laura. Was she jealous? From what I'd seen, Agatha didn't say anything at all to her mother.

So I decided to stay quiet about it. No point making Laura dislike me.

And anyway, it never came to anything. From time to time, I would ask Agatha what she was thinking about. And the answer, when she deigned to give one, was always the same: *Kah.*

I DEVELOPED A routine—or maybe it developed around me. Every day after breakfast, I put on my gardening clothes, helped settle Agatha in for her schoolwork—which meant turning to the next blank page in her notebook and writing the date and subject at the top—and then went down to work in the garden with Laura. I'd graduated from basic weeding to pruning dead leaves, checking and repairing the tiny rubber irrigation hoses, and removing bugs from the tomatoes.

One day, as we worked in silence plucking pests and clearing dead leaves out of the pumpkin patch—for which we wore long sleeves and thick gloves, because it turns out every part of a pumpkin plant wants to scratch the bejeezus out of you—I looked up at Copeland Hall looming over us, its imposing wings extending in opposite directions.

"This house is amazing," I said. "Did your family build it?"

It had taken me two weeks to summon the nerve to bring it up, because I was afraid any questions I asked would make it sound like I was asking how much everything was worth. The last thing I wanted was for the Suttons to think I cared about how much money they had. I did wonder a little, but not in a greedy way. Besides, it wasn't like knowing how rich they were was a comfort. The priceless antiques and oil paintings only reminded me on a daily basis that I was a penniless orphan.

"Yes," she said, in an almost reverent tone. "My grandfather's great-grandfather, Jerahmeel Copeland, built it for his family. He started the Eastern Central Railroad—it was one of the first to cross the Mississippi. He was a very powerful man—by the time he died, he owned buildings all over Chicago, New York, and San Francisco, as well as vast networks of train lines. Apparently he was scrupulously honest and a real stickler for the rules. Not a very fun guy to be around, according to family legends . . . but he sure knew how to build things."

"Is everything inside original?" I asked.

"Oh, no," she said. "The house was built in 1858. Most of it was remodeled and modernized in the 1930s, and since then we've just replaced some upholstery and dealt with maintenance issues as they arise . . ."

"Have you lived here your whole life?" I asked.

She leaned back. "I moved away for college, which is where I met John. We got married and he went to law school in Chicago, so we had a place in the city. But things are so busy out there. The world just spins and spins, and we wanted to be a little more still. I always knew I'd come back, and then my father died—my mother had been dead since I was two—so we packed up and came home. Then Agatha came along, and Barrett was a surprise, only a year later." She smiled sadly. "People say children keep you young, but lately I feel . . ." She shook her head. "It's a lot of pressure. Emotional pressure. I feel like I have to carry on the family legacy all by myself."

"So you're an only child?" I asked.

Her eyes locked on mine. There was a heavy, sad pause. "Yes," she said, but there was an unspoken story behind her answer.

Something landed on my heart with a gentle *thud*. Maybe Laura understood me better than I thought. "Me too," I said. "Well, now I am."

Her eyes were like tinted glass, her sadness a dark hole behind them. "Yes," she said softly. "I know."

We went back to pulling bugs off the twisting vines and dropping them into a bucket of soapy water.

"I was supposed to be a boy," she said, almost an afterthought. "I'm the first woman to inherit the house. My father's mother wept at my wedding when she realized there wouldn't be a Copeland in Copeland Hall anymore."

"She really cried? At your wedding?"

Laura smiled wryly. "Actually, she *sobbed*. Grandmother Copeland had a flair for the dramatic."

"Could you have just kept your last name?"

She laughed merrily. *Another joke, how delightful!* I could practically hear her saying. "Oh no," she said. "That kind of thing isn't done in my family. Anyway, it's okay. 'The Suttons of Copeland Hall' sounds perfectly fine to me."

My first thought was, *You* are *your family, can't you do what you want?*

But then I decided to hold my tongue. Who was I to say that if I was faced with a decision, knowing my parents would want me to do something a certain way, that I wouldn't do it their way? In fact, I probably would. Look at how committed I was to my tooth-brushing routine.

"So when my first child was a girl—Agatha—I was a little sad, but then I thought . . . what matters isn't the name, is it? It's a person's substance."

"So Agatha's the one who's going to be in charge someday?" I asked.

I had assumed from the flow of the conversation that Laura was comfortable with the direction it had taken. But now she clammed up.

"I—I had hoped," she said, her tone cooling. "But . . . I don't know. It's not worth discussing."

Mortified, I doubled my focus on our work. I picked up an earwig (a gross little bug with pincers coming out of its face) and tossed it into the water. Then I made a critical mistake—I looked into the bucket.

The earwig struggled in the soapy water, its tiny body flailing as it disappeared out of sight. Laura had told me that the soap killed them quickly . . . but this didn't look quick.

Nausea rocked my body like a shock wave.

"Margot?" Laura asked.

I scooted frantically away from the bucket, away from the dozens of innocent beings I'd heartlessly sent to dark, watery deaths. Somehow I'd failed to make the connection earlier, but now all I could think of was my whole family dying the same way.

"Margot," Laura said, a little worried. "You're flushed."

I couldn't answer. If I opened my mouth, I would throw up all over the pumpkins. Instead, I got to my feet and backed even farther away.

"Is something wrong?" she asked. "Is it too hot for you, or—"

She glanced in the bucket and the realization dawned on her.

"Oh," she said. "Oh, dear."

I heard movement behind me, and then I heard her walking away, and the splash of water as she dumped the bucket somewhere. Then she came back and stood behind me. I didn't move. I was a statue made of shattered glass.

"Margot," she said. "I'm here."

I didn't answer. I was afraid to move for fear I'd fall apart. I didn't want to cry. Not here, in the daylight, in the bright, exposed space of the garden.

Laura hesitated, as if she had more to say. Then, finally, she put her hand on my back. "The hard things are always going to be right there," she said. "Your mind is always going to be looking for reasons to bring them to the surface. Sometimes you can forget them for a little while, but at the strangest times, you'll see something—or hear a song, or . . ."

She trailed off, and I expected her to bounce back with some bland greeting-card saying, like, *But you have to look on the bright side and focus on the things going right for you!*

Only she didn't. She just left her words hanging in the air, left me with the sense that she, too, knew a little bit about the kind of loss that ripped your heart out, tied it in a knot, and then shoved it back inside your chest.

She patted me on the shoulder and walked away

to clean the tools, and after a minute or two, I went and joined her.

But she didn't try to talk any more about it, not then and not later, especially not in front of John.

The days plodded on peacefully, except for the awareness hanging over me at all times that my family had died terrible, agonizing deaths and for some reason I had not, and I was just going to have to suck it up and deal.

But hey, you have to look on the bright side and focus on the things going right for you, yes?

All in all, I was adjusting to being a resident of Copeland Hall. John seemed to come and go according to some secret lawyer schedule, but when he was home, he was friendly and courteous. I liked Laura a lot—she was almost like a friend, but with a reassuring air of authoritative momness. Her mysterious dark moments appealed to me and made me feel less alone.

And Agatha—we were getting used to each other. She still knocked Blue Bunny flat on his face every chance she got, but that wasn't going to scare me away.

Even the clothes were all right. They fit so well that nobody ever mentioned buying me something else, and that was okay. You moved differently in the structured, formal styles. You didn't flop over on the furniture; you sat up straight. It changed the way you walked, stood, and spoke. My table manners magically improved, and my hair was always brushed. What's more, it changed my thoughts and emotions. Everything seemed steadier, more manageable. Like the new persona was a suit of armor holding me together.

In a small way, I was becoming almost like one of them—not *quite* a Sutton, but no longer an alien presence in the house.

Was it amazing to be the servant-orphan of the exalted Sutton family of Copeland Hall? No. But was it as bad as being the end-of-the-hall freak of Palmer House? Or being committed to the state institution? No. If I couldn't have my old life, I would make this one work.

And something about the place—the routine, the silence, the solemn sense of history—calmed me in an unexpected way: I hadn't had a nightmare since I moved in. Not a single one.

CHAPTER
~11~

AFTER LUNCH ONE rainy Friday, Laura came to the door of my room. I was trying very hard to make myself enjoy *Tess of the d'Urbervilles*, but my eyes kept slipping shut.

"Margot, are you awake?" Laura asked, and I put the book aside and sat up. "Today is Agatha's appointment with Dr. Reed."

A mild flash of panic hit me: She was going to try to take me to the doctor, too. My potential "issues" seemed always to be on the periphery of her thoughts. Not a day went by when she didn't ask how I was doing, and the question always carried the lightest suggestion that she suspected the answer would be bad news. Maybe that was the natural consequence of having a daughter with a random, serious illness. But I still found it slightly aggravating.

I don't want to see a doctor, I whined in my head. I

was fine, really, and I kept telling her that. She just didn't seem willing to let it go.

Then she went on, frowning a little. "I would invite you, but I'm afraid today isn't a good day for it. Agatha seems a bit irritable. Also, I think you'd be bored. You might as well be comfortable here rather than sitting in a waiting room."

Oh. So it wasn't about me. In which case, the whiny voice in my head began to complain about being left behind. After being confined to the house and garden for a few solid weeks, a trip to town sounded as exciting as a mission to the moon. Even at Palmer House we got to take trips to the mall or the grocery store.

I tried not to let my displeasure show. Then, since we were already having an uncomfortable conversation, I took a chance. "Any news on the Wi-Fi password?"

She paused, and I prepared myself for yet another apology and overly detailed explanation for how it had slipped her mind because she had been negotiating with the roofers all morning, or she wasn't really sure who to call because John's office was full of paperwork that needed to be dealt with, and so on and so on. I believed her—I knew how busy she was—and I tried not to resent the fact that she had more going on in her life than just looking after me. But I *did* really want internet access. At least if I went into town with them, I could get a signal on my phone. I would happily sit in the car if it meant spending a few minutes reading about the world (and, let's be real, celebrity gossip).

"John and I had a talk about this last night. I was going to bring it up in the garden earlier, but we didn't really get a chance." She glanced away, leaving an unspoken criticism hanging in the air: my weepy episode while trimming back the lavender that morning must have sidetracked her plans. "Margot . . . we don't believe in giving children unlimited access to the internet."

"Oh, I don't need unlimited access," I said.

I guess she'd expected resistance, and my spontaneous answer caught her off guard. She pursed her lips. "I mean . . . unsupervised access."

"So I get *no* access?" I cringed at the bratty sound of my voice. *Bad orphan.*

"No, no," she said. "We just don't want you to be glued to a phone or computer all the time. Numbing your synapses with electronic stimuli is just about the worst thing that can happen in terms of your mental, emotional, and intellectual maturation. You're young, and your brain is still in a crucial developmental stage."

Even though she hadn't said it, I got the feeling she meant *my* defective brain in particular. I felt too stung to answer. Embarrassed, even. For weeks, I'd believed her when she said she was trying to find the password. And all that time, she'd been bluffing. Probably relieved that I was too dumb to question her.

"Do you actually have the internet at all?" I braced myself for a lie. I'd seen the little Wi-Fi signal on my phone—I just couldn't access it.

She cocked her head slightly. "Of course we do. There's a computer in John's office and one in mine. You can use those, if a need arises—like for school."

"But how—" I stopped myself. I'd been about to ask, *How do I get in touch with my friends if I can't even text?* Then I remembered I didn't have any friends. And living here, I had no way to make new ones.

Laura, looking quite apologetic, leaned against the doorjamb. "I'm fully aware that we aren't like most families. We're living in a bit of a bubble, out here on our own. But it's a very peaceful life. And with the books, and the garden, and all the history here . . . it's a *good* life."

Maybe there was some shadow of skepticism on my face, because her smile grew firmer, more determined to convince me.

"You'll see. All the things you think we don't have . . . it's noise. Before long, you'll understand."

I suddenly felt self-conscious under her gaze, as if she was seeing more than I wanted to show her. I turned my face away. I felt angry, but I didn't want to be angry at Laura.

"Margot, the world wants you to grab for every shiny object. But sometimes all you really need is time and space to be yourself." Then she reached down and gently smoothed my hair, the way she did with Agatha. "So what I'd like you to do is stop asking about getting online. Our answer is no, and it will always be no."

Her voice was so silky and calm that it took a moment for the impact to land. And then I felt like I'd been slapped. Scolded like a child, for what—asking to have a minor connection with the world outside of Copeland Hall? Was that a crime?

If she could tell I was seething, she didn't let on. "You may not know who you are anymore, but we see the real you. And we want to help you find yourself again. Because we like you, Margot. We like you a lot."

She slipped away before I could answer, and then I sat there reeling from about eight hundred different emotions—shock, sadness, anger, humiliation, and also a splinter of resentment against myself— resentment for being angry at Laura, when part of me thought she might be right. And hoped she was. Might I find myself again? If I was quiet enough, if life moved slowly enough, could the real me emerge from the silence?

Still, even if that were true . . . she'd been lying to me. I hated the word, and I tried to keep myself from thinking it, but I couldn't suppress it because it was so obviously true. She'd lied to me in a strange, controlling way, when it would have been easy to tell me the truth.

But that was just Laura, I thought in her defense. She was a strange and controlling person.

Yes, she was, wasn't she? She was old-fashioned, inflexible, moralistic, and demanding. And none of that had been an issue yet, because I was so eager to win her approval. The question that scared me a little was, what would she do when I finally felt at home enough to defy her? Surely that would happen one day.

How would she react? Would she send me away? Or, by the time it happened, would I be so entrenched in life here that there would be no fallout? I'd seen her annoyed at Agatha, but she never punished her. You couldn't punish someone who was so sick that she had no idea what she was even doing most of the time. And maybe you couldn't punish an orphan, either.

Barrett would be home soon, and then I could observe up close the way a normal teenager acted around Laura.

If he even *was* normal. Laura loved to go on and on

about his achievements at school: star of the lacrosse team, student government VP, honor roll . . . and how he had dated two different state senators' daughters last year, when he was only in tenth grade. I'd heard enough about the extraordinary Barrett Sutton to make me wish he would stay away for the rest of the summer.

AS DISAPPOINTED AS I was about being left behind, it was surreally relaxing to have some time by myself. On the other hand, the pressure to make good use of these few, precious hours was immense, and almost paralyzing. Should I go search the pantry for junk food? Should I fire up one of the ancient TV sets and see if it got any trashy daytime TV?

Or . . . should I see what else I could find out about Lily?

No, Margot. Don't you dare.

Right. Obviously that was a terrible idea. If Laura wanted people wandering the green wing, she wouldn't have locked the door.

Without a clear idea of where I was going, I left the nursery.

I let my hand rest on the banister, and as I did, I wondered how many people before me had touched the gleaming polished surface as they went up or down these stairs. How many of them had been important or famous? How many of them had secrets? How many had tragedies in their pasts—or futures? How many lived to be a hundred? How many died young?

An unpleasant tingle spiraled down my spine as I imagined the stairs crowded with the ghosts of all those people. Because if there *were* such things as ghosts, wasn't this where they would be—stuck in the space between spaces?

No. That was foolish. Even if I believed in ghosts, which I didn't, the last ones I'd be concerned with were rich strangers.

I imagined my own family, waiting in the shadows of the foyer, their skin the color of molding bread, puffy and moist. The image was so vivid that I could almost smell the scent of stale canal water wafting up toward me.

I stopped halfway down to catch my breath and reassure myself that this was just my crazy imagination. Obviously my family was not waiting for me in the foyer.

But what if they were?

I turned and went back upstairs.

As my eyes swept across the deserted hallway (because now I was paranoid), I saw something I hadn't noticed before: the second door on the right stood slightly open.

Agatha's real bedroom, where she lived before she became ill.

I walked toward the door, thinking I would close it. That was all—just close it.

Except I didn't close it, did I?

I went in.

A FEW STEPS past the door, I had to stop and stare. It was as if two galaxies had smashed together—Copeland Hall's stately, historical style, and a teenage girl's bedroom from a movie about how messy teenage girls are.

Its fundamentals weren't very different from the rest of the house: It was spacious, with high ceilings and tall windows. The floor was carpeted in plush pink, a shade too close to magenta to feel current, and the bed was a four-poster with a canopy of stiff, shiny fabric decorated with multicolored flowers. It exactly matched the skirt around the base of the bed and the drapes that hung grandly over the windows. There was also a matching armchair in the corner. The furniture was white wood, with little carvings tucked into the corners and crannies. The walls had lemon-yellow wallpaper in alternating lines of shiny and matte finish. And in the corner was an elaborate white vanity with a round stool that had a fluffy pink fur cushion.

It was a room built for a princess.

But no princess lived here—it looked more like the lair of a sloppy troll. Strewn, scattered, hung, and draped on all of its refined, feminine surfaces were clothes, bags, shoes, books, stuffed animals, papers, magazines, and even empty water bottles (the expensive glass kind, I couldn't help noticing).

I walked over to the vanity. There were so many photos tucked into its frame that half the mirror was blocked. I carefully pulled one out and inspected it.

Even though I'd expected to see her face, I drew in a sharp breath.

Agatha.

She was nearly unrecognizable. Even in a still image, her spirit and life shone through. It was a photograph of her and a friend standing on the deck of what must have been a very nice boat. Agatha wore a red bikini with little bows on each hip. As a cover-up, she wore a loose white button-down shirt with the sleeves rolled up. Her feet were bare, her toenails painted to match her bikini. Her hair, in a thick braid, lay casually over her shoulder like an accommodating pet snake, and under a smattering of freckles on her nose and cheeks and berry-colored lips, her face was perfectly tanned.

She had one arm lazily slung over the shoulder of the girl next to her, who might as well have been wearing an invisibility cloak. No one could have taken the spotlight off Agatha. She was too pretty, too vivacious, too exciting. Too effortlessly cool and fun.

A sick, heavy feeling filled my stomach as I slid the photo back into its spot. Then I looked at the pictures surrounding it—Agatha laughing in front of a giraffe at the zoo, Agatha staring into the distance with the Chicago skyline behind her, Agatha in a floaty white dress standing before an ivy-covered brick wall, Agatha and two other girls sitting in the bleachers of a stadium, bundled up in warm clothes with coffee cups in their gloved hands. The other people in the photos wore clothes as nice as hers, and their hairstyles and makeup were just as expert and expensive looking, but they all faded in comparison to the shining brilliance of Agatha's beauty. She was like an angel surrounded by mere mortals.

No way could I compete with her, I thought, not pausing to figure out in what way I thought she and I were competing.

I stuck the picture back in its spot, then took a slow lap around the room, pausing to touch the delicate, silky shirts that were thrown on the armchair or the floor, crumpled piles of shiny black fabric that must have been hundred-dollar yoga pants or sports bras. What struck me the most was that none of these clothes, or the ones in the photos, were at all similar to the staid, conservative style of clothing she wore now. The clothing *I* wore now.

It seemed almost like this room contained the real Agatha, her life essence, while the girl who sat by the window in the nursery was just the shell that had once held her.

Why hadn't they let her stay in here?

And why hadn't they straightened up?

The floral bedspread was bunched up on the bed, pushed to one side. The exposed sheets were rumpled, and the pillow was still askew. On the nightstand were a water glass from which the water had evaporated, leaving a light film on the inside surface; a disconnected phone charger; and a book left open on its flattened pages—*The Scarlet Letter*. Above it, on a small shelf, the line of stuffed animals had all fallen over.

I knew I should leave. I had a suspicion—more than that, really—that if Laura found me in this forbidden, forgotten room, it might fracture however much of her trust I'd managed to earn. But I wasn't that worried. I could see the front driveway and I'd have plenty of time to get out if they came back.

And I had to admit that I was starved for a glimpse of real life. I wanted to be reminded, for a moment, of what it had been like before my world imploded.

I saw a door on the far side of the room that had a hook on it, a hook that overflowed with purses in various sizes, and my brain pricked up like a dog's ears.

Her closet.

I just wanted to *peek*.

When I stepped through the door, a little sigh floated up out of me like a helium balloon. What a closet. It was about the size of my old bedroom, and the walls were lined with racks full of skirts, dresses, shirts, jeans, sweaters, and coats. The floor underneath the racks was stacked high with shoeboxes, each with a Polaroid picture on the front showing the shoes inside. Like the rest of the bedroom, it was a disaster—clothes tossed everywhere. My mom would have had a conniption fit if I'd treated my clothes like this, and that's not even taking into account how much all of it probably cost. I couldn't stop myself from picking up the most expensive-looking items and draping them over the tufted ottoman in the center of the room. There was some indescribable quality about the fabric, the stitching, the sleeves, and the hemlines that telegraphed how costly it all was.

Without meaning to, I moved to the nearest shelf, which was piled high with hats in countless materials and colors. My fingers grabbed a white straw fedora with a black velvet band, and I slipped it on my head. Then I picked up a pair of sunglasses—vintage Ray-Bans, by the look of them—and put those on.

I stared at myself in the mirror. My hair, in its choppy short layers that I hated (thank you, emergency room haircut), actually looked almost cute sticking out from under the hat's narrow brim. For a second, I pictured myself in one of those photos with Agatha, along with the other well-dressed, perfectly made-up girls.

Oh, right, Margot. Totally. That's what Agatha would do if she woke up—invite you on vacation.

I glanced at my reflection and felt ridiculous. My hands were like lead weights as I replaced the hat and sunglasses.

Then I wandered back out to the vanity. The boat picture had fallen out of its position, so I wedged it into place.

I looked over the surface of the desk and saw a spiral-bound notebook, like a journal, monogrammed with a silver-foiled *A* on the front cover.

Every muscle in my body resisted as I reached toward it. This was none of my business. This had nothing to do with me. It was a horrible violation of Agatha's privacy . . .

But I flipped it open anyway.

What I saw made me shrink back.

There was a lot of writing on the page—it was almost covered. But the penmanship was scrawling, unsteady. Words were randomly capitalized and repeated. It was the work of a person not in their right mind.

And the words on the page:

The Moral Sense of the world world world
is Reflected in the Individual SOUL, and Only
with the greatest CARE can we avoid avoid
the Descent into the DARKEST and Most Vile
tendencies of human Nature.

I slapped it shut and dropped it back onto the desk
like it was on fire.

Those were *Lily's* bizarre ramblings. But this was
Agatha's notebook.

Had she done this? Judging by the shakiness of the
script, it must have taken her hours. As for the content,
it was so creepy. Why would a person my age even
think things like that, let alone write them down?

After catching my breath, I flipped the cover open
and then fanned through the pages. Even though I'd
known what I would find, it was still awful. Page after
page was covered in the chaotic scribblings—sometimes
the same lines over and over, sometimes whole pages of
long paragraphs in her increasingly erratic handwriting.

I was contemplating this when, to my utter horror,
I heard voices in the hall.

Were they back already? I'd been so busy snooping
that I hadn't kept an eye on the driveway. How could
I have been so stupid?

Had I lost time again, been caught dazed and
unaware like that first night?

I listened, my body electrified by fear.

Only when I imagined Laura finding me in here did the magnitude of my judgment error really sink in.

But a second later, I relaxed—slightly. That wasn't Laura's voice or John's.

It was a young man. And the other person in the conversation was Mr. Albright—I was almost positive, based on the clipped, formal phrasing of his responses.

I edged closer to the door and pressed against the wall so I'd be blocked from view if they looked inside.

"Andy ran out of money in Sardinia, and his father wouldn't wire him more, so we changed our flights and left early. You know how the Bensons are," the young man said, sounding slightly disapproving.

This had to be Barrett. We'd been expecting him over the weekend, but until I stood there eavesdropping, it hadn't truly sunk in for me that there was going to be another person in the house with us. And not just a person—Mr. Albright was a person. But someone my age. A *boy*.

And now he was home early. This was bad. I wasn't prepared. Everything I'd come to know was about to be disrupted. I felt shaky and sweaty and anxious.

"I'm not surprised," Mr. Albright said. "I've heard some troubling rumors about the state of their finances. I wouldn't expect to spend any more time on that yacht."

"Too bad," Barrett replied. "I mean, it's probably for the best. Boats are a terrible investment. Well, thanks for picking me up. I can get the bags from here."

"It was perfect timing; I was coming out anyway. Oh, and your mother and Agatha are in town. They should be back within the hour."

After that they must have parted, because two sets of footsteps went in opposite directions—heavier ones headed down the stairs, and lighter ones farther down the hall.

Left to himself, the young man started to whistle—no particular tune, just a succession of notes.

Trying to regain my composure, I realized with dismay that I was still clutching Agatha's notebook. As I went to set it back down, my fingers fumbled, and it fell to the floor with a fluttering of pages like the sound of a bird's wings.

The whistling paused.

I didn't breathe—I couldn't.

Finally, after a few seconds, the whistling started back up and grew quieter, then muffled, and then there was the *click* of a door. The last door on the left—Barrett's room. Laura had pointed it out to me half a dozen times.

I bent down to pick up the notebook, glancing at the page it had fallen open to. Just one sentence was written at the top:

I am Too Weak to Fight anymore.

It was the last thing she'd written in the entire notebook.

My heart contracted with horror. Her writing had regressed even further, so it looked clumsy and awkward, like the work of a child.

But the idea itself was the worst part. To go from the brilliantly beautiful person Agatha had obviously been to the hollow shell she was now, that was bad enough—but worse was that she'd been aware of her slipping away, and at some point, exhausted from the effort, she had felt she had no choice but to give up.

I sighed, deeply, from the core of my soul.

I knew that feeling.

I set the journal back down and switched off the light, then shut the door and crossed the hall.

As I was opening the nursery door, a sudden noise made me jump.

It was the sound of someone clearing their throat.

And then he spoke. "Excuse me." His voice was cold, firm, demanding. "Who are you, and what are you doing in my house?"

CHAPTER
~12~

I TURNED AND saw that, yes, this was Barrett, the boy from the crystal-framed photograph. His attractiveness, while undeniable, was nowhere near as intimidating as Agatha's faultless perfection. He looked less like a doll and more like an ad from a catalog that sells clothes to people who talk about yachts in their spare time. His jawline was sharp, and his chin had a slight cleft. His eyebrows were dark brown and full, pressed low over his eyes as he glared at me. His hair was short but shaggy, like he hadn't had it cut in a month or two. His skin glowed toasted gold, a tan he must have picked up while traveling around Europe hitting on politicians' daughters.

I moved my mouth to answer, but could only open and shut it helplessly.

"This house is private property," he said. "You're trespassing."

"No, I'm not," I squeaked.

"What's your name?"

"It's—I'm Margot." My voice betrayed me by quavering.

"Don't move. I'm calling the police." He stepped toward me, and I ducked back toward the wall. But he was only trying to get closer to the stairs so he could yell down to the first floor. "Mr. Albright! There's an intruder here!"

Albright's footsteps came quickly—it sounded like he was jogging—and he appeared at the top of the stairs moments later, his eyes wide with surprise.

"She was in Aggie's room," Barrett said.

"Oh, no, no—Barrett, you're mistaken," Mr. Albright said. To me, he said, "I'm so sorry, Margot. This is Barrett Sutton. Barrett, your parents had planned to talk to you about Margot when you got home, but since you're here early, they obviously haven't had the chance. I didn't know she was home, or I would have said something."

Barrett's brow got even lower, his glower more pronounced. "And what exactly are you doing here?" He folded his arms across his chest. He wore a battered white polo shirt and knee-length light blue shorts with a torn hem. On his feet were leather loafers—boat shoes, I guess. They were bleached by the sun and salt water and the sole was peeling away from the leather. It was the kind of ratty outfit only an insanely rich person could feel comfortable wearing. He'd have been underdressed at Walmart.

"I *live* here," I said.

He turned to Mr. Albright for clarification.

Mr. Albright sighed. "I'll explain, Barrett. Why don't you come downstairs?"

Wait, they were going to go and have a secret conversation about me? That didn't seem fair. I felt a bit shocked myself, to be honest. Laura and John hadn't even mentioned my existence to him? This prompted a number of unpleasant theories: Maybe they hadn't thought it would work out. Maybe I'd done something to offend them.

Or maybe they didn't tell him because they predicted—correctly—he'd be upset. That was definitely starting to seem like the most likely explanation.

"It's fine, I'll wait for Dad." Barrett stared at me as if I were a household object that had come to life. "How long has she been here?"

At least he didn't call me *it*.

"Three weeks," I said, even though he hadn't addressed the question to me.

"How long are you staying?" He seemed to resent having to speak to me. "And why were you going into Aggie's room?"

"She lives in Agatha's room," Mr. Albright said.

Barrett stared at him, confused. "She does?"

"Yes," Mr. Albright said. "And she's here for the foreseeable future. She's helping your mother with Agatha."

"What? Really?" Barrett asked. He shot me a look that was . . . strange. Almost as if he was suddenly a little afraid of me.

"Yes, and she's a great comfort," Mr. Albright said.

Like the money from his friend's yacht fund, the wind had gone out of Barrett's conversational sails. Apparently fresh out of mean things to say, he took a step back.

"All right," he said. He licked his lips. "Okay."

Mr. Albright made a little salute, looked at us both with eager attentiveness, then swooshed back down the stairs.

I assumed Barrett would turn away without another word. But he stared at my feet for a second, then looked up at me. "What are you doing for Agatha? Are you a nurse?"

"I'm her companion."

"Companion," he repeated, not totally understanding. "How old are you?"

"Sixteen," I said.

"But you live here?" he said. "How does that work? Do you go to school?"

If there had been half a hint of condescension in

the question, I wouldn't have answered. But he was still strangely sheepish.

"Your parents took me in," I said, unable to keep the ice out of my voice. "My family just died, and now I'm an orphan."

He had the grace not to respond.

"And it's summer," I said, enjoying the chance to make him look dumb. "Nobody's in school right now."

"Right," he said.

Without another word, I slipped back into the nursery and left him standing in the hallway.

LATER, I HEARD Barrett going downstairs and opened the door to listen to his reunion with Laura and Agatha. I stayed where I was, thinking I'd have a chance to check in with Laura when she brought Agatha up to the nursery. But an hour passed, and another, and they didn't come up. When I heard John's voice boom a cheerful greeting, I cracked the door again and listened to their hellos.

I realized miserably that the whole family was down there without me.

It was like I didn't exist.

I passed the afternoon restlessly puttering around the nursery. I'd lived there long enough that it felt like my space, too, and so exploring didn't feel like I was getting into anyone else's business. As an excuse, I dusted and tidied as I went, fluffing the pillows on the beds, straightening Agatha's textbooks, sitting up the stuffed animals on her shelf, and tearing out the out-dated blank page from her school notebook. I thought about simply erasing today's date and writing tomorrow's in pencil—maybe doing the same every day, saving a little paper. But then I had second thoughts. Agatha's school ritual was purely artificial, and everybody (probably even Agatha) knew it. But the performance was obviously important to Laura—otherwise she wouldn't dress Agatha up like a doll and do her hair every day. When you thought about it, everything about life at Copeland Hall was a little show. Laura was the director, and we all played our parts.

So I ripped out the old page and dropped it in the trash can.

Outwardly, as I completed these chores, I was calm. But inwardly, I was an anxious mess. Angry, too. What if Barrett was, at that very moment, convincing John and Laura to send me away? Of course Laura would defend me, but I knew instinctively that Barrett's words would hold great power with his parents. Just from the way they said his name, I could tell that he was their great hope for the future. His importance was even more clear because Agatha was sick.

He was the heir now. Who was to say they wouldn't let him start to make decisions about the way things were run?

Another hour passed, and I felt like I was going crazy from the suspense. I imagined them all sitting around a table, deciding my fate.

Finally, unable to stop myself, I brushed my hair, put on some lip balm, and headed downstairs. I would go to the library, and if I came across them and was invited to join, I would do so. Surely they would hear me come downstairs. Surely they'd catch sight of me through an open door. John would say, *Come on in, Margot! Where have you been hiding?*

Except, nope. I made it all the way to the library unimpeded and then had nothing to do but roam around the room, searching the shelves for something that interested me. On the far side of the room, near a door that I'd always assumed was a closet, I stopped suddenly.

I could hear low, serious voices: Laura's, John's, and Barrett's.

So this door wasn't to a closet. It must have been a passage to another room. I got as close as I dared and focused all my energy on making out their words. Even Agatha must have been in there with them. I felt profoundly left out.

"But you must be kind," Laura was saying. "She's

very nice, and her father was a classmate of your father's from law school—Anthony Radegan."

"Anthony who?" Barrett said. "Never heard of him."

I felt a surge of anger. I was tempted to open the door and say, *Keep my father's name out of your mouth.*

"He saved my life," John said. "I almost drowned, and he pulled me from the pool."

"What? You never mentioned that," Barrett said.

"It's never come up," Laura said. "We don't tell you everything, Barrett."

He snorted. "I guess not."

"Barrett," she said sharply. "Maintain a respectful tone, please."

If Laura had spoken to me with that note of pitiless authority, I would have run away and hidden under the bed. I waited to see how Barrett would respond.

There was a pause. "I'm sorry, Mom," he said, much more quietly. "But I don't understand—doesn't she have *any* other family?"

My hands went clammy and my stomach turned cold.

"No, in fact, she doesn't," John said. "There was a great-aunt on her mother's side, but she passed away several years ago. The grandparents are all dead."

"Not a single friend?" Barrett asked.

"She *was* staying with friends . . ." Laura said

carefully. "But it didn't work out. She had nightmares. It disturbed the children."

What a polite way to say that my nightly screaming sent both of Becca's younger siblings to psychotherapy.

"Well, that sounds *great*," Barrett said, and I could hear the eye roll in his voice. "Bring her here and let her disturb us."

My back was feeling sore from the hunched position I had assumed. I straightened up and bumped into the bookshelf, knocking down a stack of books that had been hastily piled on the edge of the shelf. I hurriedly gathered them and returned them to their pile while straining to hear what was being said.

"It hasn't been an issue," Laura said firmly. "She's doing very well here. We all like her."

I felt a swell of affection for Laura. She liked me. She wouldn't let him force me out onto the streets.

"But it doesn't make sense," Barrett said. "Who is she? Was her father even respectable? So he saved your life, Dad, that's great, but couldn't—couldn't you just pay to send her to boarding school or something?"

"Barrett," John said, sounding appalled. "I didn't realize we had raised a snob. Respectable? Her father was a good man."

"Listen, darling," Laura said, sweetly conciliatory. "When your father proposed it to me, I thought it was an awful idea. The last thing I wanted was a stranger here, in our family's home—with Agatha being as fragile as she is."

Wait. Laura hadn't wanted me? I felt like I'd been sucker punched, right under the rib cage.

"Our family's home?" John repeated, with some scorn. "You two sound like you're living in a soap opera. This is a house. A large house. We have the ability and resources to help a girl who needs help, and we're going to do it. For heaven's sake, Laura, how many bedrooms are required to sit empty to preserve the precious Copeland reputation?"

"John, that's not fair," Laura said.

"Dad, you don't get what I'm saying," Barrett said. "I'm saying—it's enough work, isn't it? With Agatha. And now there's this other person to deal with, and it's got to be hard on you guys. Especially Mom."

"Your mother and Margot get along very well," said John. "In fact, I think it's doing them both a lot of good. As far as I'm concerned, the discussion is closed."

His heavy footsteps walked out of the room. I hurriedly crouched down so I was hidden from view.

There was a long pause from the other room.

"Why is Dad so attached to some guy he knew twenty years ago?"

Laura sighed. "You know your father."

"Yeah," Barrett said.

"But—it's more than that. The specialists were starting to make it sound like Agatha was going to need to be transferred to a home."

"A home?" he repeated. "She *has* a home."

"Precisely what I said," Laura said. "But your father believed them. And he was starting to make arrangements to have her sent away. Then, it just so happened that we learned of Margot's existence. And he agreed that if she were to come and keep Agatha company, we could keep your sister at home."

"Oh," Barrett said. "So . . ."

"So be nice to her, please," Laura said. "Agatha's place here may depend on it."

I felt almost as if I was choking—as if part of my throat was closing up. I was being used. I was just a tool Laura was using to protect Agatha.

"You know," Laura said, "for the first week, I didn't know what to think. But she really is a lovely girl."

There was a long silence. Then Barrett spoke again. "Well," he said, "if you like her . . ."

"I do," Laura said. "She's quite helpful with your sister. Besides, there's something pleasant about having a helper around the house."

"You mean like a servant?" He laughed. "Don't let Dad hear you talk like that."

"Oh, no, not like that," she protested.

"A pet," he suggested. "Your very own pet orphan."

His tone was teasing, and she laughed. Meanwhile, I felt completely flattened. I had thought I was one of the actors in Laura's little show, but it turned out I was a prop.

I heard a long sigh. "You do seem . . . happier," Barrett admitted.

"Happier?" Laura repeated. "She's a needy child, Barrett, not family. Why should she make me happier? Now please go change for dinner—you look like a deckhand."

They left the room and I sat in a ball on the floor, listening to the silence and trying to quell the ache in my heart. Laura, who had been my friend, now seemed like a stranger to me. Even John's kind impulse to take me in had been motivated by convenience. And now that Barrett was home, their actual child, I felt my displacement as harshly as if they'd moved my belongings to the garden shed.

I decided to count to a hundred before moving, just in case, and I rested my head on my knees and closed my eyes. But just as I reached seventy, disaster struck.

"Margot? Is that you?"

John stood in the doorway, looking down at me. I guess I hadn't realized how tall he was, that he would easily see me tucked around the corner of the green chairs.

"Oh," I said, looking up. "Yes. I just came down to get a book."

Blindly, I reached for the first book I could find—which happened to be six inches from my feet, a leftover from the stack I'd knocked to the floor.

John stared as if he didn't believe me, and I could see in the surprised wrinkle of his forehead and the embarrassed pink of his cheeks that he was wondering how long I'd been there and what I had heard.

"Can I escort you in to dinner?" he asked.

I got to my feet and held the book in front of me like a shield. "No, thank you," I said. "Actually, I feel kind of sick. I came down to excuse myself and get a book. If you don't think Laura will mind, I'll skip dinner and go to bed."

He glanced over at the door to my left, mentally calculating its soundproofing capacity. "Of course she won't mind," he said at last. "If you like, we can send something up for you."

"No," I said. "I'm really not hungry."

"I'm sorry you're not feeling well," he said, too kindly. "Feel better."

He continued down the hall, and I rushed toward the stairs, desperate to avoid encountering anyone else.

I CLOSED MY bedroom door, dropped the random book on the pile on my nightstand without looking at it, and changed into a pair of pajamas. Then I crawled into bed and covered my face with the blanket, breathing in the hot, stuffy air like it was my punishment for existing.

Everything was ruined. My shaky peace was destroyed by the knowledge that Laura saw me as little more than a servant. Why couldn't she have just treated me with cold disinterest instead of making me think we were friends? Instead of pretending she cared about me? And worse was the fact that Barrett knew how Laura felt. Any time we were together, he would be looking at me and thinking, *She's a needy child.*

My eyelids grew heavy and my vision began to swim. It was probably too early to go to sleep, but I was exhausted. So when my eyes closed, I let them.

I guess it was only natural, after such emotional turmoil, that my brain would take that darkness and use it to create the first nightmare I'd had in weeks. I'd forgotten that the things that seemed horrible in the light of day became monsters when I let my guard down.

And that was how I found myself sinking into the dark layers of a dream world that was as black as charcoal, where I was trapped in a windowless, doorless room between walls that seemed to move closer and farther away from me at random. A person stood in the corner with a veil over her face and hair, and as I walked closer, she hunched down, cowering away from me.

"Agatha?" I asked.

There was no answer, and it dawned on me that this wasn't Agatha at all. It was someone else, someone I wasn't sure I wanted to be locked alone in a dark room with. So I stopped and looked for a way out, and while I was facing away, a hand came to rest on my shoulder. I could see the fingers, grayish and lined with dirt, with bulging knuckles and shredded fingernails.

"I'm here," whispered a soft voice. "I'm always here."

In the dream I held my breath and tried not to move, hoping this would make her leave me alone.

"Margot," the voice said more insistently. And the hand clamped onto my shoulder. *"Margot."*

But I couldn't look, because if I looked I would see her face, and I didn't want to see her face.

"Margot?"

With a gasp, I opened my eyes and found myself staring up at Laura, who was watching me with concern.

"Are you all right?" she asked. She reached her hand down as if to press it on my forehead, and I jerked away.

I started to catch my breath.

"Was it a nightmare?" she asked. "You look pale."

I nodded, my eyes darting around the room, taking stock of reality. More than once I'd thought I had awakened from a dream only to find myself in a second layer of unreality, and I didn't want to take any chances.

Finally, my senses had gathered sufficient data to convince me that this was actually happening, and I propped myself up on my elbow. "Yes," I said. "Yes, a dream."

"I came to say good night," she said, nodding at the steaming mug on the small tea tray on my nightstand. "But you were already asleep. I wouldn't have woken you, but you seemed restless."

"Yeah," I said. "Thanks."

She took a half step closer. "Would you like to talk about it?"

"No, thanks." It wasn't just my desire not to live up to her expectations of my neediness; it was that I wouldn't have known what to say about my dreams even if I did want to talk them over. It was embarrassing that my brain plucked inspiration from everyday life. It was disturbing that I had thought the scary veiled figure was Agatha. And it was frustrating that I still didn't know who exactly it had been.

Absolutely zero percent of that was anything I wanted to share with Laura. Today of all days.

"Well, why don't you have a little tea and read for a bit?" she asked. "I can bring you some toast if you're hungry."

Her words were so kind. Her manner was so polite. And that made it worse.

"I'm not hungry, thank you," I said. "But I'll drink some tea."

"That's good," she said approvingly. "Calm down a little."

I nodded, then reached for the top book in the stack next to me and scooted up to a sitting position. Laura switched on the reading light and then headed for the door.

"Good night," she said gently.

"Good night."

And then she left, and I sighed and leaned back against the pillows. I had no desire for tea, or for reading in bed as if nothing in my life had changed. But I was afraid to shut my eyes and find myself back in that dark room, trying to figure out whose desiccated hand I'd been looking at.

So I opened the book to the title page:

Philosophical Foundations for Personal Morality:
The Rights and Responsibilities of the Privileged Class

Okay. Well, I had gone and picked out the absolute most boring-sounding book in the whole house. But I flipped it open anyway and read some of the text:

The proof of virtue is the ability to obey in the face of inner resistance. A demand for obedience performed against the will is the ultimate test of rectitude. A child is led to righteousness by the lantern of his parents' steadfastness and must by firm hands be molded into a creature of exemplary humility and worth. Abandoned to the darkness of parental deficiency, the child's quality of character will assuredly be as weak as a lily grown in shade.

Inwardly, I recoiled at the words, then flipped back to see the chapter title:

Management of Children and Youth

I was curious enough to go back and look at who the author was, and to my surprise it was a woman named Loretta Copeland. There was no author biography, so I was left wondering if she was a family member or just coincidentally shared their name. What was weirder was that there was no copyright date, but the book was made of blue fabric, threadbare on its edges, and the pages, though not falling out or cracking, were a light brown color that seemed very old.

It was a vanity project, perhaps. Loretta Copeland had been bored enough to write a creepy book telling people how to mold their children.

Gross.

I paused my examination of the book and drank some tea, grateful for the distraction from the drama of the evening. Then I opened the book again and gently thumbed through the pages, reading the chapter headings, which were all like something from a museum: *Public Decorum*, *Standards for Servants*, *Spiritual Purity*, *The Dangers of Education*, and my personal favorite, *The Particular Tendency Toward Wickedness in the Young Female*.

I browsed that chapter, hoping for some funny bits about what a disaster it was to teach your daughters to read and write and use their brains, but it ended up being an unfunny mix of dire warnings about the natural desire of young women to pursue sin and entrap men, and harsh instructions on what to do if you suspected your daughter was flirting with the devil, so to speak—or, I don't know, maybe literally.

One of the recommendations was to isolate her from evil influences. Another was to distract her with domestic labor. If that failed, you could marry her off and just make it somebody else's problem.

At the end of the chapter, there was a short summary.

I stopped short when I scanned the paragraph:

The moral sense of the world is reflected in the individual soul, and only with the greatest care can we avoid the descent into the darkest and most vile tendencies of human nature.

I knew that sentence. That was the sentence both Agatha and Lily had written over and over.

And the last sentence of the chapter sent a chill through my body:

Be ever mindful that the female of the species was the direct cause of the fall of man from divine grace. Do not allow her to bring similar devastation to your family and its reputation. Undoubtedly she will try.

I shut the book and set it down, feeling weirdly like I'd done something wrong by looking at it. Its tone was so hostile and unkind—especially toward girls—that I wanted to bleach my eyes.

I thought of Laura's grandmother sobbing at her wedding. And the portrait of the Widow Copeland. And the designer of the garden—how had Laura described her? *Preoccupied with the fall of man?*

No wonder Laura was the way she was, growing up in a family like this.

But why had Lily copied those words? And why had Agatha—especially when she was facing a serious illness?

I sipped my tea and tried to browse a gardening book, but thinking about gardening just made me think about how little I wanted to get back to gardening with Laura. So I stared at the wall and tried to keep my mind blank.

Then I thought about Barrett. I tried to imagine him at some fancy boarding school, surrounded by friends with names like Chet and Trip and Woodward, or whatever ridiculously rich people named their kids. Whatever lacrosse was, they were all experts, and the beautiful daughters of lesser politicians wore pastel sweaters and tasteful loafers and waited in a line to date them.

The whole idea was pleasantly revolting, and it kept me occupied until I finally fell asleep.

CHAPTER
~13~

SOMETHING TOUCHED MY shoulder.

I awoke slightly, sure that whatever it was had only been a too-real part of a dream—and then I realized that I hadn't been dreaming.

Agatha sat on the edge of my mattress, her hand hovering over my shoulder.

I gasped and jerked back in my bed so fast that I almost fell off the other side.

"What are you doing?" I whispered.

She jabbed me again. Her eyes, clear in the moonlight, contained not a trace of passion. She might as well have been a bored shopper poking her fingers into a display of throw pillows.

"Okay, stop," I said, sitting up and rubbing my arm. "I'm awake."

She took her hand away and turned to face the closet door.

"What do you want?" I asked. "Do you need the bathroom?"

No answer.

"Are you thirsty?"

No answer.

"Bad dream?" I asked.

She walked to the main doorway of the nursery and paused.

"Are you going back to bed?" I asked hopefully.

She stepped aside, holding the door open for me.

It's amazing what you can project onto someone who's staring impassively at you. You can project that though they're silent and still on the outside, on the inside they're trying desperately to get you to help them with something mysterious and interesting.

"Fine," I whispered.

I walked past her, and then she went around me to the locked entrance of the green wing.

To my shock, she grabbed the doorknob, pushed against the door with her shoulder, and then bumped it with her hip. It opened easily, and then she led me into the forbidden hall.

I'd already been in the first bedroom on the right, and I had no interest in going back . . . but that was where she stopped. She pulled that door open, too, and stepped away from it, revealing the darkened interior. Almost as if she was making room so *I* could go in. Alone.

Oh, come on. My fear found a tremulous voice and spoke for me. "Nope," I said. "Sorry."

She continued to stare at me, as tranquil as a statue of an angel.

The whole situation was so bizarre that I actually hated to say no. But no, no, no. I had no desire to go back into that room. I'd already spent several hours there. Just the stale smell wafting out was enough to make me feel a thrill of fear.

"I *can't*, Agatha," I said. I could hear a note in my voice that was almost pleading. "I don't like it in there."

She reached up and tucked her hair behind her ear as she turned her face away.

"You go in," I said. "I'll wait here."

Nothing.

I took a deep breath and let it out with a little hint of melodrama, to show her I wasn't happy. Then I walked in.

She followed close behind me, but when I got to the center of the room and stopped, she kept walking—toward the window that had been open that first night. A few feet away she stopped and stared at the floor, like something was missing.

"What are you looking for?" I asked, not expecting an answer.

Her shoulders slumped a little, a posture of disappointment.

"Wait," I said. "Hang on." I went to the desk and retrieved the trash can I'd put away. "This?"

She watched me, with no clear expression of interest but also not with complete blankness, while I carried it over and set it down.

Then she knocked it over.

"Oh, come on," I said. I reached down and set it back up.

She knocked it over again.

"Okay, fine, I'll leave it," I said. But that wasn't right, either. So finally, I reached down and slowly flipped it so it was upside down. Now that I thought about it, that was how I'd found it the first night. "Now what?"

She stared up at the window frame, made of thick, dark wood.

"Yeah? I closed it. Did you like it open?" That didn't require an overturned trash can, though . . . "Agatha, is there something up there?"

No answer. She simply stared.

But why would she need me for this?

Maybe she just wasn't confident enough in her ability to climb? I thought of the way she always hesitated at the stairs, how her hand always gripped the banister tightly.

I dragged the metal trash can closer to the window, and then, praying that its load-bearing capacity didn't max out at Agatha's weight, I stepped carefully up onto it.

The top of the window was still almost out of my reach. I stretched my arm to the point where my shoulder began to cramp, and the very tips of my fingers brushed against something up against the wall.

"What is it?" I asked her. But she'd stopped watching me. She was staring at the hall.

A few more swipes and my fingers finally pulled it toward me. It was a string, and I managed to loop a fingertip through it and pull. To my surprise, it was a tiny black velvet bag.

"Ha!" I said, holding it out to her. "I got it!"

Suddenly, she went stiff.

"Ags?" I asked.

She grabbed my arm and yanked me off the trash can. I almost fell to the floor but managed to land upright—barely—just in time for her to pull me toward the door and drag me down the hall and out the double doors.

We rushed across the hall and stopped just outside the nursery. I had my hand on the doorknob when Laura's voice called up from the bottom of the stairs.

"Girls?" She sounded alarmed. Her footsteps approached rapidly. "Girls, what are you doing out of bed?"

She'd said *girls*, but she clearly meant the question for me. She reached the top of the steps.

I didn't have time to think. I lied as fast as I could. "I was just coming to find you," I said, hoping words would form themselves. "Agatha was—"

On cue, Agatha bent over and threw up all over the floor.

"—um, sick," I said.

"Oh my goodness!" Laura cried. "Run into the bathroom and get some towels, please."

As I was hurrying back from the bathroom, the door at the end of the hall opened, and Barrett stepped out, wearing flannel pajama pants and a T-shirt.

"What's going on?" he asked blearily.

"Nothing," Laura said. "We're fine. Go back to bed."

She shepherded Agatha past me, and I heard the shower turn on. So it was just me, Barrett, and a gross mess on the floor.

"What happened?" he asked.

"Your sister's sick." I tossed a towel over the dirty spot.

"I can clean that," he said, stepping closer. "You shouldn't have to."

"It's fine," I said, even though it was actually very gross. He came closer, and I instinctively backed away. I couldn't even stand to be near him; his presence made me irrationally angry. He was a snob, a bad person.

But even if he was those things, he suppressed them long enough to clean up the mess on the floor, for which I felt a twinge of gratitude.

"Does this happen a lot?" he asked, balling up the towels.

I shrugged. "Not since I got here."

"Poor Aggie," he said, and the quiet kindness of his words momentarily disarmed me. "It must be confusing for her."

"I guess," I said, glancing over to the nursery door. Should I tell him good night and make my escape?

"What else does she need?" he asked. "Did she throw up in the nursery, too? Does she—"

"She's okay," I said. "Your mom is with her. The nursery's fine."

"I just—" He looked around helplessly. "I feel bad."

"It's fine. It's not your fault she's sick."

He stared at me, and in the dark, where our faces were shaded, I felt like I was seeing a totally different side of him. He seemed vulnerable. Almost scared.

Interesting, I thought. Not that it made me like him any more. But it was interesting.

He glanced away. "Okay, well . . . I guess I'll go back to bed."

I nodded.

Without saying good night, he ducked into his room and closed the door.

I waited off to the side of the nursery while Laura re-settled Agatha in her bed and spent the next several minutes fussing over her. Finally, when Agatha was tucked in and seemed to be asleep, Laura left—but she made me promise to come and get her if anything else happened.

I walked into my bedroom. I had shoved the tiny bag into my pajama pocket, and now I took it out and inspected it in the low light. The fabric was black, but very dusty. I loosened the drawstring and dumped the contents onto my bed. There were three items: a key—largeish with a pattern of leaves and an ornate letter *C* on it; a small plastic vial with clear liquid inside it; and a tiny origami-like triangle of folded money.

Why did Agatha want these things so badly? What did the key unlock? What was in the vial? It looked almost like a perfume sample, but I didn't open it to sniff. And the money? If I thought I might be able to refold it, I would have unfolded it and looked. But I'd never been good at origami.

I crept back out to the nursery, which seemed artificially silent. I could hear the second hand of the old clock on the wall over the desk.

"Agatha," I whispered. "Are you awake?"

Yes, she was awake; she turned toward me—her skin was rather gray, probably from the effort of regurgitating everything she'd eaten since lunch—and her eyes seemed to work to focus on my face.

"I'll keep your stuff for you in my room," I said. "Okay?"

She stared at me for another long moment, and then her eyes closed as if they didn't have the strength to stay open any longer.

THE NEXT FEW days were tense. Worried about Agatha's "illness," Laura made her stay in bed and rest, which was frustrating and difficult for all of us. Agatha didn't *want* to spend all her time in bed, which meant that she needed to be distracted and entertained. I spent hours reading to her from books she showed no interest in—books that, to be honest, I had no interest in, either. Laura had chosen them, and they were all bland stories with a dull educational bent.

As I read, I would sometimes hear Barrett walk by in the hall, and I'd be overcome by resentment and envy. He could come and go as he pleased. And

I hated the thought that he could overhear me awkwardly reading to Agatha.

Because of the time I spent confined to the nursery, I put aside my insecurities and jumped at the chance to work in the garden with Laura on the first day she deemed Agatha well enough to get up and spend the morning in John's office. Our next big project was cleaning out the greenhouse, which meant hauling old plants to the compost bins and organizing the shelves of dormant bulbs and boxes of unplanted seed packets. We also washed and squeegeed the glass walls, and unscrewed and scrubbed out the insulation vents, which were coated with dust and grime. After we finished that, Laura's grand plan was to replace every bit of quarter-inch drip-line sprinkler tubing, which would take the better part of a week.

Don't get me wrong—the existing quarter-inch drip-line tubing was in an appalling state and needed replacing. But by the end of the week, the amplified sun and steamy heat of the greenhouse were wearing me out.

Still, there was an upside: Laura seemed to take satisfaction not only in the quality of the work I did, but in the fact that I was strong enough to keep up with her feverish pace. After the first couple of days, she stopped asking me every few hours about headaches and whether I'd had any odd mental episodes.

"You're strong," she said to me once, watching me drag a pot with a dead palm tree in it across the walkway. "Did you play sports?"

"Cross-country," I said. "But I wasn't fast. I'm not very athletic."

"Ah," she said.

I had a memory of the coach saying to me, *So this is just résumé padding for you, right? I don't want to push you harder than you want to be pushed.* (Which at the time I found insulting, but in hindsight was a pretty reasonable question.)

"My sisters were athletic, though," I said. "They were both cheerleaders at their middle school."

She smiled, but it was an uneasy smile.

I was caught up in the sudden surge of memories. "Siena was really good, technically—I mean, her technique. She was thirteen. Dina was just okay at tumbling, but she had crazy stage presence. She was always smiling. She truly believed in the greatness of the sixth-grade-girls' volleyball team. You never looked at any of the other cheerleaders, because Dina was, like, glowing."

Laura didn't reply, which was fine, because I had lost myself in the memory of watching them from the stands. Dina was on the junior squad and Siena was the co-captain of the advanced squad. She was definitely going to make junior varsity when she got to high school, and I was proud of her. Not because it meant she would be popular or anything like that—at my school the cheerleaders were a mixed bag, cool girls and normal girls and a few totally irritating try-hards—but because she worked so hard and she had real talent.

Laura worked in silence, permitting me to be alone with my thoughts and the tears that began to spill down my cheeks. After a minute, she clucked kindly and moved away to the table of orchids.

When I felt collected enough to join her, I went to her side and started pulling pots toward me.

"Did you play sports?" I asked. I figured she must have some connection to it, if she'd brought it up.

To my surprise, she narrowed her eyes—not pleased by the question but not bothered by it, either. "No," she said. "I could have, but . . . forces conspired against me."

I didn't even know how to begin responding to that.

"I would have been good," she said, staring steadily at a leathery dead leaf. "I would have been very good. But I never got the chance."

Then she carried the plant away, and I decided to stop trying to make conversation. I stayed out to re-coil the hose after she went inside, and when I finished, I was filthy, sweaty, and sort of miserable.

The last thing I wanted to see, as I came to the garden entrance, was Barrett sitting on one of the benches, reading. He was lost in the book, and I startled him as I rounded the corner. My appearance seemed to alarm him. I saw the confusion in his eyes as he looked at my dirt-streaked clothes and skin.

"Are you okay?" he asked. As if I looked like this because I'd been in a fistfight or something.

"Of course I am," I said. "I'm just dirty."

"Oh," he said. "Where's my mom?"

"She went inside."

He glanced back at the house. "You're just . . . out here . . . by yourself?"

"What's wrong with that? Are you afraid I'm going to steal something?"

Instantly, I regretted snarking at him. All I needed was to make him hate me and tell his parents I was unacceptable.

"No," he said, looking shocked. "That's not what I meant. Obviously you're not stealing. But why are you doing all the work yourself?"

"I'm sure you've noticed that I'm a penniless orphan, Barrett," I said. "I don't have the luxury of belonging here like you do. So I try to do my part."

I turned to walk away, but he set his book down and stood up. "Why do you hate me?"

"I don't hate you," I said. "I don't know you."

"That's because every time I try to start a conversation, you—"

"Oh, like when you accused me of trespassing?"

He raised his palms helplessly. "I was confused. There was a stranger in my house. We don't get a lot of visitors—what was I supposed to think?"

I hated that I heard the logic of his statement.

"Anyway, I said I was sorry—"

I laughed. "No. No, you didn't. You asked me why I was an orphan, and then you said my dad wasn't respectable."

His forehead wrinkled, and he shook his head. He had the helpless look of wanting to deny having said it but knowing it was true.

"You did. I heard you. You said it to your parents." I swallowed hard. I couldn't cry. If I cried, I would hate myself. "I heard you guys talking that night. I heard everything you said."

He took a huge breath and then had the grace to remain silent.

"I don't care what you think about me. I do care what your mom thinks, though."

"So that's why you do all this manual labor for her?" he asked.

"I don't mind helping out." I glanced away. The sun was beginning to sink toward the horizon. "In fact, I should get back to it."

"But you don't have to do so much work," he said. "I mean, they don't expect it."

That was a lie. He didn't believe what he was saying. He knew as well as I did that Laura did expect it.

"I have to finish up a few things," I said.

There was a pile of pots near the benches, and I tried to lift it. A few of the smaller ones fell off the top, and Barrett rushed to pick them up.

"Here," he said, trying to take the others from me, but I turned away.

"I've got them," I said.

Then he followed me to the storage area near the iron gate, and we set the pots down near the older stacks.

Barrett stood looking around, and then turned his attention to the gate. "This is really cool, isn't it?"

I found it a little tacky that he was complimenting the house that he would someday inherit, but I let that slide. "Yeah," I said. "Have you ever been through it?"

He shook his head. "I don't spend a lot of time in the garden. It's Mom's thing."

I studied the ironwork, its intricate details—the top of the gate was the tree, with hundreds of individual leaves. The trunk of the tree was the middle of the gate, where it opened. On one side was Adam, looking slightly confused, and on the other side were

Eve and the snake. Eve's expression as she studied the apple was probably meant to be wicked, but she, too, looked a little confused.

Barrett tried to press the lever to open it, but it wouldn't open.

"It's locked," I said, and as I said it, I looked at the lock.

A pattern of leaves, and a fancy letter *C* . . .

Was this the lock that went with Agatha's key?

But why would she have the key to this place? And why would it be so important to her that she would wake me up to find it in the middle of the night?

I realized, as I stared, that Barrett was staring at me staring at the lock. So I turned away.

"I'm going inside," I announced. "See you later."

He shrugged. "I'm going, too."

So we had to walk next to each other, which made me self-conscious about the frumpiness of my clothes and the dirt on my face and arms.

Barrett cleared his throat. "If you need help with anything, let me know."

"Why would I need help?"

"I mean, if there's anything you don't feel like doing."

"I don't mind doing stuff," I said. "The whole reason I'm here is to help."

He looked mildly disgusted, which hurt my feelings. "That's not true," he said. "Or it shouldn't be. You don't take in an orphan to have free labor."

Oh, so he wasn't disgusted with *me*. That soothed my feelings a little.

"I should talk to Dad about it," he said.

"Please don't," I said.

"Why not?"

"Because," I said. "I literally have nowhere else to go. That may sound like I'm being dramatic, but I'm not. It's here, or the state institution."

Now he was alarmed. "Why the institution?"

"Because there aren't a lot of places for people who wake up screaming every night."

"I haven't heard any screaming."

"Well, it doesn't happen here," I said. "Which is another reason I want to stay, okay? Just please do me a favor and don't try to help. I'm fine. I don't need to be rescued."

He sighed. "I guess it's temporary, anyway. Things will change when school starts."

"I don't even know when that is."

"Five weeks," he said. "It's the same day my school starts. I saw the sign in town."

"Oh," I said, and a waterfall of feelings and thoughts crashed down over me. "Okay."

Five weeks? That didn't seem like enough time. I didn't know anything about the school. I needed to prepare for meeting people. How would I get there? Would I have to ride a bus? Would the bus pass by dark canals? What if it slid off the road? The image of a giant tin can full of drowning kids filled my head, and my stomach turned. What if I didn't want to go to school? What would I wear? I couldn't show up dressed in Agatha's clothes. People would assume I was in a cult or something.

We made it to the back door of the house, and Barrett moved aside for me to pass.

"Hey," I said. "Who's Lily?"

"Lily?" he repeated. "Lily who?"

"Copeland," I said. Duh.

He frowned. "There's a Lily Copeland?"

I was frozen. I didn't want to give away the fact that I'd been sneaking around the house at night. "Yeah," I said simply.

"Well, I don't know," he said. "Sorry."

"Okay," I said, eager to drop the subject.

"Where'd you hear about her?"

"I'm not sure," I lied. "I just saw the name somewhere."

Then, before he could ask any more questions, I hurried upstairs and into the nursery, closing the door behind me.

AT DINNER, IT was clear that something had changed between Barrett and me. It was harder to actively dislike someone I'd just had a conversation with—someone who'd let me scold him without protest. And even though I hadn't particularly wanted his help, the fact that he'd helped me without being asked forced me to award him some okay-maybe-I-don't-*hate-you*-hate-you points.

Plus, I was intrigued. The way he talked about his parents wasn't the way I would have guessed a person would talk about John and Laura. He wasn't the obedient robot I had expected. Which made me wonder about Agatha. What was her true personality? All along I'd assumed she was just a clone of Laura—but what if she was more like Barrett? After all, she'd been a normal teenage girl. Her bedroom was evidence of that, even if there was none of it left in her behavior.

We only exchanged a sentence or two, but I didn't find myself automatically irritated by what he said; I felt neutral, like it was fine if he chose to say things in my presence, which was decidedly not how I'd felt at previous meals.

THAT NIGHT, LAURA brought my tea but hardly drank hers; I knew she saved most of it for her visit to Barrett's room, and it bothered me a little, but not as much as usual. Barrett was her son, after all.

A deep rumble came from outside, and Laura gave a happy little shiver. "Big storm coming in tonight," she said. "I love storms. I love feeling safe inside the house while it's so wild outside."

I nodded. I wasn't quite as enthusiastic about the elements—to be honest, my sense of adventure in general had been pretty suppressed since the accident. But I could see the appeal of being sheltered in this fortresslike place while the wind thrashed and the rain fell in buckets.

I wasn't very thirsty, so after she left, I set down the teacup and closed my eyes. My head was full of thoughts of Barrett and the garden and my sisters and Laura's strange mood change. Then I remembered the elaborately decorated lock and the key that seemed to match it. And once I started thinking about that, I couldn't think of anything else.

The first fat drops of rain hit the window, and I took the key out of my bottom drawer, where I'd stashed the small bag, and stared at it as I finished my lukewarm tea. I was trying to calm myself with my evening ritual, despite knowing that I wasn't going to properly relax until I'd had a chance to put the key in the lock and see if it turned.

The only thing was . . . when? If Agatha had hidden the key, and hadn't wanted Laura aware of our mission to recover it, then maybe Laura wouldn't approve of my having the key at all. I would have felt worse about possessing it if Agatha hadn't been the one to give it to me. That wasn't my fault, was it? It wasn't anything I'd done wrong. I was her companion; I'd accompanied her somewhere in the middle of the night, that was all.

So when, then? Certainly not when Laura and I were working in the garden. And there were no other times of the day when there would be the freedom to roam around unnoticed. Laura didn't micromanage my every movement, but she did seem to have a sixth sense about where I was at any given time. If I went to the garden outside of our typical time, she'd want to know why. And I was a pretty bad liar. Besides, I didn't want to lie. *Lies pile up until they bury you,* Dad used to say. Better to avoid having to tell the truth than to come up with a lie, no matter how believable it seemed.

I held the key in my hand. I would just have to wait until the right opportunity presented itself.

CHAPTER
~14~

WATER STREAMED DOWN my face. A sudden arc of blue-white light cut the world in half and then disappeared, leaving its imprint on my vision. I blinked hard, and the air around me filled with the roar of thunder.

What on earth?

I turned in a slow circle, looking for anything that might give me a clue about where I was or what was happening.

I was outside, in a place I'd never seen before— there were trees stretching overhead, but they did nothing to stop the rain from beating down on me. There were walls—walls?—dark boundaries of some sort, maybe stone or shrubs. It was too dark to see, until another shock of lightning turned everything briefly to daylight.

Shrubbery, the walls were shrubbery.

Under my tender, bare feet, a gravel path. To each side, a long swath of dirt.

Up ahead, there was something in the path. A small structure.

I should look for the exit, I should get back inside—I was thoroughly freaked out by the fact that I had no idea where I was or how I'd gotten here. But I also felt drawn to the structure. I wanted to know what it was. And it wasn't very far away—

As I approached, my emotions grew heavier. Nothing good was tucked away in a walled-off dirt patch. Nothing good was outlined by a low iron gate, the size of a bed.

No, it wasn't anything good—it was a grave.

This was a cemetery. Beyond this grave, there were more—the path wandered under the trees in an ambling circle, and I could see more low, tomblike structures.

I was close enough to see the white stone statue of an angel at the end of the gated enclosure, and I leaned in to see the text:

BEVERLY TURNER COPELAND

CHERISHED WIFE AND MOTHER

1946–1975

Was this Laura's mother's grave?

Thunder rolled and lightning flashed, and I realized that even though I didn't know how I'd gotten here, I wanted very badly to leave, so I turned and followed the path toward what I hoped was the way out.

Oh God, I couldn't spend the night in a cemetery. Not a night like this, with rain pounding the ground so hard that you couldn't hear—so loud you'd never know if someone was coming up behind you and preparing to grab your shoulder—

Someone grabbed my shoulder.

I screamed, a bloodcurdling scream, and swung my arm, knocking the hand off my shoulder and managing to smack Barrett pretty sturdily up the side of the head. Which, I decided, as I panted madly, he deserved.

"What are you *doing*?" we both shouted at the exact same time.

His eyes were wide, his face and clothes soaked all the way through.

"Seriously, why did you do that?" I demanded.

"Why are you out here?" he shot back.

I wanted to continue yelling at him, but I had to draw in a breath of air. "I don't know," I said. "Why are *you* out here?"

"I followed you," he said. "And before you accuse

me of thinking you're trying to steal something, I was worried about you."

"Why?" I asked, although I had to admit that the situation could easily seem a little worrying. "I mean . . . what happened? I don't remember . . . anything."

"You don't remember coming out here?" he asked.

I shook my head.

A massive web of blue lightning spread over the sky, and the thunder that followed sounded like it was on top of us.

"Come on," Barrett said. "Let's go back to the house."

I kept pace with him, although the gravel hurt my feet, and I tried not to notice how many graves there were. I especially tried not to notice the very small ones.

"This place is so creepy," I said.

"Yeah, it is," he said. "I had no idea it was even here. How did you know?"

"I didn't," I insisted. "Honestly, I was in bed one minute, and then . . ."

And then what? A memory flashed into my mind. The key. I'd been holding the key, thinking about using it.

"Did we come through the Adam and Eve gate?" I asked.

"You honestly don't remember?"

"No," I said. "Honestly."

"Yeah," he said. "I followed you down and you went straight to the gate, unlocked it, and came inside. It was like you were looking for something."

I gazed around, perplexed. "How did you even know I was awake?"

"You were making a ton of noise," he said. "Probably putting together that outfit. My closet wall backs up to your bedroom, and I heard you thumping around."

I suddenly remembered to worry that I was wearing thin cotton pajamas in the dumping rain, but when I took a second to notice my outfit, I was relieved—sort of—to find that I had apparently dressed myself before embarking on this little adventure. Over my pajama top, I wore the I LEFT MY HEAPT IN FLORID shirt, and over that I had put on a tan blazer that Laura had given me.

Okay, I may have looked like I dressed myself in the dark, but at least I was covered up. Which was more than could be said for Barrett, whose wet shirt clung to the muscles of his chest—*very nicely,* I thought, and then gave myself a mental pinch.

"I must have been sleepwalking," I said. "I don't remember any of that."

"Weird," he said. "Has it happened before?"

The path rounded a corner, and under a weeping willow tree whose branches reached almost to the ground, I saw a small, flat grave marker. Its placement was so out of the way, its presentation so humble compared to the soaring, carved stones and walled-off spaces of the other graves that I felt drawn to it.

Barrett fidgeted as I walked closer. "Don't you think we should go back?"

"Yes," I said. "This will only take a second."

The raised letters on the marker, which was hardly more than a square of metal, were hard to make out in the shadow cast by the tree. Luckily, a flash of lightning brightened the words just long enough for me to make out some of the writing:

LILY COPELAND

BELOVED DAUGHTER AND SISTER

But that wasn't the part that shocked me. What shocked me were the years printed below her name:

1971–1988

"What is it?" Barrett asked.

"It's Lily," I said, turning to look up at him. "I think she was your mom's sister."

WE WALKED TO the gate in silence, passing a few more scattered graves. Barrett seemed like he was turning something over in his head, and I didn't want to disturb him. When Adam and Eve came into view, I felt a strange little flip-flop in my stomach. Why couldn't I remember coming out here?

I silently shut the gate and removed the key. The raised pattern felt familiar under my fingertips.

"I had no idea this was here," Barrett said, and he sounded almost hurt. "I had no idea Mom had a sister . . . Why would she keep that from us?"

"I kind of get it," I said. "When you were little, it probably seemed too heavy. And then when you got older, she probably didn't know how to bring it up."

Lily's grave site was so small and unassuming.

"She died really young," I said. "Our age. I wonder what she died from?"

Barrett stared up at the gray expanse of the house's walls looming over us. The rain had slowed to a light drizzle, which hardly felt like anything on my already-wet face.

"I'm going to ask my mom about it tomorrow," he said.

"No—" I said. "Please don't."

"There's a *graveyard* on the property," he said. "And she never even told me about it."

"Sure, yes," I said. "But—I don't think we were supposed to find it."

And then I explained—without mentioning the part about sneaking around at night—that the key had come from a secret bag of Agatha's.

I half expected him to start demanding answers, but as soon as I mentioned his sister, he softened.

"Agatha gave it to you?" he asked. "I didn't think she could do things like that."

"I didn't, either," I said. "I mean, I know she's not totally catatonic, but this was kind of next-level."

"But you didn't mention it to my parents?"

I thought of Agatha dragging me through the house, forcing herself to throw up to deflect Laura's suspicion.

I shrugged. "I just . . . kind of got the idea that she wanted it to be our secret."

"I didn't know she had secrets," he mused. "I didn't know she was awake enough."

We made it to the reflecting ball, which was dotted with water droplets. I wiped them off and stared into it. At my side, I could see Barrett staring at his own reflection.

"I'm sorry," he said, looking down. "I'm sorry for making you feel unwelcome."

"It's okay," I said.

"My parents aren't perfect—God knows—but I've always had a place to go. I never even stopped to think what it would be like not to have that."

"I never did, either," I said. "It would have been weird to spend much time thinking about it, actually."

We were having this conversation with each other's distorted reflections.

"I'm glad you're here," he said, with a firmness behind the words that was almost emotional. "Agatha likes you. She trusts you."

I turned to the real Barrett in surprise. "You think so?"

"Definitely." His eyes darted away. For the first time, I got the idea that Barrett may have been shy. Maybe at school he wasn't the princely snob I'd assumed. He probably still had a line of girls waiting for him, but maybe they all liked him because he was quiet and thoughtful. And cute.

"I like her, too," I said. "It was a little rocky at the beginning, but we get along now. What was she like before she got sick?"

"She was kind of wild," he said. "I mean, by Mom's standards."

"I feel like everybody's wild by your mother's standards."

He laughed, but it was short and there wasn't much humor behind it. "Yeah, she's pretty strict. When she and Agatha got into it . . . you could hear them yelling all over the house."

"Really?" I asked.

"You're surprised?" he asked. "Well . . . I guess you would be. You didn't know Agatha."

"Yeah," I said. "It's kind of weird to think that she and I would never have met if both our lives hadn't gotten totally messed up."

"She would have liked you," he said. Then, quieter, with a hint of guilty embarrassment behind it: "I mean, she does. But—"

"I know what you mean," I said. "But I don't believe you."

"Why not?"

"Because look at me," I said. "And look at her."

He literally looked me up and down. "Well, your fashion choices are kind of eccentric, but other than that . . . I don't get what you mean."

He was teasing me, which was fair. My outfit was absurd.

"Forget it," I said. "It's late. We should get inside."

As if to underscore my words, the sky lit up overhead, and the flash of light was followed instantly by a deafening crack of thunder. It was so close and so loud that I felt my skin tingle. Barrett and I both ducked, and then we stared at each other.

In the distance, I could hear the rumble of pouring

rain coming toward us like a stampeding herd of antelope.

"Let's go!" he cried. Grabbing my hand, he began to run. We made it about ten feet before the water came down on us in sheets. We had fifty yards of ground to cover before making it to the house, and it felt like running through a dream world—everything was shiny, gleaming, flashing with light and punctuated by menacing rumbles of thunder. As we rushed into the back hall, and Barrett pulled the door shut, the sudden quiet seemed like something from another world.

We stared at each other, panting and out of breath, and then we both began to laugh—relieved laughter, triumphant laughter, *we-made-it* laughter.

"Wow," he said, glancing at the small window on the back door. "I can't believe we didn't get struck."

I nodded, feeling exhilarated by the thrill of sharing an exciting experience with another human being. I couldn't think of anything to say, and I felt my mouth take the shape of a huge, goofy grin. Barrett grinned back.

As the seconds ticked by, the somberness of the house fell over us like a veil, and we peered out toward the main hall. Neither of us spoke, but we were both questioning whether Laura was out there, wandering the house. Had she checked our bedrooms and found us missing?

Then I wondered for the first time what she would think if she found us both gone, in the middle of the night. And what she would think if she found us together.

Before tonight, in my mind, Barrett had only existed in the context of his place in the Sutton family, so he had felt more like a brother than a *boy*. I'd never stopped to consider him for what he actually was, outside of picturing the girlfriends I'd imagined he'd left weeping in his past.

Now, suddenly, he was standing before me in three dimensions, more real to me than Laura and John, and a separate person from Agatha altogether.

And in that moment, it became crystal clear to me. He was a boy. And I was a girl.

Possibly to him, too, because when we had grabbed a few towels from the kitchen pantry—trying to mop up the puddles we'd made on the floor, and dry ourselves off as well as we could—he bumped lightly into me and then jumped back like he'd been burned, with a mumbled apology and a flush flooding his neck and cheeks.

I felt myself blush, too. something—maybe everything—had changed between us.

Maybe the storm had masked any sounds we'd made, or maybe the raindrops provided the perfect white noise Laura needed to sleep through the night, but whatever the reason, she didn't wake up. Barrett and I purposefully minimized our goodbyes—no meaningful looks or thoughtful discussions, thanks, just a quick wave and turning our separate ways—and then I found myself safely back in the nursery.

I glanced at Agatha's bed, confident that I'd find her sleeping soundly. To my horror, the bed was empty, the sheets and blankets hanging off the side.

"Agatha?" I called, and as my eyes swept over the room, I saw her motionless figure sitting at the window.

She didn't turn when I said her name, but when I walked over to her, her eyes made a quick motion to acknowledge my presence before returning to the view.

Out this window, you could see the walk that led to the garden.

Had she seen us outside? She must have.

Did she know I'd used her key? Did she know what lay behind that gate? "I'll tell you about it tomorrow. Go back to bed now, okay?" Then I went into the bathroom to dry off and change.

When I emerged from the bathroom, she was in her bed, with the covers neatly pulled over herself—just the way Laura would have arranged them. Her eyes were closed, but I whispered, "Good night," and went into my own room.

Once I was in there, I looked around blankly. It was a disaster. There were clothes everywhere, the bedsheets were tangled, the teacup was on the floor in pieces. On the far wall, the small window was wide open and rain and wind were blowing inside, filling the air with the smell of wet stone and moss. The dresser drawers were open, all of them—it was a miracle the dresser hadn't face-planted onto the foot of the bed.

But the worst thing was the wall next to the dresser. In streaky black letters two feet tall was written:

GO

CHAPTER
~15~

"YOU'RE SLEEPY TODAY," Laura said as I tried in vain to stifle a yawn.

Yep. I was. It had taken me an hour to get the room cleaned up, the floor dried, the wall wiped down. And then I'd lain in bed staring at the ceiling, too wired to sleep, too curious, too freaked out, too everything. I knew I'd managed to drift in and out of a light, fuzzily dreamless state, but I basically felt like I'd been awake all night.

Now Laura studied me. "You look pale, too," she said, worry creeping into her voice. "Maybe you've been working too hard this week."

"No," I said. "It's not that. I just didn't sleep well last night, for some reason."

"Oh, I see," she said, unconvinced.

"Maybe I'll take a nap or something, while Agatha does her homework."

She smiled. "That's a good idea."

She proceeded to watch me so closely that I lost my appetite and couldn't finish my food. I excused myself and went upstairs, made my bed, and inspected the wall where the writing had been.

The obvious explanation was that Agatha had done it. She had the time, she had access to my room . . . Did she have a motive? It hurt to think that, after all the time we'd spent, after developing what seemed almost like an easy familiarity, she still wanted me to leave. Then again, who knew what simmered beneath her silent surface? Just because she'd given me a little break didn't mean she had accepted me. Maybe all this time she'd been formulating a plan to chase me away.

I'd cast a couple of searching glances her way during breakfast, which she'd returned with blank neutrality.

And then there was the part of my thoughts that kept returning to Barrett. So slowly that I hardly even noticed it, his face and voice and the whole boyness of him would crowd everything else out.

It hardly seemed like the previous night had even happened, except that there were still wet clothes hanging behind the closed curtain of my shower. The whole thing was dreamlike—the rain, the graves, the sky lighting up around us. And especially the sudden, shocking feeling of being close to another human again—close like a friend, close in the sense of wanting to know what he was doing and what he was thinking about. I wanted to see him and be near him, and talk about life, and family, and whatever. I wanted to be near enough to speak in a low voice and say things only he could hear.

It was like my loneliness was an empty jar I'd been carrying around, and all at once the promise of Barrett's friendship had rushed in and filled it.

Of course, there was still the mortifying question of whether he felt the same way. Maybe last night had been too weird. Or he found me annoying, or dull.

But I didn't think so. A slideshow of images flicked by in my mind: his eyes, rimmed by dark lashes with drops of water balanced on them like tiny jewels. Water streaming down his face. And then, as if I'd seen it on a movie screen, him taking my hand as we ran for cover.

No, he didn't think I was dull. I didn't know what he thought.

I LAY IN my bed, eyes closed, and tried to make myself fall asleep. But I felt as if I'd chugged two cups of coffee; my heart was pounding and my thoughts raced. I knew Laura would send me back to bed if she found me wandering around, so I decided to be proactive and hope I would eventually fall asleep in spite of myself.

It didn't happen. But I did use the time to think carefully over the previous night's events. Every time I looked at Laura now, I would think: *You had a sister and she died.* It's what I would have thought about anyone at all who might have shared an understanding of what I'd been through.

I had to proceed carefully. Clearly, Laura didn't feel comfortable talking about Lily, but it seemed like she was the kind of person who carried around her secrets like a heavy burden on her shoulders. The obvious cause would be Agatha's illness, but what if it went deeper than that? Barrett made it sound like she'd *never* been a particularly happy person. What if she'd been mourning her sister in silence all these years?

Well, it wasn't like she was going to want to talk to me about it, although I thought I might make a pretty good confidante on the topic. It was something I knew a little bit about, anyway. But maybe I could just help her feel more comfortable with the memories, so she could think of Lily with a sense of peace.

Maybe I was wrong, and she had processed the grief in a perfectly healthy manner. But I seriously doubted it. Otherwise, why wouldn't she have told her own kids about Lily? Why would she keep the grave-yard locked and hidden?

Just to unlock that gate would be such a huge step for her. Just to open up those memories—or just provide a place for all those memories to rest. Because obviously you could never really let this kind of burden go.

What if I could give her a safe place to go when the past caught up with her?

BARRETT AND JOHN had gone to John's law office for the day, and they reappeared in time for dinner. At first, Barrett had come to the table in his shorts and a dark blue CAMDEN LACROSSE T-shirt, but Laura sent him back upstairs to dress properly. He glanced at me with an almost-smile as he left the room, and I felt a delirious rush of connection.

When he came back, we proceeded with our meal in the usual way, with polite conversation. I tried not to speak directly to Barrett, for reasons I couldn't quite name, but our eyes kept meeting and I couldn't stop myself from feeling happy just to be around him.

I felt Laura watching me, but that was nothing new, and she asked enough questions about my nap and my level of sleepiness that I thought it was just her normal interest in my health, amplified a bit because of my tiredness that morning.

Afterward, I carried the stack of plates over to the sink and handed them to Barrett one at a time, to rinse under the firm spray of the faucet.

"Hey," he said. "Any midnight adventures planned?"

"Actually," I said, and the plate he was holding nearly slipped out of his grip.

"What? Really?"

"It's not supposed to storm tonight," I said. "Want to meet me out there?"

He hesitated, and I suddenly felt my cheeks redden furiously as I realized how that had sounded.

"There's a project," I said. "Something for your mom—"

"Oh," he said. "What kind of project?"

It was like there was heat radiating off his arm, inches from my own. I took a sidestep away from him. "A gardening project."

"In the middle of the night," he said.

"Sure."

"Does Mom know about it?"

"Of course not."

He paused, the plate under the stream of water, and looked down at me. "Do you think that's a good idea?"

I didn't know what to say.

"Yeah, I'll meet you," he said. "What time?"

"Um . . . I don't know. I could just knock on your door. It'll have to be after everyone's asleep."

"Okay," he said.

"Yeah?" As much as I wanted to spend time with him, the truth was that I really needed his help if this was going to work. I couldn't do it alone.

"Yeah, sure," he said. "What's the worst that could happen? Mom gets mad and punishes us?"

I almost laughed, then said, "What are her punishments like?"

"Oh, don't worry," he said breezily, slipping the plate into the dishwasher and taking the next one from my hand. "She won't hit you. She's more into psychological warfare."

I stared at him, trying to read his expression. "I can't tell if you're joking."

He looked at me and raised his eyebrows. "I don't know if I am."

IT WENT PERFECTLY according to plan. I sipped my tea when Laura came in, but as soon as she left, I set it aside. It was too strong an association by now—I couldn't afford to let myself relax if I was going to stay awake for a few more hours. Instead, I read carefully through the gardening book I'd pulled from the library that afternoon. When that got boring, I started reading what seemed to be the tawdriest romance novel I'd been able to find in the house, a slim red-bound book from the 1930s called *The Girl Least Likely*, which ended up not being tawdry at all, just the story of some "bad" girls who eventually reform and throw out their cigarettes and slang talk and marry their bosses. Then I reorganized my closet by color. Then I changed out of my pajamas into a set of gardening clothes, minus the apron and grandma hat. When that was done, I pulled out my phone and played a game for a while.

Finally, it was time. I slipped the key into one of my pants pockets and went to Barrett's room. I knocked lightly, and a few seconds later, he opened the door.

Looking me up and down, he smiled like I'd just told the world's most hilarious joke.

"Don't," I said. "Don't say a word."

"Couldn't you wear normal clothes?" He, for instance, was still wearing his khaki pants and collared shirt from dinner.

"I don't *have* normal clothes," I said. "This is what I wear in the garden. Don't laugh at me."

"It's fine," he said. "I'm sorry."

"You're still laughing," I hissed.

"I'm not," he said. "I swear."

"If I get my everyday clothes dirty, your mom will want to know what happened," I said.

He was suddenly serious. "Really? She pays that much attention to what you wear?"

"Well, yeah," I said. "She pays that much attention to what you wear, too. She just figures you're a lost cause, is all."

IT WAS EASY to find what I was looking for in the greenhouse, since we'd just reorganized the whole place. The wooden crates of bulbs were on the back shelves, each labeled with the type of bulb it contained. Some were done neatly, with stencils, and some were scribbled on with black marker.

Lilies was scrawled, almost as an afterthought, in small print in the upper corner of one of the crates. I pulled it out, and Barrett carried it outside while I gathered the gardening tools from the shed. Then he unlocked the Adam and Eve gate and we followed the winding path through the graveyard to Lily's isolated corner.

It looked different tonight, and the sight gave me a chill. In the rain, it had seemed . . . I don't know, connected somehow to the rest of the garden. Now, though, her grave seemed isolated, even desolate. I hadn't realized how far it was from the others, which were arranged in a neat pattern closer to the entrance.

Barrett felt the unease, too. He peered back toward the entrance. "Do you think . . . do you think Mom wants us all to be buried here?"

"Not me," I said. Nope. I had a grave already, in a cemetery four hours away. The company that owned the cemetery where my family was buried had thrown mine in as a freebie, and I hadn't been able to find the words to refuse and tell them how horrible that was. But now that I'd gotten used to the idea, I didn't mind so much.

"Sorry," he said. "I meant her, and Dad, and Agatha and me."

"Maybe you'll want to be buried somewhere else," I said. "I'm sure that's a decision you can make for yourself someday."

"I guess," he said.

"Put some gloves on," I said. "Let's get to work."

For the next two hours, we dug into the soil, churning it with water and fertilizer, and arranged the bulbs in a horseshoe shape around Lily's grave. We were both careful never to kneel on the grave itself, instead working from the outside. But it was still extremely creepy—and quiet. Our conversation was about planting, and nothing else. If we weren't talking about logistics, we weren't talking. It didn't seem respectful to carry on small talk here, in this dark, sad little place.

After we finished, we cleaned the tools and put them back, then slid the empty crate onto the shelf. We'd planted something like two hundred bulbs, and it would be weeks before we knew if anything had come of it. But even if nothing happened, it felt good to have a project like this—something meaningful.

I just hoped Laura would find it equally meaningful.

I pictured us working in the garden together some morning, Laura sitting back and looking at me and then deciding to trust me enough to start talking about Lily. About how it felt to lose your sister. All because these lilies had reminded her that your memories could be beautiful in spite of the pain they stirred inside you.

She doesn't have to like me, I thought as we walked in silence back to the house and upstairs to our rooms. *But if I can help her, she might respect me a little.*

This time, when I went back into the nursery, Agatha was in her bed, sound asleep. And my room was just as I'd left it.

I washed the dirt from under my fingernails, changed into my pajamas, and got into bed, expecting to fall asleep as soon as my head hit the pillow. But I found myself lying on my side, eyes closed, listening to my own breath and feeling my heartbeat gently pulse through my body. I sat up and tried a sip of my tea, but it was cold.

After another long stretch of helpless wakefulness, I took my teacup and went down to the kitchen.

I considered brewing myself a fresh cup, but ended up sticking the cold tea in the microwave instead. Afterward, I wandered out of the kitchen, taking small sips. I had intended to go right back to bed, but as I came out of the kitchen, I glanced across the hall into the drawing room. Through the open doorway, I could see the far side of the room, where there was a line of paintings—family portraits.

I went in and flipped on the gallery lights aimed at the walls, and the portraits were suddenly illumi-nated. They went from left to right, oldest to new-est, featuring each successive generation of Copeland heirs and their children.

The leftmost one was Jerahmeel, who was thin and unhappy looking, his face strangely birdlike with a small chin and heavy brow. His wife, next to him, looked just as unhappy, but stockier in her wide-skirted and bell-sleeved dress; her mouth was set grimly. Their five children, three boys and two girls, all looked like they'd just realized how unfun their parents were.

The next painting was of Jerahmeel's oldest son and his wife, who was rather pretty and looked familiar to me—and then I realized that she was the future Widow Copeland, whose portrait hung upstairs in the hall. She was already wearing black, even before she was a widow—a high-collared blouse and a high-waisted skirt. At first, I thought they had only two children, boys. Then I realized that Mrs. Copeland held something in her arms—something that was the size and shape of an infant, but draped in gauzy black fabric.

I hurried onward.

The next guy and his wife looked bored, which could hardly have been possible considering the sheer volume of children seated around them—I counted eight. The youngest was a boy, and the rest were girls. The girls all wore dull-colored, shapeless dresses that reminded me of paper lunch bags.

I was about to pause before the next picture when a familiar face caught my eye in the final painting in the row. This one contained exactly two people: Laura and a man who must have been her father. Laura looked rather grown-up, wearing an off-the-shoulder black top and a string of pearls around her neck. She stood in front of her father, who was staring into the distance, with his hand resting on her shoulder. Laura stared directly out at the room. It was a lovely likeness of her.

Her mother would have been long dead by that point. But where was Lily?

The next spot was empty, waiting for the next generation. I wondered if they would continue the tradition. Maybe they were waiting for Agatha to get better first.

I stared at Laura, feeling the emptiness of her loss, and finished my tea.

"Can't you sleep?"

I managed to hold on to my teacup, but only barely. I turned around and found Laura, in her old-fashioned high-necked nightgown, standing in the doorway watching me.

I shook my head. "Sorry, I just came down to heat up my tea."

"I can make you a fresh cup," she said, reaching for the cup.

"I finished it," I said. "Sorry."

"You don't need to apologize," she said. "This is your home, too."

It was a lovely sentiment, although I didn't completely believe her. But why ruin the mood?

She stared at the portrait of herself. "I felt so grown-up when it was time to have this painted. I guess I had some old-fashioned idea that Dad and I would spend a few weeks posing for the artist . . . it turns out we weren't even in the same room. He came and took our photos. It felt like cheating."

"But it's a nice painting anyway," I said.

"Oh yes," she said, leaning a little closer. "I've always liked it. Dad and I were quite a team."

"It was just the two of you?" I asked.

My question hung in the air.

"Yes," she said. "My mother had passed away years before."

"Oh," I said. "Right."

She walked back to the previous picture. "Grandfather and Grandmother—Matthew and Edna. My grandfather passed in a car accident when I was a baby. It was very sad for my father."

Matthew and Edna stood with two young children, a boy and a girl. The whole family looked serious, like they knew what was coming.

"This is the one who cried at the wedding?" I asked.

Laura laughed, a sweet, surprised laugh. "I mentioned that? Yes, Edna, bless her heart. This painting makes her look well-behaved, but she was a terror. And here are David and Maude—although her given name was Agatha, can you imagine deciding to go by Maude?—my great-grandparents. I don't know that she ever forgave herself for having seven girls and only one boy. The kings of Europe couldn't have been less interested in turning their empires over to a female. And she only *married* into the family! She came from some high-society old-money family who ran out of money. Thank God Matthew came along at last."

At first I thought she was joking, but there was almost a little too much sincerity in her voice.

"And over here is the designer of the gardens."

"The Widow Copeland?" I asked.

"Yes, very astute! Loretta Copeland. She married Jerahmeel's oldest son, Abel. He passed away quite young—probably right around when this painting was finished. Loretta took over and ruled the house and the railroad with an iron fist until my great-grandfather came of age. Then she managed the house for him, hand-picked Maude to be his wife, and conveniently dropped dead three days after my grandfather was born."

"Wow," I said.

Laura's gaze swept over the wall. "It seems so impressive . . . until you look at all of them as individual people. They were all flawed. None of them was very much fun, I'm afraid. I guess I'm not, either."

"You've been through a lot," I said.

"I have," she said. "But that doesn't mean you have to turn hard, does it? Look at you. Think what you've lost, and you still seem so . . ."

Her voice sank to nothing. The tone had turned sad.

She straightened her shoulders. "Still, they all did great things. And the family will continue to do great things. Even after my generation. And my children's generation."

She sounded like she was trying to convince both of us.

I nodded.

Then she turned to me, her eyes shining with a strange intensity. "Do you like it here, Margot?"

"Yes, of course," I said. Because I would no sooner have expressed ambivalence than I would have stuck my hand into a lion's cage.

"What if you stayed?" she asked.

"I—" I stared at her, baffled. I thought I *was* staying.

"No, no," she said, like she'd read my mind. "I mean . . . the Albrights have always worked for us. For generations. But Tom—Mr. Albright—his daughter, Colleen, has decided to do something else. Art school." She said *art school* like the words themselves were coated in a thin layer of acid. "And so . . . there is no next generation of Albrights. That's sad, but it's not about the name as much as it is about the idea of it. The loyalty. And so what if you went to business school and then apprenticed with Mr. Albright? What if you stayed? Stayed with us?"

"Oh, wow," I said. "That's so generous."

Was it? I had no idea. I was all muddled, and growing painfully sleepy.

Laura's smile seemed blindingly bright. The points of her white teeth gleamed.

"It would be perfect," she said. "Then, when Barrett takes over, you—"

"Or Agatha," I said.

She didn't speak.

"If Agatha gets better," I said.

"Yes—of course." She tightened the silky sash around her waist. "Yes. Agatha. Or Barrett. But the important thing is that the affairs of the family would be in the hands of someone we trust implicitly."

This was strange. This was overwhelming. How could Laura trust me implicitly? She'd only known me for a month. The room seemed too warm.

She put her arm around me and her thin fingers wrapped around my shoulder. I could feel the pressure of each individual fingertip through the fabric of my pajamas.

I began to feel slightly queasy.

"Oh, Margot, think how nice that would be," she said. "Think—"

I OPENED MY eyes.

I was in bed.

How did I get here?

The last thing I remembered was talking to Laura in

the drawing room. What had we been talking about? What was the last thing she said?

What on earth was happening to me?

It was still dark outside, which was good because I wanted to go back to sleep. I felt like I could sleep for ten more hours. But as I turned over and began to shut my eyes, I saw, written on the wall:

GO

CHAPTER
~16~

"GOOD MORNING," LAURA said, her voice a happy singsong.

And then—to my utter amazement—she stood up from the breakfast table and hugged me quickly.

"Agatha has an appointment with her specialist in Chicago today, so I need to scoot if we're going to be ready to go." She glanced at her watch, and her eyes popped almost comically. "Oh, goodness, it's later than I thought."

"Do you need help with Agatha?" I asked.

Her smile was so warm that it made me slightly uneasy for a moment. Who was this version of Laura?

"I was telling John this morning, before he left, how thoughtful you are. How is it possible for a sixteen-year-old to be so thoughtful? But no. I'll be fine. Agatha ate already, so it's just a matter of getting her dressed and doing her hair."

"Okay," I said.

Her gaze lingered on me. "But thank you."

"You're welcome," I said.

She looked like there was something she was dying to say, but then she thought better of it and started to leave the room.

I headed for the table, a little relieved. The unfamiliar brightness of her energy was a little too much for me this early in the day.

Then I felt a hand on my shoulder. It made me jump, and Laura let out a tinkling little laugh.

"I startled you," she said. "I apologize. I just wanted to say, Margot . . . I hope you know how much you mean to us. To me."

What was I supposed to say to that?

Her eyes were searching, pinning me in place. Her voice got lower, whispery, excited. "And the thought that you'll always be with us . . . that you're really one of the family now . . . I'm thrilled."

Then she scurried out, as if trying to save me from having to come up with a reply.

I stared after her, openmouthed, like a cartoon character who's just seen a cartoon alien appear out of a cartoon flying saucer.

What was she talking about? Always with them? One of the family? I racked my brain, trying to remember our conversation. I remembered looking at the paintings with her the previous night. I remembered her saying something . . . What was it?

For a panicked moment, I was afraid I had agreed to be adopted. I had no interest in being adopted by the Suttons—none.

But that didn't feel right.

No, it was something else.

Art school? No. What did art school have to do with anything?

Something to do with Mr. Albright? Working for Mr. Albright?

No . . . working for the Suttons. *Being* Mr. Albright.

An absurd image of myself flashed into my head, me in one of Mr. Albright's suits, with a necktie and a briefcase, sweeping into the house with his robotic good cheer.

That was it, I was sure of it. Laura had asked me if I wanted to take over for Mr. Albright . . . someday.

And I said *yes*?

I plopped down into a chair, staring at the plate of pastries. Suddenly I wasn't hungry anymore. I felt like I'd already had breakfast—something made of dust, that had left a dry coating over the inside of my whole body.

I said *yes*?

I couldn't have said yes. I would never have said yes. Living here with the Suttons for a couple of years while I finished high school was one thing. But living with them—being part of this world forever—no, I couldn't do that. I knew it without thinking about it. I'd go crazy. I'd lose my mind.

But if I hadn't said yes, Laura wouldn't have said any of what she'd said just now.

If I hadn't said yes, she wouldn't be happy—she would be hurt.

She would be angry.

I DIDN'T USUALLY go looking for Barrett during the day. I knew he spent part of the day in his room, doing summer homework. Sometimes he went out for a jog around the perimeter of the property—presumably to stay in shape for lacrosse. And he spent another part of the day with his father. The rest of his time was a mystery to me, and it had never occurred to me to find him.

Now it occurred to me. Because I was restless and bored, and Agatha and Laura would be gone until dinnertime. Reading was okay, but after I finished a book, I had trouble getting up the motivation to immediately pick up another one.

I would have done some tidying, but there was nothing that needed to be tidied.

I stood outside the nursery, freshly showered and

dressed, and wondered whether he was in his room thinking about me and wondering what *I* was up to. . Probably not, right?

No matter how lonely I was, it wasn't my style to stand around waiting for a boy to remember my existence. So I picked up another book, stationed myself in the library where I would hear him come down the stairs, and waited. I mean, read. I read so much that I fell asleep almost instantly.

I was awakened later by a sound, a rolling peal of music that reverberated through the halls. I stood up, feeling like a rat following the Pied Piper, and went to find its source.

I had seen the music room a couple of times—a cozy tucked-away space at the far end of the hall, where the music wouldn't dominate the house—but I'd never seen a human being in there. But now I followed the sound of the piano and rounded the corner to see Barrett sitting on the piano bench, his face frozen in concentration.

For a few seconds, he didn't notice me, and then he glanced up toward the door—maybe he'd sensed a change in the light. When he saw me, his frown softened, and he gave me a faint smile, but it didn't break the fluid rhythm of his playing. He went back to the keys, and I stood leaning against the doorway and watched and listened.

The piece he played was quick and light, but with slower, meditative parts. I was embarrassed by my lack of musical knowledge and hoped I wouldn't be called on to say something intelligent about it.

But that wasn't really what I was focused on.

I was focused on the absolute tension of his body, the way his hands and fingers always seemed to be playing the next notes before I even took in the last ones. I couldn't keep my eyes off the angles of his shoulders, the way he held his head.

He loved this. It was important to him. And he was *so* good at it. I held my breath, as if that could keep his fingers dancing, help push him along the lines of the melody. As if I was part of it.

Finally, the song ended, and he plucked out a playful little flourish and then turned and grinned at me.

Oh, *help*.

"What . . ." I began. "What is this?"

"This," he said, standing up and giving the keys another little twizzling riff, "is called a piano."

"No, but seriously," I said. "How did I not know you played? Where do you practice?"

"In my room, mostly," he said. "I have a keyboard and a pair of headphones. Mom doesn't like the noise."

"How could she not like that?" I asked. "I could listen to it all day."

A soft smile curved his lips. "That's sweet," he said.

"I don't understand." I couldn't stop myself from moving closer.

He shrugged. "She just doesn't like music very much. I don't get it, either, but it's her house."

"Do you play at school?"

"Yeah," he said. "I'm starting in the conservatory program this fall."

"Wow."

"Well." He shrugged. "It's not hard to get into, but it should be fun."

"Does Agatha like to hear you play?"

He shrugged. "I don't know. She used to. But she hasn't heard me for a while."

"We should try sometime," I said. "I've been wondering about music. Whether it helps her."

He sighed. "Like I said, Mom's kind of into silence."

"We could get a headphone splitter."

His expression suddenly got a little brighter. "Yeah, actually. We could. That's a great idea."

I stared at the piano, which was gleaming black and six feet long. "I've never seen a piano this big."

"Do you play?"

I shook my head. "I took lessons until third grade, but I complained so much I broke my mother's will."

"I was the opposite," he said. "She finally gave in and let me take lessons in town. And Dad bought me the keyboard."

"Play something else?" I asked.

"I will, but I'm starving," he said. "Did you have lunch yet?"

I shook my head.

We went to the kitchen and, without discussing it, made lunch together. Just sandwiches with sliced apples on the side, but standing shoulder-to-shoulder with him, working in quiet, intimate silence, made me almost breathless.

I took my plate and started for the breakfast room, but he said, "Let me show you something," and headed back through the kitchen into a dim, plain hallway. Near the end was a door leading to a set of stairs in an almost pitch-dark stairwell. We took them up and then went out the door at the top into the light of the afternoon.

It was a cloudy day, but the light was still comparatively blinding. It took a minute for my eyes to adjust, and then I looked around.

We were on the roof of the house, but it wasn't a normal part of the roof. It was fancy, with black-and-white-tile flooring and old patio furniture strewn about, shoved into irregular pairings.

"There used to be a stairway over there," Barrett said, indicating a place where the waist-high ledge looked patched. "But I think they took it out before Mom was born. Now the service entrance is the only way up here."

One of the enormous trees that grew next to the house shaded a small corner of the deck, so we pulled a couple of incredibly heavy chairs under there and sat down to eat. You could see the whole property from here—except the graveyard, well hidden behind its walls and overgrown hedge.

The wind blew softly, and I tried to eat like a normal person, which was hard because my body seemed to want to devote all my attention to Barrett. A musician. He'd been hiding this secret part of himself like a person hunched over to conceal the soft, brilliant light of a candle.

"I think it's so amazing," I couldn't help saying. I felt at this point like I was costing myself all of my cool points, but I wasn't too afraid that Barrett would care. After all, he'd seen me all dressed up in the garden, and he'd watched me meekly follow his mother's every order.

"Yeah," he said. "It's beautiful, isn't it?"

I looked over at him, thinking he was complimenting himself.

"I do love this property," he said. "But I just like it so much more if I . . . if I know I'm leaving soon."

Leaving soon. I forced myself to ignore that part for now. "But you may inherit the whole thing," I said. "You might live here one day."

"No," he said, his face stony-serious. "Never."

I couldn't hide my surprise.

He looked almost pained, squinting out over the soft hills. "I . . . respect my family. What my ancestors did. But their legacy is dead now. My mom stays here and tries to keep everything exactly the same as it always has been. But that's like . . . it's like if you worked at a factory, and one day it stopped making things, but you still showed up for work every day. That's how my mom is. There's nothing left here. It's all history. There's no future."

"But how . . ." I had to tread lightly. "How can you guys afford to stay here?"

"Oh," he said. "There are investments . . . my mom's really smart with money, actually. And she's pretty frugal. We could stay here indefinitely, even with more staff. But I don't care about that. I don't want to spend my life babysitting the family fortune."

"What do you want to do?"

He ducked his head a little, shrugging his shoulders. "Play piano, if I could."

I sat up. "Oh, you could. You're so talented. The house is fine, but it's . . ."

"What?" he asked, looking at me carefully. "You don't like it?"

I looked out at the breathtaking view. "It's beautiful," I said. "But I don't feel like myself here. Not that

I even know who I am anymore, but . . . whoever I am here, it's not quite right."

"It'll be better when the school year starts," he said.

"Yeah," I said.

"You'll make friends and stuff. Mom can't lock you away when you have people wanting to hang out."

"I hope so. Anyway—I don't mean to complain. Your parents have been really nice to me." I couldn't help veering off topic. "I was so surprised to see you playing before. I can't believe I didn't know."

"What did you think I was doing all day?" he asked.

"I don't know," I said. "What do you think I do all day?"

He leaned back in his chair and looked up into the interlaced branches of the tree overhead. "Well, you come down to breakfast and then you go upstairs and help Agatha. You go out and work in the garden, but you're always clean at lunch, so I assume you shower and get dressed before eating. In the afternoon, you take my sister upstairs and read. Before dinner, you always ask Mom if she needs help with anything, which she never does. Then you go to the library."

I stared at him.

He gave me a smirk. "And you thought I sat in my room and stared at my lacrosse trophies all day."

"I'm sorry," I said. I couldn't stop myself from

smiling. "I should have known you contained hidden depths."

"They're so hidden and so deep that most people assume I'm a dumb jock," he said. "And they're basically right."

"Except for one little secret," I teased.

"I'm entitled to one, right?"

"Sure," I said. "Everybody gets one free secret."

He nodded and looked away. I could feel my heart fluttering wildly, like a tiny bird in my chest.

"Do me a favor?" I asked.

"Whatever you want," he said.

Kiss me, I wanted to say.

"Play for me," I said.

CHAPTER
~17~

WE WASHED THE dishes and cleaned the kitchen, and then he played for another hour and a half. The music room was small, with a low ceiling. The piano was in the center of the room and there were other instruments in cases along the walls. In one corner was a miniature harp on a stand. Barrett sat on the red-upholstered piano bench and I lay sprawled on an ivory curve-backed sofa feeling like Marie Antoinette. Even the design of the chair made me feel self-conscious—it was the kind of furniture you would drape yourself over, posing attractively to catch the attention of some tasty morsel you were trying to seduce. I was surprised Laura allowed it in the house, actually—to me it seemed to be asking for scandal. (*Kiss me,* I continued to not say to Barrett.)

I closed my eyes and let myself float away on the

music. But after a while, I began to worry about his hands. Were they getting tired? So when he came to the end of the song he was playing, I said, "Let's take a break."

He looked up, and I swear he'd forgotten I was there. "I'm sorry," he said. "Is it boring?"

"No," I said. "Oh my God, no. But your fingers must need a rest."

He sat back and wiggled them. "They're okay." But I noticed how he rubbed his palms together.

"Your mom will be back soon," I said, reluctantly getting to my feet. "She'll probably be tired. I should stay with Agatha until dinner."

He nodded, stretched his arms over his head, and then sighed. "Thanks for listening."

I was struck by the realization that I might not get another chance to sit in this room and listen to him play, and that made me want to cry. We had several weeks left, but would there be more time without Laura's presence? Without John? Even without Agatha? His music had felt like a connection to something in myself I hadn't quite known was there—not my old self who no longer existed, and not some mysterious future self I could possibly become. But the thread of me that had always been and would always be there inside me, unchanged and unchanging. The part of me that was a good sister, that cared for Agatha, that longed to help Laura make sense of her sister's death. In the music I heard myself.

"Wait," I said, and he looked up at me. "One more?"

He nodded again, then waited for me to settle. He watched me and kept watching me even when I expected his eyes to turn to the keys of the piano. He was studying me, and even though I wanted to flinch, I didn't.

"Okay," he said quietly. "I know what to play."

He began to play a song that was slow and gentle, each note thoughtful and soft and in a quiet harmony with the others. It made me think of swans floating on a quiet lake. It was happy but sad.

It was over too soon, and the last note still seemed to be echoing in the air.

"Did you like it?" Barrett asked.

I did. More than I'd ever liked or appreciated any piece of music in my life. But I didn't feel like answering. Being there with him made me feel strangely, awfully alone.

"It was lovely," I said, standing up. "I have to get going. I need to—put away my clean laundry."

"Wait—" he called as I hurried down the hall. "Margot, I'm sorry—"

I held myself together all the way upstairs, until I

made it into the nursery and closed the door behind me. I knew he would never knock.

Then I sank onto my bed and let tears roll down my face.

There were no hysterics. There was no bitter wailing, no heartbroken agony.

It was just me, sitting there, already missing him.

I was so good at missing people. What was one more bit of sorrow?

"MARGOT? BARRETT?"

The sound of John's voice in the upstairs hallway was so unusual that I ran to the door and opened it, breathless. Twenty feet away, Barrett did the same.

"Dad?" he asked. "What's wrong?"

"Nothing," John said, looking from Barrett to me. "Everything's okay. You both look like you've seen a ghost. I just came up to say that Laura and Agatha are staying overnight in Chicago. So I was thinking pizza for dinner. Does that work?"

"Oh," Barrett said, and I felt his eyes on me. "Sure. Great."

"Do you like pizza, Margot?" John asked. "No eggplant."

I was touched that he remembered. "Yeah, I love it."

"Great. I'll order in a few minutes, it'll probably get here in an hour." With an awkward smile, he thumped back down the stairs.

Barrett looked at me, and I looked at him.

"See you at dinner," I said, and closed my door.

DINNER WAS FUN. Without Laura there barely veiling her disapproval of the informal ambience, John was lighthearted and a little goofy. He told many dad jokes worthy of my own father's considerable dad-joke repertoire (*Why do they call them French fries when they're cooked in Greece?*) and acted really interested in Barrett's stories about life at school.

Afterward, he excused himself to finish up some work, and I carried the rest of the pizza to the kitchen to wrap it up and put it in the fridge.

"I can do that," Barrett said, coming in and finding me wrestling with the plastic wrap.

"I can also do it," I said. "Hence the doing of it that I . . . am."

"I wasn't trying to imply that you can't," he said.

"Just that I shouldn't be oppressed by your parents' insistence that I personally wrap all the leftover food."

"Exactly," he said. "Fight the power."

"The power bought me dinner," I said. "So I can put the dinner away."

"Well, I can take the box to the trash," he said, snatching it off the counter and disappearing. He seemed to be gone for a long time, and I grew uneasy. Finally, I'd given up and started back toward the nursery. I hadn't shed the melancholy that had settled on me, and it made me sensitive to every detail of our interactions. I began to think his long absence was intentional.

"Margot, wait, please," he said, jogging down the hall behind me. This time, unlike earlier, he caught up. "Sorry, the box didn't fit in the normal trash. I had to take it over to the garage . . . I was wondering if you wanted to go for a walk."

"Where?" I asked.

"Just around," he said. "Not to any specific place to do any specific thing—"

"Oh, we can water the bulbs," I said.

He laughed. "Or that."

"I'll go get the key," I said.

WE EMERGED FROM the house into a world on the verge of nightfall. The sky was darkening swiftly, the last gasps of sunlight shooting into the clouds and painting them shades of rose pink and orange.

We were strangely quiet as we made our way out through the garden and into the graveyard. I think we were contemplating the absolute insanity that could ensue if we ever admitted that we wanted to be together in any way. I know I was.

After my conversation with Laura, the names on the gravestones suddenly made sense, which also made them supremely creepy. Abel? Yes, I remembered Abel. Well, here he is. Loretta, the old battle-ax. Here she is. Agatha (a.k.a. Maude), Matthew. Here they all were, arrayed in orderly, picturesque little graves, spread out among the trees yet still all part of the whole.

But not Lily. Her grave was one curve of the path too far from the others. Maybe they'd decided to start the new generation back here, spread things out a little. That made me imagine the current generation of Suttons lying still and silent underground someday, their bodies cold and their muscles melting away, bones fading to dust, and that turned my stomach.

"Are you okay?" Barrett asked.

"I really don't like it in here," I said.

"Yeah, me neither," he said. "Should we go?"

"It's okay," I said. I carried a hose looped over my shoulder, one of the extras from the back of the greenhouse, and I planned to hook it up to one of the spigots that had been installed by whoever built the wall.

We rounded the corner and I was busy inspecting

the rubber washer at the end of the hose. I hoped it wasn't too corroded. The dry rot got to the rubber if you didn't keep it moist enough.

"Margot," Barrett said, quietly and quickly.

"Yeah?" I asked, turning to face him. But halfway through the turn, I stopped.

I stared.

"No," Barrett said. "Right?"

He meant, *No way are we seeing what we think we're seeing*.

The bulbs we had planted the previous night, if we were lucky, should have been soaking in water and getting a feel for the warmth and weight of the soil. If all went according to plan, in about two weeks, the first tiny green shoots should creep out of the papery layers of the bulb and poke out of the soil. In a month, maybe a plant would be on its way to flowering.

But now—less than a full day later—the grave was completely surrounded by brilliant dark red lilies, fully grown and open, yawning and leaning and swaying on their slender stems. Their leaves, like oversize blades of grass, bent gracefully toward the ground.

"No way," I said.

This was a complete impossibility. This was the kind of thing that didn't happen in reality.

"I don't understand," Barrett said. He knelt to inspect one of the flowers, lightly touching its velvet-soft petal as if he half expected it to snap shut on his fingers.

I knelt next to him, feeling weirdly afraid.

"It's like magic," I whispered, and then I stood up and backed away.

Barrett stayed there, looking at the grave, which now seemed so small—like a child's bed, its edges defined by the lush crowd of lilies.

Then he looked over his shoulder at me and laughed in amazement, and for a moment the sound of it transported me back through time to my old life, days spent sitting in the cafeteria at school with Becca and CJ and the others, the hum of happy/stressed/tired chatter all around us. And punctuating it from random corners of the room, laughter. Warm, bright, happy laughter.

"How could this have happened overnight?" Barrett asked.

I didn't answer. I stared in wonder at the sight. The flowers were beautiful, a deep burgundy with yellow centers and ruffles along the edges of their petals.

A hush seemed to fall over the garden, over us.

The evening's last light edging in over the wall had turned dazzling gold. It shone on Barrett's face and turned him into a bronze statue.

"This house . . ." I said.

He came closer. "What about it?"

"Did you like growing up here?"

"It's what I knew," he said. "I thought it was normal."

"When I first came here, I thought your mom was just kind of anxious," I said.

"She is," he said.

"No, but . . . it's more than that. It's like she's worried all the time. It's not just about Agatha."

"You think that has something to do with her sister dying?" he asked.

I shrugged. "Depends on how she died."

"We never played with other kids," Barrett said thoughtfully. "And when we did, we weren't allowed to go into the closed-off wings. Mom's big on not letting the cold air out, or the hot air in, or whatever, I don't know." He frowned, his forehead creasing. "I had one friend for a while—a kid we met at the grocery store in town. I basically forced Mom to invite him over. His mother drove him here, and the moms sat and talked while we played. We were having fun, but Mom called for us and we didn't come right away— and then she yelled at us both. So his mom got mad at my mom, and we never saw them again."

"Why did she yell?" I asked.

He shrugged. "At the time I didn't know. But there are a lot of weird things in a house like this. Exposed wiring, random places you could get stuck. There used to be a dumbwaiter, like a tiny elevator, in the storage room off the kitchen—well, it's still there but we don't use it. Apparently when my grandfather was a kid, one of the maids lost a finger trying to send a mop and bucket to the second floor, and Mom forbade us from even opening the doors. She caught me trying to climb in once and freaked out. Like, shaking, she was so scared."

"Sometimes I wonder how everybody's not scared all the time," I said. "When you have a family you love and everybody leaves the house in the morning—don't you think, *What if that's the last time I ever see them?*"

He was frowning deeply. "I never did before. But . . . when Agatha got sick, I think I did feel that way. Only it was too late. The last time I talked to her, we were arguing. And then it was like she changed into a different person. I go over that conversation in my head every day."

"What were you arguing about?"

He seemed to stare directly into the orange light, which was quickly fading and leaving a pale indigo shadow in its place. "She was sneaking away from school for the weekend—she'd forged herself a permission slip and she and her friends went to somebody's lake house. I told her not to go. And then she fell off the dock and cut her foot, and the doctors think some weird bacteria got into her bloodstream. She came home so Mom could keep an eye on her, and she never got better. That was October . . . by the time I got home for Christmas, she was . . . like she is now." He stared at the ground. "They said she's lucky she didn't lose her arms and legs—or die. But she lost plenty."

I'll say.

"I know it's nothing compared to your life. And it sounds terrible to say it. But it's like the sister I knew . . . died." He sighed heavily. "I could have talked her out of it. I should have tried harder. She's somebody else now, and it's too late to say sorry."

"You don't have anything to be sorry for."

He was quiet for a long time. He stared at Lily's grave, but it was like he was seeing something else.

"I told her . . ." he said, and his voice wavered. "I told her she was just asking for something bad to happen."

I didn't say anything.

"And she said . . . 'You probably want something bad to happen to me. So I can learn my lesson.' But I didn't. I swear I didn't."

"Of course you didn't," I said.

"But when she was getting sicker . . ." He stared at the ground. "Did she know? Did she know I didn't really want something bad to happen to her? Or did she think I was glad?"

"She would never think that," I said. "No sane person would ever think that."

"And then . . . I left," he said. "She was so sick at Christmas, and I still went back to school."

"You had to. You couldn't quit school."

"But what if she'd died?"

"She's not that sick." I thought about Agatha. "She doesn't seem sick at all, actually. Just zoned out."

"I've abandoned her, though. I don't think I realized that until I met you." His eyes turned to meet mine reluctantly. "If I was rude to you in the beginning, that's why. Because I'm . . . I'm ashamed. I'm a bad brother. And you being the way you are just makes it so much more obvious."

"The way I am?" I asked, a little alarmed and hurt. "What am I doing wrong?"

"No, Margot," he said, looking down at me. "I mean . . . you're great."

Oh, whispered my heart.

I looked up at him.

I liked the way his floppy hair lay on his forehead. I liked the softness of his brown eyes.

His hand was reaching down toward mine, an invitation, and I touched him and felt strong fingers wrap around mine.

"Your hands are so cold," he said.

"It's okay," I managed to choke out. "They always are."

"Here." He pressed my hands against the heat of his chest and covered them with his warm palms. I could feel his heartbeat as if I held his heart in my fingers.

"Thanks," I whispered.

He smiled.

The air around us seemed to blur into something glittering and dreamlike.

"What I wanted you to hear in the song I played for you," he said, in a voice as low as the murmuring of the leaves in the trees overhead, "is that it was about you. It was about the way you walk, and talk, and—"

Before he could finish the sentence, I had pulled my hands free and used them to bring his face down to meet mine. Our lips touched softly, as softly as a feather floating to meet the silent ground. And then they parted, and touched again, hesitantly—and then the kiss took flight and the dreamy air swirled in around us, enveloped us like a tornado.

Mutually dazed, we pulled apart. But his hands were wrapped around my lower back, just above my waist, and he didn't let go.

I leaned toward his chest and laid my cheek against his shirt, breathing in the air around him. It was that boy smell, warm and spicy and clean and dirty at the same time. I wanted to memorize his scent and carry it around with me forever.

"Margot, Margot," Barrett whispered, and I turned back to his lips.

We kissed for a few minutes while the daylight fluttered its eyelashes and finally sank away. The aroma of wet soil rose around us. I read somewhere once that the scent of a freshly mown lawn is actually the cut grass screaming for help, and I felt something deep inside my body screaming:

Help, help, help.

But what kind of help did I need?

This kind, I thought, pulling him closer.

We kissed for a little while longer, until it felt natural to stop, although our hands were clasped together and we stood maybe eight inches apart.

"Wow," he said.

"Yeah," I said.

His lips pressed against my hair.

"We should go inside," I said.

He nodded, and we walked hand in hand to the entrance of the garden. We closed the gates, but when I went to turn the key, it wasn't there.

"Weird," Barrett said, and we both looked around. "Did you put it in your pocket?"

"These pants don't have pockets," I said, sliding my hands over the places where any normal human would have sewn pockets into their design. "I'm sure I left it in the lock."

I looked around, feeling suddenly sorry to be out here, in the fresh, dewy night.

"We can just leave it," he said. "It's okay."

That suggestion, so mild and harmless, sent a wave of anxiety through me. "No," I said. "We have to lock the gate."

I began searching the ground around us—perhaps it had simply slipped out and was lying at our feet. But a quick visual sweep showed nothing, and even when Barrett took out his phone and turned on the flashlight, we couldn't find the key.

I wandered a few steps away, drawn toward the pile of empty pots and spindly tomato cages sitting nearby.

"It couldn't be that far," Barrett said, but I knelt anyway and looked in the dirt. He came over behind me and held up his phone, moving it around.

"There," I said, seeing the flash of metal barely sticking out of the soil. I reached over and grabbed it, but instead of the metal key, my fingers were clasped around a small buckle. I tugged it, and it reluctantly came out of the dirt. The metal part was attached to a thin strip of cracked, filthy leather.

"What's that?" Barrett asked, leaning closer. His arm brushed my arm and I forgot what I was doing for a moment. "A collar?"

"Did you guys use to have a cat?" I asked. The

band was so short it would barely have made it around my wrist. "Or a really small dog?"

"No, never," he said. "Mom hates cats. And she thinks dogs are dirty."

"It was probably a cat," I said. I knocked loose a clump of mud, revealing a filthy bell. "Definitely a cat." Then I rubbed away the caked dirt from the little tag, revealing a name: MISSY.

"It must be really old," he said.

I sighed. What I really wanted was to find the key so we could lock the graveyard and go inside.

Barrett shone the phone around in one last defeated movement.

"There—" I crossed the path and walked down to the closest flowering plant, clusters of tiny purple and white flowers on thin, weedy stalks. Lying in front of it, as neatly as if it had been placed there, was the key.

"How did it get there?" Barrett asked.

I looked around. "Must have been the wind," I said.

He didn't answer.

I was relieved just to have found it, so I tried not to dwell on the weirdness as I locked the gate and held the key in my hand.

We walked slowly back to the house, our hands linked together.

As we came around the corner, the back door of the house opened.

I dropped Barrett's hand like it was a buttered eel.

Laura stepped outside. Next to me, Barrett stood straighter and took a deep, nervous breath.

"Well, hello," she said pleasantly as we came closer. "What are you two up to?"

"Just out for a walk," Barrett said. "I thought you were going to be in town tonight."

"I planned to," she said, leading us back inside. "I'd even booked a hotel room. But the pharmacy was able to finish the formulation three minutes before closing. Wasn't that lucky?"

"I'm glad Agatha can sleep in her own bed," I said.

"Yes." Laura gave me an appreciative smile. "Me too."

As we came into the hall, she said, "Well, Barrett, I'm sure you have a lot of reading to get to."

"I do," he said, heading for the stairs. I hoped he wouldn't even glance at me—Laura saw everything—but he did, one tiny look over his shoulder.

I felt her noticing, and inwardly I cringed.

Then she glanced down at her gold watch.

"I'm so sorry, Margot," she said. "I just don't think I'm going to have time to drop in and see you before bed. My schedule's all thrown off because of the delay in town. And I have a headache, so I'd like to get to bed. Is that all right?"

"Of course," I said. No offense to Laura, but it wasn't like I relied on our talks to calm down. In fact, most of the time I found myself tensing up while anticipating her arrival. Laura could turn even bedtime into a formal affair.

When I got to the top of the stairs, Barrett stuck his head out of his bedroom, like a gopher, and grinned.

In spite of myself, I smiled back.

"What did she say?" he asked.

"Nothing important."

Keeping an eye over my shoulder, he came out and walked over to me. I could feel the nearness of his body like a fire.

I glanced at his hands and then I couldn't stop thinking about how it felt to have his fingers pressing gently on my back. As it was, I settled for holding his hand. His thumb moved across my fingers and sent shivers down my spine.

I wanted to lean in and kiss him. Then I thought better of it and pulled my hand away.

"See you at breakfast?" he asked.

"Yeah," I said. "Good night."

"Good night."

I watched him disappear into his room. As soon as he was out of sight, something inside me sank a little. How could we do this with Laura around? It was obvious that she knew everything that went on under her roof. I didn't have enough faith in my acting abilities to think I could hide the change in the circumstances between Barrett and me. I pictured myself trying not to make googly eyes at him over the breakfast table, and the image was horrifying.

Still, how delicious was it to have someone to kiss?

Very.

So delicious that I couldn't stop myself from smiling from the time I went back into the nursery until I got in bed. I read for a while, growing sleepier and sleepier, until I realized that I was waiting for Laura's entrance. I heard her and Agatha come in, but she didn't even knock on my door.

It's okay, I told myself. She's just busy.

The next time my eyes started to slide closed, I set aside my book and switched off the light.

I fell asleep with Barrett's gold-tinted profile projected in my head like a movie.

It was lovely.

Until the screaming started.

CHAPTER
~18~

IN MY DREAM, I was wandering around the graveyard by myself, looking for something . . . someone?
Fingers of light reached through the trees and lit my
path. I passed the stately memorials and elegant stat-
ues without taking much notice of them.

Who am I looking for? I wondered.

Suddenly, ahead, a flash of movement across the
narrow path—a cat?

"Missy!" I cried, beginning to run. "Missy!"

I kept catching sight of her, even when the trees
got so close together that I had to turn my body sideways to keep going. A shadow here, the flick of a tail
there—

"Missy, wait!" I had to catch up with her—she
wanted to show me something. But what?

I came around the corner and found Lily's grave,

completely covered in flowers. On the far side, the cat waited, perched on the grave marker.

I began to wade through the lilies toward her, but halfway there I realized that I'd made a huge mistake.

My feet were beginning to sink into the soft ground. Every step required a massive effort to lift them free. But before I could turn around and go back, I had sunk too far to pull myself out. For a moment, I thought the flowers were growing freakishly high, but then I realized that I was the problem—I was being dragged underground.

Soon I was up to my waist, grabbing for the flowers, as if they would help me. I imagined I could feel slender fingers in a vise grip on my ankles, helping the process along, and all the while, the cat sat just out of reach and primly cleaned her paws.

At one point, I tried to dig in the earth and my hands came up filled with tiny bones—and then I heard muffled ringing and saw the collar dangling from the fistful of mud I was holding. These were *Missy's* bones. I frantically shook my hands and the bones went flying, lost among the lilies.

Suddenly, I felt the cold, wet grit of the soil on the back of my neck, and my shoulders and arms were completely submerged. The mud, inches below my nose, smelled of death and ruin.

Then the cat looked up and dashed away, and I turned my head to see what had frightened her.

There was someone lurching toward me, through the trees—moving not with the easy gait of the living, but the stilted, horrific stagger of the dead.

And just before the mud poured into my mouth— I screamed.

I screamed, and I screamed, and I screamed.

I WAS SHAKEN awake, and the person who leaned over me in the darkness was so like the stumbling figure from my nightmare that I drew in a breath to scream again.

But then she slapped her hand over my mouth and leaned closer.

It was Agatha.

When she saw that I recognized her, she pulled her hand away, and then wiped it on my pillow in a gesture that would have been funny if I weren't slowly getting used to the idea that I wasn't about to be swallowed by the earth or hunted down by a zombie.

Then she watched me. After a second, she reached over and turned the nightstand light on, and I could see her face.

She looked normal, basically, but there did seem

to be something—a minute spark of interest more than she usually showed.

"I'm sorry," I whispered. "I get nightmares sometimes . . ."

She watched me evenly.

"I was getting pulled under," I said. I had to say it aloud, to make it less real. "Down into the dirt."

And then something incredible happened.

Agatha's eyes meandered to my face. Then they locked together with my eyes.

And she opened her mouth.

"I," she said.

Suddenly, the door opened behind her, and she shut her mouth.

With dread, I thought, *I've woken Laura.*

It wasn't Laura, though.

It was Barrett.

"Hey," he said. "What's going on?"

I was still watching Agatha; though her expression had changed, her attention drifted. Whatever she had been about to say, it was gone. Finally, I looked up at Barrett.

"Bad dream," I said. "I think I scared Agatha. She came in and woke me up."

"Do you want me to go get Mom?"

That was the opposite of what I wanted. I shook my head. I was relieved that she wasn't there already—

how could she have missed the screaming? "No, don't bother her," I said. "She had a headache."

"Oh, yeah," he said. "Her headache medicine is really strong. You could probably scream in the same room and it wouldn't wake her." He touched his sister's shoulder. "It's okay, Aggie, go back to bed."

She waited a few seconds. Having spent as much time with her as I had, I knew this was a choice. She didn't really want to leave. I felt a pang of affection and gratitude toward her.

Eventually, though, she did go. And then I was alone, in my bedroom, with Barrett standing over me. I felt distinctly aware of how close his body was to my body.

The room was dark and quiet; the nightmare still lurked in the back of my mind like a specter.

"Are you okay?" he asked.

"I don't know," I said. "I mean, yes, but . . . I can't go back to sleep right now. It'll just start right where it left off. I'll end up screaming again."

"Do you want me to get a chair and sit with you?"

No. I didn't want him in a chair. I wanted him to sit *next* to me. I wanted him to put his arm around me and let me put my head on his shoulder. I wanted to put my hand inside both of his hands. I wanted him to slowly turn his face down toward mine, and I wanted him to kiss me.

I patted the bed, and he hesitantly lowered himself. I reached over and took his hand, which felt dangerous and wild.

He took a deep breath. "Do you want to talk about your dream?"

I shrugged.

"Was it about . . . your family?"

"No, it was . . ." *It was about* your *family.* "It was . . . vague." I took a shuddering sigh. "I guess I forgot how bad they can be, since I don't have as many as I used to."

"That's a good thing," he said.

"I guess. In a way, it makes it worse, because I got used to them. Now I'm just going to worry every night that they've come back. And wake up your sister. And make your mom hate me."

I expected him to say she wouldn't hate me, and I was prepared not to believe him. But he didn't say anything.

I closed my eyes. "I miss *my* mom."

"What was she like?"

"Funny. And smart. And strict, but kind of a pushover, too. Like, if we did what she said most of the time, we could always get away with stuff the rest of the time." Mom's face appeared in my thoughts, her curly hair, her double-pierced ears that I found so embarrassing—like some part of her had never out-grown her edgy teenage years, even though she was a middle-aged dentist. The freckle that was centered above her left eyebrow and always made her look weirdly like she had a secret. "I miss her so much. I miss them all."

"What . . . um . . . do you mind if I . . . no, sorry. Never mind."

"It's okay," I said. "I can tell you about it."

"I don't want to make things worse by making you think about it."

"Barrett," I said. "It's like ninety percent of what I think about. It's not worse to talk about it. Besides, I don't remember that much. There's a bunch that's just . . . gone."

So then I described the accident—what I remembered. He held my hand the whole time, and when I got to the part about crawling onto the shore and simply waiting to freeze to death, I felt his grip tighten and saw his jaw clench.

"I'm sorry, Margot," he said breathlessly when I had finished. "It's terrible. I'm so sorry."

I nodded. I couldn't say It's okay because it wasn't okay. It would probably never be okay.

But it was better . . . because he was there.

He leaned over and gently kissed my forehead.

In a weird way, I was happy to have this conversation. Happy to return to familiar territory. Sadness about my family was like a well-fitting old sweater. I knew how to wrap myself in it.

"Is Agatha okay?" I asked. "Can you check on her and make sure she's back in bed?"

"Yeah, of course," he said. He got up and went out to the big room, then returned a few seconds later. "She's fine."

"Okay, good."

"It's so sweet," he said. "How you look out for her."

"She came to help me," I said. "So it goes both ways."

His smile was weirdly uneasy. "I think . . . I'm not a good brother."

"Barrett, there's a limit to what a person can do. You have school, you have—"

"No," he said. "I mean, I could leave school—maybe I should leave school—but even before this, I never connected with her. We were more like acquaintances. I thought she was annoying. Shallow."

I didn't interrupt him. It seemed like there was more he needed to say.

"And now I'm stealing her inheritance," he said. "Mom is acting like it's all decided."

"Well, she can't exactly run this place the way she is."

"She was never going to run it," he said. "And Mom knew that. Sometimes I think Mom is relieved Agatha got sick, because it keeps her from having to break tradition."

That was a horrific idea.

"Not happy," he said quickly. "But relieved."

"Right," I said.

"But I don't want to live here, either." He spoke the words as if they left a bitter taste in his mouth. "I'm not going to spend my life trapped here." He looked at me. "Dad feels the same way. But he can't do anything, since Agatha's so sick. They used to argue about it. He wanted to move to Chicago. Or at least into town."

I imagined them buying a regular house somewhere more ordinary. Someplace I could get outside and walk around and see other people. It seemed too good to be true.

"To be honest, I think that's why he works so much. He doesn't have to. Before Agatha got sick, I thought they were going to get a divorce. That's why he spends so much time at the office and in the city. Sometimes he'll be gone for a week at a time. Mom pretends it's because he's a legal superstar, but it's because he feels like an animal in a zoo when he's here."

I thought about John's wiry tension, the way he never, ever seemed relaxed or happy. And suddenly his long stretches away from home—which Laura never even mentioned—made sense.

He let out a huge sigh. "When I inherit this place—if I do—which I hope I don't—but if I do—I'm going to sell it as fast as I can. I'll use the money to make sure Agatha's taken care of, and then I'll go live my life for real somewhere else."

"You can't tell your mom that," I said.

"I know." After a long pause, he asked, "Do you think I'm a bad person?"

"No, I don't," I said. "I don't even know what it means to be a bad person. People definitely do bad things, but maybe it's because they're scared or sad or hurt."

"But I'm not those things."

I looked at him, and wanted to ask: *Are you sure?* "But it's not bad to want to live your own life. If this place isn't right for you, then it's not right for you. Your mom should want you to be happy."

"I'm not sure she knows very much about happiness."

"You make her happy," I said. Although even as I said it, I wasn't sure it was true. I thought about the way my parents used to talk to my sisters and me. They liked us. They thought we were fun. But Laura seemed to see her kids as part of a preplanned existence. Her version of happiness looked more like being satisfied by a job well done.

"I don't want to leave you here," Barrett whispered.

"I can hide in your suitcase," I said.

He sat up. "I'll talk to Dad. They can send you to Camden. They have plenty of money, and—"

"I can't," I said. "I can't leave Agatha."

His shoulders sank.

A huge yawn shook my body.

"You should go back to sleep," Barrett said. "Do you think you can?"

"Yeah," I said. "That's not the problem. The problem is more bad dreams."

"I can stay here. Wake you up if you seem to be having a hard time."

I pulled his hand to my cheek and rested it there. "Imagine if you fell asleep in here," I said. "What would your mother say?"

"She'd implode," he said.

I nodded.

"But I can stay for a little while. Until you fall asleep again—if you want."

His fingers gently combed the hair out of my face.

"Okay," I said. "Thanks."

Then he leaned down and kissed my lips—a sweet, sad, concerned, protective kiss. The kind of kiss that says more than words. That speaks of regrets and fears and hopes that we would never be able to verbalize. I wanted it to go on forever, but of course that was impossible.

He sat up, placed the covers over my shoulders, and then sighed. "I wish I could make things easier for you."

I was growing so sleepy I almost didn't answer. But after a few seconds, my brain matched up the words to the thoughts, and I said, "You do."

I WOKE WITH the soft morning light. I turned and stretched, and then opened my eyes.

Barrett was still in my room, asleep in the chair in the corner, his chin touching his chest.

I scrambled out of bed. "Barrett!" I whispered. "Barrett, wake up!"

His eyes opened, and as soon as he realized where he was, they went wide in panic. "Oh, God," he said. "Is Mom out there?"

"I don't think so." I went to the door and pressed my ear against it. "What time is it?"

"I don't have my phone," he said, so I reached over and looked at mine, flashing the screen at him.

It was 5:59 a.m.

"What time does she come in?" Barrett asked.

"Six o'clock."

He seemed to turn to stone.

"Come on," I said. "You can't stay in here. If she

finds you in the hall, you can say you woke up early."

He nodded.

I pulled the door open, looking out into the nursery. Agatha was asleep. The door to the hall was ten feet away.

I turned to Barrett. "I'll go downstairs. If she finds me, I'll keep her talking. You only need fifteen seconds, right?"

"Right."

If he'd just left immediately, we would have been fine. "Okay, no problem. I'll see you at breakfast?"

"Yeah," he said.

"Don't come into the hall until I'm downstairs."

He nodded.

I turned around and gave him a kiss—a quick one—and then slipped out the door and into the hall. It was quiet, and for a second I felt foolish. All he had to do was walk to his bedroom. That wasn't a huge deal. It wasn't worth acting like we were spies in enemy territory.

But as soon as I started down the stairs, I realized how close we'd come to being caught.

Laura was approaching. I could hear her humming softly to herself.

I rushed down the stairs—too fast. She stopped short and looked at me in surprise.

"Margot," she said. "Is everything all right? Is Agatha—"

"No," I said. "I mean, yes. Everything is fine. I just—I was wondering—do you have anything I could take for a headache?"

"A headache?" Her eyes narrowed in concern. "Oh, goodness. It must be a bad one for you to come down so early."

"Um." I closed my eyes. "It's okay. It's just . . . I just woke up with it."

"Oh, dear. Come with me."

She led the way to the kitchen and then pulled a small key ring from her pocket and unlocked a cabinet in the corner.

I tried to hide my surprise—she basically had a full-fledged pharmacy. Every shelf was lined with neatly organized clusters of medicines: pill bottles, liquid bottles, even some syringes.

"It looks like a lot," she said, smiling. "But most of it is basic stuff—for colds, allergies—because it's hard to find those things in town sometimes."

That made sense, although I kind of wondered what the rest of it was. I knew Agatha took a lot of pills, but this couldn't *all* be for her.

She pulled down a simple white bottle and shook a couple of small brown tablets out of it, then held them out to me.

I stared at her open palm.

"It's ibuprofen," she said. "I buy generic. Would

you rather take just one? If it's a bad headache, you should take two."

"It's not *so* bad," I said, handing one back. Then I got myself a cup of water and, because Laura was watching me, swallowed the pill.

"Why don't you go back to bed?" she asked, locking the cabinet. "Get some more sleep and come down when you feel better."

I'd gotten plenty of sleep, so obeying her would mean staring at the ceiling until enough time had passed that I could pretend to feel better.

But it was too late to back out now, so upstairs I went.

Agatha sat up and looked at me in alarm as I came in.

"It's okay," I said. "Your mom will be up in a minute. I'm just going to rest for a while."

She kept watching me.

"Are you okay?" I asked.

I walked closer to her bed. "Ags, are you all right? Are you worried about something?"

Her gaze remained intent on my face.

"About me? Don't worry about me. I'm okay. Are you okay?"

No answer.

"You were trying to talk last night," I said. "You said *I*. I what?"

Behind me, the sound of the door being decisively opened.

Then, sharply, Laura said, "Margot, get away from her!"

I was too confused not to jump back, and then I stared at Laura, thinking something was wrong.

Something *was* wrong. It was me.

Laura stared me down. "Did I, or did I not, ask you to come upstairs and get in bed?"

"Yes, but Agatha seemed—"

"Please don't talk back to me," she said, closing her eyes for a moment as if I'd physically pained her. "I cannot abide it. I am very disappointed that, being ill, you would risk Agatha's health by putting yourself in such close proximity."

Inwardly, I rebelled—I wasn't even actually sick—but of course, I couldn't say that to Laura.

"I'm sorry," I said. "I would never risk her health—"

"To bed, please," she said coolly. "I think you'd better rest for the whole morning."

My cheeks felt like fire as I slinked into my room and closed the door (which I was tempted to slam—but who, besides Agatha, would dare slam a door with Laura in the vicinity?). I had to stay in bed the whole morning? Because I stood too close to Agatha when I had a *headache*?

I flounced onto my bed and sat there stewing until

I heard them leave, and then I went to the bathroom and took a shower (if she commented, I could say it helped my headache).

When I came out, I found a stack of books on my bed, as well as a handwritten note on Laura's fancy stationery.

I'm sorry I was short with you. Please rest and I'll see you at lunch. Here's some reading if you can't sleep.

I appreciated the gesture, even though her note made it clear that she expected me to stay quarantined up here for the whole first half of the day.

At least Barrett got out safely.

I didn't even want to think about what her reaction would have been if she'd found him in my room.

CHAPTER

~19~

THE DAY PLODDED along. I nearly died of boredom—the books Laura had left me ended up being punishingly dull. Barrett was at lunch, but I felt Laura's eyes on me and avoided talking to him. I could sense his confusion after my first snub, but by a few minutes in, he seemed to understand. He made small talk with Laura about the upcoming school year, while I listened and felt bitterly jealous of everyone who got to be around him. As soon as the meal was over, I escaped to the garden so she couldn't send me back to bed.

He was mysteriously missing at dinner, but I thought asking about him would give me away somehow. Then, halfway through, I thought not asking about him might be worse, so I asked Laura if she knew where he was.

It was a mistake—she caught on immediately,

even though she didn't say anything. And by the end of dinner, I was more than ready to go to bed just to have an excuse to stop trying to look innocent (while trying not to look like I was trying to look innocent). I didn't get an answer about Barrett's whereabouts until later, when she came to say good night.

I'd pulled a more interesting book from the library and was in bed reading when Laura came in with our tea. She smiled apologetically and apologized again for being snippy with me that morning—that was how she described it, *being snippy*.

She sat down and handed me my cup, and I drank some.

"Maybe you'll sleep better tonight," she said.

I took another few sips.

I'd been replaying my conversations with Laura in my head all day . . .

And I couldn't remember telling her that I hadn't slept well.

Why would she think that? Why would she even suspect it?

"I hope so," I said, because one didn't not answer Laura.

She gave me a smile and then slowly stood. "See you in the morning? Sleep in. No reason to risk another headache."

I nodded.

She glanced down. "Finish your tea. It'll help you relax."

I AWOKE WITH a jerk, vaguely aware of being coated in a light layer of sweat.

What had woken me?

I pushed my blanket off and stood up, but as I got to my feet, a rush of dizziness forced me back down. I took a few deep breaths and rubbed my eyes to clear the blur, then tried again.

My feet were still unsteady beneath me as I walked to the door, but by the time I reached the bathroom, I felt better. I gulped a few handfuls of water and used a washcloth to wipe down my face, neck, and arms. Now that I was out of bed, I was getting chilly. I draped the washcloth over the faucet and started back for my room.

As I was stepping out of the bathroom, I saw a figure standing in the middle of the room.

"Agatha?" I asked.

She was so perfectly still that even if I hadn't been in a state of dizzy confusion, it would have been unnerving. But now I found it downright creepy.

She stepped toward me, and I reared back. But her

hand caught my wrist, and then she started walking, pulling me behind her.

What was I going to do, fight her? She seemed to know exactly where she was headed.

I didn't even have time to put on my shoes. We hurried down the hall, and then down to the first floor.

"Where are we going?" I whispered.

Out the back door. Past the parking area.

Toward the garden.

As we entered the garden, she slowed. I glanced down and saw my distorted reflection in the gazing ball, then almost giggled. But Agatha gave me a hard tug, and the buoyant feeling disappeared back under the confusion.

"Agatha, slow down!" I hissed, trying to rush but feeling another wave of dizziness overtake me. I dragged her to a stop and put my hand on her shoulder to keep from toppling over. She gave me a moment to get my bearings and then we were off again.

I'd never seen her move so quickly. There was none of the usual wooden stiffness in her body, none of the passive slowness. She didn't even seem like the same person. I had the surreal thought that we'd switched roles, that I was the sick one and she was the steadfast companion.

Finally, we made our way down the barren stretch of path that led to the graveyard.

The gates ahead of us were wide open.

We weren't going in there, were we? After my nightmare, I wasn't exactly eager to visit Lily's grave. Any grave, really.

"I don't—" I began to protest, but she spun on me, silencing me with an intense stare.

Oh, she's mad, I thought. *She's upset that I planted flowers for her mother.*

So upset that she brought me down to look at them in the middle of the night?

And also . . . how would she even know I'd planted the flowers?

We went more slowly now—taking our time and moving between the trees, using them as cover. Agatha seemed to be carefully considering each bit of forward progress. I gave up on the idea of resisting— she was strong, and any struggle would have broken the silence that seemed to be an important part of this undertaking.

Finally, we passed the last of the large, gated memorials, and reached the part where the path wound like a snake around a thicket of low, dense bushes. Beyond this, I knew, was Lily's grave.

I started shivering, and felt Agatha's hand tighten around my arm. Was she reassuring me—or grasping me harder so I wouldn't run away?

Then she stopped short and sidestepped, dragging me off the path to stand behind one of the tree trunks. Forty feet away from where we hid was Lily's isolated grave site.

I blinked. Even from this distance, I could see that there was something . . . weird about it.

I looked back at Agatha. She was frozen, staring straight at the grave. Her right hand released my wrist and then hovered in the air, still, as if caught mid-gesture.

Suddenly in the darkness, movement.

A pale figure standing over the grave, luminous in the sliver of moonlight cutting down through the trees.

A ghost?

I gasped, and Agatha grabbed my hand again to express her disapproval.

Right. Quiet.

Don't disturb the ghost.

Then the figure began to move almost frantically, bending and twisting. I held my breath, trying to figure out what I was seeing.

And that was when the fear began to seep through my skin. It started at the top of my head, and the coldness of it slid down my face, my neck, my shoulders, my back . . . but it was more than fear. I also felt a ferocious need to know what I was seeing. Was it Lily's ghost?

I wrenched my hand free and darted to the next closer tree. I glanced back over my shoulder at Agatha, who stared at me, appalled by my lack of caution.

But I was glad I'd moved closer, because from this distance, I realized that I wasn't seeing a ghost.

I was seeing . . . Laura?

And she was . . . digging up the flowers?

She grabbed them by the fistful and yanked, and even from this far away I could sense the violence and anger behind her movements.

But why?

We stood and watched in silence as Laura manically but methodically worked to unearth the entire blanket of lilies.

I felt hypnotized by the scene, and Agatha must have known she was going to startle me no matter what—which is why, when Laura was nearly finished, Agatha slapped her hand over my mouth before grabbing my arm. (Good thing, too. I *definitely* would have screamed.)

Once she saw that I was going to behave and stay quiet, she moved her hand and then pulled me away.

Standing still had made my feet go numb and my thoughts go small and hyperfocused. I swayed a bit, and Agatha propped me up and then got me moving. As we walked, I felt better.

After we passed through the iron gate, she let

go of me, and then we walked together back to the house. There was so much I wanted to ask her—but I didn't know where to start. And I knew I wouldn't get answers, anyway.

So I settled for just one question:

"Do you know about Lily?"

She shot me a sharp look, her eyes shockingly bright.

I sighed. By now we were inside the house, headed up to our room. Agatha seemed to have lost interest in me, and I was feeling exhausted and cold and dizzy. Plus my feet were sore from running through the gravel and along the rough dirt path without shoes.

She slid back into her bed as I closed the door, and then I went into my own room. The delicately flowered teacup on the nightstand seemed ominous and stern, like it was judging me.

That doesn't make sense, I thought. A teacup can't judge you.

But I still moved it to the dresser.

Then I climbed into bed and reached for the switch to shut the light off—

And I saw, written on the back of the door, in streaky black:

GO

I pressed my eyes shut. I couldn't deal with this tonight.

But as I began to drift off to sleep, my fuzzy brain began to wonder if, all this time, who or whatever had seemed to be telling me to go hadn't just been trying to make me feel unwelcome.

Maybe they were trying to warn me.

CHAPTER
~20~

AT BREAKFAST THE next morning, Laura looked like her normal self—which is to say, she didn't have the look of a person who had been awake all night digging up flowers in a graveyard.

She gave me a pleasant smile as I came in. "How are we today?"

"Right as rain," I said. It was an old silly saying of my dad's.

But something about it struck Laura wrong. It was as if a shadow briefly passed over her features, and then it was gone.

"I've never liked that phrase," she said. "It's overly colloquial. Please don't use it anymore."

Uh . . . okay?

I sat down next to Agatha, who didn't look up from her food, and pulled a slice of toast onto my plate.

"What's that?" Laura asked. "That mark on your arm."

I twisted my forearm to see what she was looking at—a black mark. While I was cleaning the letters from the door, I must have rested my arm against it.

"Oh," I said. "I don't know."

Her brow furrowed. "Is it a bruise of some sort?"

I rubbed it away with my hand. "Nope. Just . . . maybe ink or something?"

The mark was gone, but her suspicion lingered.

I waited for Barrett to show up—my whole body waited for the sight of him the way you wait for Thanksgiving dinner when the smell of food starts wafting out of the kitchen—but he never did.

In the void, my mind turned back to the strange events of the previous night.

GO.

Should I?

Was this place, its isolation, its utter weirdness, Laura's intensity, Agatha's silence, so bad that I needed to get out? Even if getting out meant taking myself to the state institution?

She wouldn't let me take the clothes, I thought. And while it felt small and petty, I knew it was the truth. Laura would pack me off with the rags I'd brought with me. Maybe a nicer backpack, if there was an old one stuffed into a closet somewhere. But the cashmere sweaters, the tasteful trousers, the thin-soled shoes that fit my feet like they'd been made for me? Nah.

Laura was weird, and my future was uncertain— would I *ever* have anything approaching a normal life?

But were those things reason enough for me to leave? No. No, they weren't. Maybe someone braver than me, but not me.

I wasn't going anywhere.

It wasn't just the threat of the institution—it was having to leave behind another home. As bizarre as life was at Copeland Hall, I understood how it worked (well, mostly) and I knew who I was there. I had Agatha. I had Barrett. Even Laura and John were reassuring presences.

Out there? In the real world? I would have to start over. Alone.

And I just couldn't bring myself to do that.

And then the quiet voice in my head surprised me. It said, *Yet*.

KNOCK KNOCK.

I sat up in my bed and smoothed my hair. "Yes? Come in."

Barrett pushed the bedroom door open. When he saw me, he smiled, bemused. "The nursery was open . . . Do you always just sit around in your bedroom with perfect posture?"

"No—I thought you might be your mother."

His eyes crinkled. "And . . . you sit like this when she comes in?"

I felt acutely the squareness of my shoulders and forced them to slump a little. "I don't know. Maybe. Why are you posture-shaming me?"

"I'm not," he said, wide-eyed. "You look very nice."

"Thanks."

"Helpful," he said. "Like a trained poodle. Eager to zip away and . . . fetch something."

"You can fetch my butt," I said.

"I would love to."

I threw my pillow at him. "Are you just here to make fun of me? Or can I . . ." I was going to say *help you*, but I stopped. I'm no poodle.

Kiss you was the next thing that came to mind. But that wasn't possible. Agatha was doing her homework right on the other side of the wall.

Nope. We would just have to wait until—

But then Barrett was slipping inside, closing the door behind him.

"This is dumb," I whispered. "You're being so dumb."

"That's okay," he said. "You're right. Be dumb with me."

He reached for my hand. When I gave it to him, he pulled me close. I turned my face up and our mouths found each other, and for a couple of blissful, dumb, incredible minutes, we clung to each other and kissed.

At last, we forced ourselves apart, and Barrett took a deep gulping breath. "Come on, let's get out of here," he said.

"Out of where?" I asked.

"The house."

"Permanently?"

"Ha." He shook his head. "I actually came to see if you wanted to go for a walk."

"Oh, and here I thought you came here to compare me to a dog."

"I came here to kiss you," he said, and then our bodies were so close, and his lips were whispering across the place where my neck met my shoulders and I would have been happy to just lie down and die.

But no. This wasn't the time or place. With a frustrated grunt, I pulled away, then swung out of reach as he tried to duck his face toward mine again.

"Agatha is *right there*," I said. "Literally on the other side of the wall."

He sighed.

"Would you want *her* making out with someone five feet away from you?"

He made a face, and I knew I'd successfully killed the mood. "Okay," he said. "Fine. How about the walk?"

"I can't leave Agatha," I said. "Your mom went grocery shopping, and I said I'd stay with her." Was that how it had happened, or had Laura told me I *should* stay with her? I swatted the question out of my mind. What difference did it make?

"Well, Aggie can come, too." He opened my door and walked over to the chair where his expressionless sister sat looking out the window. "Want to go for a walk, Aggie? Huh?"

"Hey," I said, sharper than I intended. A flare of protectiveness had ignited inside me. "She's not a dog, either."

"I didn't mean it that way." Barrett looked crestfallen. "I'm sorry, Agatha. Do you want to get outside for a bit?"

She didn't reply.

"Is she mad?" he asked me.

"No," I said.

"Are you sure?"

"Are you mad, Ags?" I asked, and she ignored me. "See? She's not mad. But it's okay, really," I said to

Barrett. "I'll stay in with her. Even if she wanted to come, she couldn't keep up."

"Wait," Barrett said. "I have an idea."

JOHN HAD BROKEN a femur ten years earlier on a ski trip and had to spend four weeks in a wheelchair, which had since been stored in a random closet. (Whatever a "double black diamond" was, I never needed to go near one, since it apparently led to your bones cracking like mishandled candy canes.)

I was afraid Agatha would balk, but when Barrett wheeled the chair over to where we waited on the front steps, she sat down as cooperatively as if it had been her favorite chair by the window. Then she waited patiently while I applied sunscreen to her face.

Despite his protesting that we would be back at the house well before Laura returned, I made Barrett leave a note in the morning room. And then we were off.

I felt a strange tremor in my body as we followed a brick-lined path across the front lawn, the feeling a bird might get if its cage door was left open. At some point, I had adjusted to the pace of life at Copeland Hall. The security of the house and its established, ancient-feeling routines were oddly comforting.

We weren't going to the outside world, I reminded myself. We were staying on the property. So I walked alongside Barrett and tried to enjoy the fresh air.

It was a beautiful day, warm but not hot. Most of the paths we took were sheltered under the dappled shade of the gorgeous old trees scattered generously around the property. Off in the distance, a riding lawn mower growled in slow laps across the gentle hills. A breeze meandered around us, carrying with it the pleasantly tart green scent of mown grass (screaming in protest of its grisly fate).

For the first few minutes, Barrett was in a state of quiet contemplation, while Agatha kept her chin slightly raised into the breeze. When we passed through small patches of sun, she closed her eyes and seemed to be trying to memorize the feeling of the sunlight on her cheeks.

Their tranquility eluded me; I felt like I was walking on a precipice, about to fall off.

Just before we reached the main driveway gate, another brick path appeared in a break of the high decorative grasses. This one was slightly overgrown, and the bricks looked older, worn into roundness with age. Some of them had settled, and the whole thing seemed to undulate slightly. But if that made it harder to push the wheelchair, Barrett didn't complain. And Agatha didn't seem to mind the bumpy ride.

This part of the yard was lovely, but its isolation made me uneasy. We came to a fence made of white boards that were peeling and falling down. On the other side of the fence were lush, tangled green woods. Shoots of the plants reached into our path like the bony arms of hungry witches looking for lost children to eat.

I was starting to think I preferred the garden.

"What are you thinking about?" Barrett asked. "You're so quiet."

I couldn't very well tell him that I was imagining his family's property as fairy-tale villainy brought to life. And I wanted to spill the beans about Laura's disturbing midnight jaunt to the graveyard, but I couldn't figure out how to begin. "Just things," I said. "Um . . . your mom."

He sighed.

"So last night, Agatha woke me up and—"

"She did? How?"

"She . . ." Well, hmm. Did she wake me up? "She just did. And we went out to the garden—"

"You took her to the garden in the middle of the night?"

"No," I said. "She took me."

He looked doubtful.

"I swear!" I said, more offended than I'd expected. "I had no desire to go. She led me out there. And we went into the graveyard, and that's where we saw . . . your mom."

I explained what she'd been doing.

"You hid and watched her?" he asked.

"I didn't want Agatha to get in trouble."

"Agatha doesn't get in trouble," Barrett said. "Mom knows Aggie is . . . isn't all there."

I didn't answer.

"I mean, *you* might have gotten in trouble," he said uncertainly.

"Barrett, I swear, I only went because Agatha basically dragged me. But that's not the part we should focus on. The part that's weird is that your mom was down there ripping out all the flowers we planted. And she was *angry*."

He shrugged. "Maybe she's protective of Lily's grave?"

"Maybe," I said. "I guess . . ."

"Well, what else would it be?"

"Why isn't Lily in the portrait?" I asked. "Of your mom and her dad."

"What?"

"In the drawing room. It's just the two of them. Doesn't it seem like Lily should have been included? The other families had all their kids painted." *Even the dead ones.*

"I—I don't know. You kind of lost me with the going outside in the middle of the night."

"You've done that, too."

"But not with my sister," he said. "What if she caught a cold?"

"She's not sick," I said.

He looked at me like I was out of my mind.

"Not like that, I mean. Not like she's at more of a risk for a cold." I looked down at Agatha, who stared straight ahead.

"Are you sure?" Barrett asked. "Mom made it sound like her immunity could be messed up."

"I'm trying to tell you." I fought to keep the seething frustration out of my voice. "I didn't take her out there. She took me."

He nodded shortly.

"What?" I asked.

"You didn't have to go," he said. "You could have told her to stay inside. You could have said no."

I sighed.

He sighed. "Forget it."

I did want to forget it, but I also didn't. "If you don't believe me, go look. The flowers will all be gone. Why would she do that?"

"I have no idea," he said. "Maybe she hates lilies. Maybe she had other plans for that space."

"But in the middle of the night?"

"What are you trying to get me to say, Margot?" he asked. "That Mom's crazy? She's intense, yeah, and she makes me angry sometimes, but I don't think she was out in the moonlight acting like a maniac."

But she *was*.

"And I don't think you should let Agatha go outside at night," he said stiffly.

"Okay," I said.

"Don't be mad at me."

I shook my head. Don't be mad? He'd just implied that I was a negligent liar.

"Let's talk about something else," he said. "Please?"

Like how there's part of me that would rather live at the state institution than Copeland Hall?

We walked on in an uncomfortable silence.

"Agatha tried to talk," I said, before I had a chance to stop and think. "Last night. She said *I*. I think she's tried to say it before, but I'm not sure. But last night, I'm sure."

I waited for him to find some way to twist this around and make me look bad, make me doubt myself.

But finally, he said, "When I came home for Christmas, I spent so much time with her, trying to get her to communicate. I just couldn't believe she was . . . gone."

The walk got nicer as we went on. Trees provided a shady canopy, and mushrooms grew lushly on a few of the tree trunks, like little gnome houses. Wildflowers dotted the sides of the path, and the breeze returned.

It was lovely. But it was ruined. The mood between us was tense, and I felt hot, indignant embarrassment at the thought that he'd accused me of taking Agatha into an unsafe situation.

CHAPTER
~21~

WE PASSED A gazebo in quaint disrepair and a still, dappled glade where a fat mallard snoozed on a bed of dried grasses. We passed a pair of benches that had phrases carved into their sides in Greek that neither Barrett nor I could remotely understand.

I took over pushing the wheelchair for a while, to give him a break.

"I'm sorry," he said finally.

"Don't worry about it," I said.

"But I like you. A lot. And I hurt your feelings."

I didn't answer.

"Didn't I?" he asked.

"Does it matter? When you think about it, we don't even know each other."

He sputtered out a laugh. "We don't?"

"What's my favorite book?" I asked. "What's my favorite color?"

His forehead creased in concern. "There's time to figure that stuff out."

"No, actually, there's not," I said. "You're leaving."

Aren't I just a genius at killing the mood? Barrett seemed to pull his whole being, body and spirit, away from me—without even moving.

"I'm just being realistic," I said. "What are we going to do, try to keep some kind of relationship going while you're back at school and I'm here?"

"It might be complicated," he said. "But I don't see why we couldn't try, at least."

"I can't even get the Wi-Fi password, Barrett. My phone gets no signal."

His mouth turned down at the corners. "You should have a working phone."

I shrugged. "What does it matter? Who would I even text?"

"Me!" he said. "Your old friends. Santa Claus. It doesn't matter—you should have a way to communicate with people."

"But not having internet doesn't seem to bother *you*."

"I'm only here for a week or two at a time. And I usually spend part of that in the city with Dad. I mean, I'm *used* to it, and it's starting to drive me crazy. It's not okay to expect you to live like this forever."

"I don't want to cause any trouble," I said.

"Trouble doesn't bother me. I'm going to ask my

mom about it. Today." His expression was serious, and there was a darkness in his eyes I'd never seen before.

"Please don't," I said. "It might upset her."

"Why should it upset her?" he asked.

Talk about a landmine of a question. I wasn't even going to attempt an answer.

We reached a shady spot with another Greek-themed bench, and I steered Agatha's wheelchair so she could see the view. Then Barrett and I sat down. He scooted closer—not quite touching me, but almost. The leaves above us shuddered in the wind and made tiny, ever-changing patterns of light and shadows on our faces. I turned to Barrett and touched the little shag of hair hanging down over his forehead.

Forgiveness was creeping up on me. What was the point of staying mad?

"I know my mother," he said, more quietly. "If someone doesn't force her to make a change, she may never do it."

"I know her, too," I said softly. "We've spent a lot of time together. And she's been really nice to me when she didn't have to be."

He looked at me incredulously. "Of course she has to be nice to you. They brought you here."

"Because she had to. But that's okay."

"You're so good for Agatha," he said softly. "And Mom. And me. But . . ."

"What?" I asked.

"You shouldn't live like this. Out in the country, alone. When you're in school, are you even going to be able to meet up with friends?"

I shrugged. "Maybe that doesn't matter. It's only for a couple of years."

"A couple of years is a long time," he said. "You need friends."

I thought about that. If you'd asked me a week or two earlier, I would have said that Laura was my friend. Now I wasn't so sure. Barrett was my friend, but he'd be gone soon.

"Agatha's my friend," I said.

He sniffed skeptically.

"No, really," I said. "She can't say it, but she likes me."

He reached a tentative hand up to my face. "*I* like you," he said softly.

"I like you, too," I said.

He pulled me closer. We'd kissed enough by now that there was a warmth, a familiarity between us. It didn't lessen the happy little vibrations that ran through me, head to toe, when we touched, but it added a dimension that made this feel deeper than just a random hookup. It made the kisses more urgent, more important.

I'd told him we didn't know each other, but we did know some things.

I knew he was a good brother, a dutiful son. I knew how much it pained him to be torn between what Laura wanted for him and what he wanted for himself.

I wanted to know more. I pulled back, slightly breathless. "Tell me a secret about yourself," I said.

He looked a little bewildered. "A secret?" he repeated. "Okay, uh . . . I used to think my mom was a witch. I was afraid of her. She thinks I was a really well-behaved kid, but I just didn't want to end up in a soup."

I laughed. "Why would you think that?"

"She has this lab—she makes things there—"

"Oh, her perfume?" I said. "Body wash?"

"Yeah," he said. "But I didn't know that. I thought she was making witches' brew."

"A witches' brew that smells like roses?" I teased. "When did you discover the truth?"

"I walked in on her once, and she let me help her make soap." He shrugged.

"That's hilarious," I said. "But it's more of a secret about your mom."

He tried to smile, but his expression changed, and his smile was strained. "I didn't make the varsity lacrosse team," he said. "They posted the list and most of my friends were on it, and they were all joking around, and I laughed about it—I don't even like lacrosse, seriously—but after that . . . I went back to my room and I cried."

I didn't make a sound.

"I think I was just worried about upsetting my mom," he said. "When she's already dealing with so much. She really cares about lacrosse."

"*Was* she upset?" I asked. To be honest, I couldn't imagine Laura caring about sports.

He didn't answer.

"Oh," I said. He hadn't told her.

He shook his head. "Never came up."

Never came up? Laura mentioned lacrosse on a weekly basis. Unless I was imagining things, she'd just ordered him an expensive pair of cleats.

"When will you tell her?" I asked.

His expression darkened. "I don't know."

"You might as well get it over with."

Barrett sighed. "So what's *your* secret?"

"I don't think I . . ." I swallowed hard.

There was something, one thing, that nobody knew. That I could hardly even admit to myself.

"I think my mom was alive," I said, my heart

banging in my chest. "In the car. And I think I left anyway."

Barrett stared at me.

"I don't remember, exactly," I said. "It's just a feeling."

He didn't speak.

"I mean, I could have stayed and saved her."

He placed his hand on the side of my face. "You don't even know what happened," he said. "Don't make that kind of assumption."

Then he softly kissed me. We parted and stared at each other, about to lean back in for another kiss.

Agatha was facing away, looking back down the hill, which is why she didn't warn us.

"Barrett!" Laura's voice cut like a knife through the perfect tranquility of the moment. "What are you doing?"

We jumped apart and stared at her, stunned and guilty. This was nightmare territory.

"It's much too hot for your sister to be outside today!" Laura snapped.

Oh. So she hadn't seen us kissing? The path leading to this spot curved briefly behind a small patch of trees. If the timing had been perfect, she might have been behind the foliage at the perfect moment.

"Mom, it's okay—" he began.

She held up her hand, and he fell silent.

I waited for her to say something to me, but she was glaring at Barrett and didn't seem to know or care that I existed.

Finally, without even glancing at me, she said, "Margot. Please take Agatha back into the house. Get her a glass of water and make sure she's not overly warm."

"Okay," I said, and it came out thin and scared and I kind of hated myself for being such a scaredy-cat. On the other hand, I'd possibly just been caught kissing the son and heir of the mighty Sutton family, so for all I knew, I was about to get dropped down a trapdoor into the dungeon.

I glanced back at Barrett and found both him and Laura looking at me, so I whipped my head around and focused on pushing the wheelchair toward the house. There was a slight uphill climb that got steeper as I approached the driveway. I started to sweat, and my breath came in tired puffs.

As soon as we were out of Laura's line of sight, Agatha held up her hand.

I stopped. "Are you okay?"

She got out of the wheelchair.

"Are you sure?" I asked. "Your mom said it's too hot—"

She was only staring into my eyes, but I got the distinct impression of an eye roll.

"Okay," I said. "Thanks."

We walked together up the hill.

"What do you think?" I asked. "Do you think she's going to send me away?"

It was hard to read her expression—maybe I was assuming too much, but it seemed somewhere on the spectrum of pity and *Well, what did you expect?*

"DO YOU HAVE a minute, Margot?" Laura asked.

I looked up, stunned, from where I lay on my bed, trying (and failing) to focus on a book. "Does Agatha need—"

She cut me off, a note of impatience slipping into her voice. "Agatha's fine."

After we came in, I'd set her up with her school-work and brought her a tall glass of cold water. Then I'd retreated to my room to lick my wounds and feel sorry for myself. I'd kind of expected (hoped?) that Laura would ignore me. But here she was.

"Oh," I said. "Okay, yeah. Yes. Of course."

She led the way to the morning room, then sat on one of the mauve sofas and patted the spot next to her. I hesitated, because this was new—usually when we spoke in here, she sat behind her desk and I sat in one of the chairs like we were conducting business. Finally, a split second before it got awkward, I sat down.

She leaned toward me. "How *are* you, Margot?"

Um. Bad? "I'm great," I said weakly.

"How do you find life at Copeland Hall? Are you happy here? Have you been lonely? Bored?"

I'd prepared for cold, snobbish anger. I had *not* prepared for a painstaking examination of my emotional state.

"No," I said. "Yeah. I mean, I'm happy. Yeah."

She sat up and looked at me, a trace of regret in her expression. "I've noticed something, and I hope this doesn't make you uncomfortable."

Oh, sure, no chance of that. I sat frozen in place.

"It's Barrett," she said. "You seem to be spending a lot of time together lately."

But not the kissing, I thought. She didn't complain about the kissing.

"I know he's . . . charming. But I don't want you to feel you have to entertain him."

"No," I said. "I don't feel that way."

"It's sweet of you to 'hang out' with him." She said the phrase *hang out* as if it was alien slang she'd just read about on the internet. "But if he's always lurking around and bothering you, please feel free to tell him you're occupied with other things."

The thought of Barrett lurking, like some mad

scientist's assistant, almost made me laugh. But that was a blip, because most of me was highly aware that there was nothing, not one thing, that was actually funny about this.

Sitting there, so close to Laura, with her studying my face, I realized what it was that I was detecting under her outwardly warm and caring manner—and it was the same thing that some little part of me was always aware of but never wanted to acknowledge. It was a shadow of something.

Something scary.

I wanted to think that I was mistaken, but I couldn't talk myself out of it. I was too attuned to Laura's moods, her whims, her looks. I'd spent so much time trying to please her that I knew when she was happy and when she wasn't. And what was happening now was that she was pretending. Pretending at something big. And underneath that something, she was . . .

She was . . . sharp. Like the tip of a knife.

"It's fine," I said, trying to make it sound like I didn't really care. "He's nice."

"He really is," Laura said, sounding pleased. And I almost thought that was going to be it. But then she went on. "And you're so sweet and easy to talk to . . . It must be quite a change from the sophisticated girls he dates when he's at school. It *is* a shame that he gets so bored here. Any little amusement that catches his attention will do—for the short term. One summer, he took up bird-watching. Do you know how much proper bird-watching binoculars cost? A lot."

She was rambling cheerfully on, but we both knew she'd already said the important part.

He gets so bored here.

Any little amusement.

"And one year, it was baseball cards. That was quite sweet, because John got his old collection out of storage. Barrett loved it. He loves little, useless curiosities. You know—one man's trash is another man's treasure."

I nodded.

"Margot," she said simply, "what I'm trying to tell you is . . . don't get too attached."

Danger. Danger. Danger.

"If you get too attached, you might let him try to kiss you." She took my hand. She stared into my eyes. "And I think we can both agree that would be inappropriate."

Her concerned expression gave way to a warm, wide smile. "But why am I saying these things to you? You're part of the family now. You get it."

Her breath smelled like roses.

Whose breath smells like roses?

"You do get it," she said. "Don't you?"

My throat felt so dry I wondered if I could even speak.

"Yes," I said. "Perfectly."

AFTER I ESCAPED upstairs, Barrett tried to talk to me in the hallway, but I shook my head, and he stared at me. "What did she say?" he asked.

"Nothing," I said.

"Margot." His voice was dark. He knew. "Please. What did she say?"

I shook my head. It wasn't so much this idea of him using me for amusement—a convenient way to relieve his boredom. It was being hyperaware that Laura saw things that way. And yes, maybe she'd been exaggerating, used crueler terms than necessary, but she never did anything accidentally: She was sending me a message. One I couldn't possibly fail to understand.

I felt ill.

He came closer. Now he looked terribly worried. "Please tell me what's wrong."

"Nothing." I managed a smile that I knew came out looking sickly. "I'll see you later."

WHEN I ENTERED the nursery, Agatha was still at her desk, but her position was slightly different from her usual one—she wasn't sitting straight up in her chair, facing directly toward the desk. Instead, she was slightly turned toward the center of the room, as if something had caught her attention.

"Are you okay?" I asked.

She didn't respond.

"It's almost time for dinner," I said. "Why don't you go wash your hands? I'll put your stuff back."

She got up and walked away without looking at me.

I straightened her chair and reached for her notebook to rip out today's page and prepare tomorrow's.

I stopped. The blood turned hot in my veins as I stared down at the page.

The whole thing was filled with one word, written over and over in an impossibly shaky, childlike hand:

GO GO GO GO GO GO GO GO GO GO GO
GO GO GO GO GO GO GO GO GO GO GO
GO GO GO GO GO GO GO GO GO GO GO

I tore the sheet out and froze.

The next page was full, too.

And the next one. And the next one.

All in all, seven pages were completely filled with the word—

Why had she done this?

"Kah," said a voice behind me, and Agatha stood there, her expression *almost* blank . . . but not quite.

"What?" I asked. "What is it? Please tell me, Agatha."

She wanted to. I saw her draw in a breath, as if she was going to just spit out the word. But then, halfway through her exhalation, her attention wandered. She drifted away.

CHAPTER
~22~

FOR A LITTLE while, I was so distracted by Agatha's scribblings that I didn't pause to dwell on any of the things Laura had said to me about Barrett. But during dinner, I felt plainly that something had changed between us. It wasn't anything I could put into words, only a feeling of unmistakable discomfort. And most of it was coming from me.

Barrett seemed to get the message and stayed silent for the meal, except for a few single-word answers to some of Laura's questions about how his summer reading was going, whether he'd gotten his room assignment yet, and whether he needed to order new uniforms for next year. (Good, no, and probably.)

Now I had the time to really wallow in the things Laura had said earlier. And, of course, the things she hadn't quite said—how I failed, in every way, to measure up to the dozens of girls Barrett crossed paths with at his fancy school. How she and John thought I was a treasure, but to Barrett I was probably just . . .

Trash? Impossible. But Laura had basically come out and said it. Would she lie? She was trying to protect my feelings, that was all. And despite the old-school *boys will be boys* tone of the conversation, I sensed that she really thought she was doing me a favor.

What use was my judgment these days, anyway? It was better to think I was just . . . tired and confused. I'd lost my head because Barrett, who was good-looking and smart and rich and important, had parked his stupid body near my stupid body and touched my lips with his stupid lips.

After dinner, I showered and changed into my pajamas, then sat down in bed and tried to read. I'd decided I would finish the gardening book. Until school started, I would focus on working outside. Fresh air and a lack of (Barrett) distractions would do me good. I could still improve my relationship with Laura and show the family my gratitude by helping out as much as possible. I could start cooking, too. And cleaning. I would just immerse myself in being a penniless orphan, collecting the checkmarks.

As usual, the gardening book got the better of me within about three pages. As I was setting it on my nightstand, Laura came to the door, teacups in hand, and sat on the edge of my bed.

"How are you?" she asked softly. "I noticed you were quiet at dinner."

"I'm fine," I said. "A little sleepy."

She handed me my teacup. I inhaled the soft, spicy aroma and then took a sip. "Sleepy? Do you think you're coming down with something?"

Great, I was making it worse. "No, no," I said, rubbing the skin just above my eyebrows as if there was an ache behind them. "It's just . . . my sinuses, I think. Allergies."

She visibly relaxed. "I wanted to tell you that Barrett is leaving."

I almost dropped my teacup.

She was very careful not to look at me. "He's going to stay with a friend until the new school year starts. It's so hard for him to be here. Our pace of life is too slow for a dynamic teenage boy."

Oh, but it was fine for me? Was I not dynamic?

After moving past the perceived insult (aided in part by admitting to myself that I was not, in fact, dynamic), I had time to think about what she was actually saying. Barrett would be gone. I felt a sudden stab of loss—not just because of the kissing, but because when we weren't kissing, he was a nice person to talk to. The only person, in fact, for me to talk to in any real way.

For a moment, I wondered—was she doing this

because she knew he liked me? Was that why she had said the things she'd said? That seemed like it was assuming too much—making myself too important. I was nothing, remember? An amusement?

"John will drive him over to Glencoe tomorrow," she said.

Tomorrow?

I made an attempt to hide my surprise and drink my tea as if nothing was wrong. But I inhaled some and ended up coughing and sputtering while Laura took my teacup and held it.

"Goodness," she said. "Coughing like that, you should stay in bed tomorrow."

"No," I said. "I just got some tea down the wrong pipe."

She looked at me doubtfully.

I was trying to be cool, but I was still inwardly freaking out. Barrett couldn't leave tomorrow. That wasn't enough time to say goodbye.

"All the same," she said, "why don't you stay in bed and rest in the morning? I'll bring you breakfast, and you can come down in the afternoon with plenty of time to see Barrett off."

I didn't answer. I wasn't committing to her plan because I thought it was a dumb plan. Much better just to get up and get out of bed the next day like normal, and if she asked, tell her I felt perfectly fine.

"Sound good?" she asked, handing the teacup back.

"Mm," I said, looking away.

"Good girl, Margot," she said, patting my leg. "Finish your tea and get some rest."

I'D CURSED MYSELF. The next morning, my body and brain felt vaguely fuzzy. My vision blurred around the edges, making windows and light bulbs look like they were surrounded by pale auras. My mouth felt like I'd been chewing cotton balls all night. And my hands and feet were clumsy and tingly, as if my fingers were wrapped in gauze.

So when Laura showed up with a trayful of food, I was grateful. I sat up and ate the toast, the bowl of yogurt with berries in it, the little wedges of fancy cheese, and I felt less hostile toward her than I had the previous night. I went along with her plan, staying in bed and dozing all morning, and then before lunchtime I got up and dressed.

Agatha was nowhere to be found—she must have been downstairs—and I was combing my hair when there was a loud knock at the door.

I pulled it open and found Barrett, looking somewhat frantic.

He slipped inside and took my hands.

"I'm leaving," he said.

"I know." I was proud of myself for not betraying any emotion. *You show him, Margot.*

But my cool delivery clearly pained him. "What did she say to you about me?"

I bit my lip.

"Please, Margot," he said. "Whatever she said, don't believe her. She doesn't understand me at all."

"She's right, though," I said. "You wouldn't look twice at me if we weren't stuck here together. When you're back at school, you'll forget I exist."

"You think that?" he asked. The disbelief in his voice made my heart hiccup. "Really? Seriously? I get that my mom might think that way, but . . . it doesn't seem like you'd believe her."

I shrugged, a little embarrassed. "Look at you," I said. "Look at your life. And then look at me."

"I see you," he said. "And I don't know anyone else like you."

"But that's part of it," I said. "I'm a curiosity. I'm something to think about while you're bored and stuck here."

He shook his head. "You think I'm 'stuck' here? I was only planning to be home for four days. But after I met you, I canceled my trip to California. Even when you hated me—I didn't want to leave."

I stared up at him. "Are you serious?"

"I don't lie to you," he said.

"Who *do* you lie to?" I asked with a small half laugh.

"Basically everyone," he said. "If lying means not showing people what you're really thinking. What you really care about."

I sighed.

"Do you believe me?"

"Yeah," I said. "But why would your mother tell me those things? It was horrible."

"Mom thinks she can will things into existence." He seemed troubled. He stared at the floor. "But really, it's because she can't control us, and she knows it. And she can't *stand* not controlling what happens here."

"That's kind of messed up," I said softly.

"I'm going to talk to my father," he said. "I'm worried about you. You need to be around people."

"It's okay," I said. "Once school starts—"

"That's more than a month from now."

"It'll go fast." Suddenly it hit me. He was really leaving. My voice was hollow. "When will you be back?"

"Fall break." His eyes met mine. "Middle of October."

I nodded. And nodded and nodded. Okay, Margot, okay. You knew he was going away at some point. You knew it wasn't going to be like some fairy tale where you're the princess in the tower and the prince comes and kisses you and suddenly everything is great.

It was more like he came to the castle, found me in the tower, kissed me and woke me up, and then left without slaying the dragon.

The dragon . . . Why did I think there was a dragon?

He leaned down and kissed me softly. "You know I don't want to go, right?" he asked. "She's sending me away."

"Because of us?" I asked. "Does she know about us?"

He shook his head. "Maybe. Maybe not. She's just really angry with me in general. She says she can't trust me."

"Because you took your sister out for a walk?" I asked. "That's ridiculous."

"No, it's more than that. She found out about lacrosse."

"That's *sports*," I said. "She's mad about sports?"

"She thinks I messed up the tryouts on purpose. She knows I've never really liked playing."

"If you don't like playing, why play? Why does she care?"

He shrugged. *"Obedience performed against the will is the ultimate test of rectitude."*

I stared at him. "What's that from?"

"It's a thing Mom always said." He rolled his eyes. "Some old family saying."

"From Loretta?"

He looked confused. "You know about Loretta?"

"As much as I want to know. I found the book in the library. *You* know about Loretta?"

"That book was the bane of my childhood. We used to have to copy passages from it when we got in trouble." He tried to smile reassuringly, but the misery shone in his eyes like dying embers. "Don't worry, she'll never do it to you. You're not duty bound to the family like I am."

But Laura *wanted* me to be.

Barrett glanced back out at the hall. "I'm supposed to be packing. I don't want her to find me in here."

It felt like there was a hole in my heart that went all the way to another dimension. "I hate this," I said.

"Me too."

His fingers wrapped around mine. His skin was warm and a little rough, and it took all my strength not to yank him toward me and smother him with sympathetic kisses—and be smothered by them, myself. Moment by moment, it was sinking in that he would be gone soon. He was being punished, but his punishment was as bad for me as it was for him.

Or worse. Because he would be free of this place—and I was stuck here.

We were both at lunch, but neither of us spoke. There was nothing I wanted to say to him that I was willing to say in front of Laura. Instead, they made small talk about what he would do when he got to his friend's house.

At one point, Laura made some comment about a girl—somebody's sister. Judging by her tone and the things she said about her ("I've heard she's destined for Ivy League"), I guessed that this was a person Laura considered to be an appropriate match for Barrett.

But his answers were clipped, almost rude.

So Laura turned her attention to me, fussing at me for being out of bed and suggesting that I go back and rest so I had enough energy to come out and say goodbye to Barrett.

Initially I resisted, but she wore me down. She made me a cup of tea and I went upstairs, preparing myself for a dull afternoon in bed.

PATTER PATTER PATTER PATTER.

I opened my eyes and squinted.

The room was dark, and the shock of the darkness and the confusion of not knowing what time it was propelled me up to a seated position.

The sound came from thick raindrops splatting

against the window. The darkness, I thought, must have come from the storm.

Or was it nighttime?

I yipped like a hurt dog and raced out to the hallway. The house was quiet. I hurried down the stairs and toward the only room lit up in the darkness—Laura's office.

She sat at her desk, and Agatha sat nearby in a tufted chair.

"Goodness, Margot," Laura said. "Are you all right?"

"Are they gone?" I asked.

She blinked. "I'm sorry—do you mean John and Barrett?"

No, I mean Mickey Mouse and Wonder Woman.

I nodded.

"Yes, of course. They left after dinner."

"But I didn't get to say goodbye!" I was too distraught to keep my voice low. "Why didn't someone wake me up?"

She glanced at me with reproach in her eyes, on the verge of reprimanding me. "I *tried*, Margot," she said. "You said that I should tell them goodbye for you."

I wavered. I didn't want to believe her, but I couldn't even remember falling asleep.

"You don't remember?" she asked, sounding worried.

I didn't answer.

Laura frowned.

Forget it. I needed to be alone. I needed to go back to my room and cry my eyes out over the fact that not only had I missed a chance to see Barrett one last time, but that he thought I'd chosen a nap over being there when they left.

"Are you hungry?" Laura said. "I saved some dinner for you."

"No, thank you," I choked out.

Her lips flattened, but she nodded. "I'm very sorry. I know you and Barrett were friendly."

By the time I reached the stairs, I was crying so hard I couldn't see.

I went back to my room, changed into my pajamas, and climbed under the covers. I didn't even wash my face or brush my teeth. I just wanted to fall asleep and forget about everything.

MY DREAM WAS simple: Barrett and I were sitting on the bench, looking out over the grounds. It was lovely to be so near him, to be holding his hand.

"Look," he said. "Here they come."

I looked around, suddenly uneasy. Who was coming? For some reason, I expected to see my family—in their usual deadness, slack-muscled and vacant-eyed.

But for once it wasn't them.

And then I saw what he meant—all over the ground around us, and as far as the eye could see, tiny green shoots were poking through the grass. They grew as thickly as a plague of locusts, and I pulled my legs up onto the bench to keep them from touching my legs.

"I don't like this," I said. "Your mother doesn't like the lilies."

"It's not about what she likes," Barrett said. "She hates everything."

I watched the green stalks climb into the air as if they were the product of magic beans, and my chest began to feel tight. I gripped Barrett's hand harder, but he pulled free and stood up. "I have to go now," he said. "See you in October."

"But what if I need your help?" I asked.

He was already walking away. The lilies were gigantic around him, like stalks of corn, and just before he vanished into the thick forest of them, he said, "I'm not the one who stands up to her."

I wanted to ask what he meant, but then he was gone.

I turned to look for an escape route, but the bench was surrounded. I started to worry about being late for dinner. Laura would be angry. And where was Agatha? Oh, God, we'd lost Agatha! The last time I'd seen her, she'd been in her wheelchair. And now she'd been swallowed by the lilies.

Then, suddenly, there was movement to my left.

Agatha came out of the flowers.

She stared down at me impassively.

"Go back to the green wing," she said.

My eyes popped open.

I was alone in my dark little room. It was nearly midnight.

Go back to the green wing.

The words had sounded too real in the dream, like they'd crossed over into my sleep from the real, waking world. But of course I was alone, so that was impossible.

I crept across the nursery to the door and went to turn the knob—

But it was locked.

I stared at it, trying to figure out if I was right or wrong and if I was right, why? Why had Laura locked us in?

Barrett was gone. Her son was safe from my peasant wiles.

What trouble could I possibly get into now?

CHAPTER
~23~

"I'VE BEEN THINKING that what we need is a change," Laura said. "Would you like more eggs?"

She held the platter out to me in midair, so I had no choice but to take some more eggs, although I'd already eaten a full serving.

"Agatha has her doctor's appointment today," she said. "But after that, let's do something fun. We could have a dance party. Or play cards."

This was the part where a bad orphan would answer sullenly, distracted from her duties by her brooding sadness. Or demand to know why the bedroom door had been locked—if it even had been locked. It opened easily enough that morning.

But me? I'm a good orphan. "Yeah," I said. "Sounds fun."

Laura beamed at me. "It's such a gift to have you here with us. You're really just like family, you know."

"I was actually wondering if we could figure out some things today," I said. "Maybe my school enrollment. I might need a physical—although that would be ridiculous, considering how much time I've spent in hospitals this year."

It was meant to be a joke. But it didn't land.

"I'm sorry," she said. "I don't understand."

"Oh—I just mean, you'd think they'd learned everything they needed to back after the accident." Way to wreck a joke, Laura.

"No," Laura said. "About the enrollment? We don't have anything to do. It's all set up."

"It is? Oh, wow, okay. Great." That was something to wrap my head around. And worry about. "When's the first day?"

She smiled. "Whenever you like."

Uh.

"No, I mean—when does the school year start? I can just start when everyone else starts."

"Oh, that doesn't matter," she said. "You shouldn't worry so much about what other people are up to. It will disturb your inner balance."

"But . . ." I sat in helpless confusion. How could I clarify this without insulting her? "But I need to be . . . where the teachers are."

Now she frowned slightly. "I don't follow. Perhaps it will be clearer if I just say that the curriculum is ready, and anytime you'd like to begin your studies, you're welcome to. Did you know there's even a schoolroom in the house? It hasn't been used for probably a hundred years, but we can set it up for you—if you feel you need that kind of environment. Who knows, it might be a good change for Agatha, as well."

Now I was starting to get it. "Are you talking about homeschooling?" I asked.

"Of course."

"I . . ." I found myself utterly speechless. "I'm sorry, I don't think . . . I don't . . . I don't want to do homeschool. I'd like to go to the regular school. The one in town. With people."

"Margot, we talked about this." She stared at me like I'd started making animal noises and declared myself to be in the process of transforming into a frog. "We had a conversation. It was decided weeks ago."

"No," I said. "No, we didn't. I would remember that. Because I think it's a terrible idea."

"Well, I'm sorry," she said, too offended to be sorry. "But this issue has been settled for some time now. I wouldn't have ordered an expensive curriculum if I'd thought there was any doubt."

I felt panicky. "Laura, I seriously did not agree to this."

She set down her silverware and pursed her lips. "Are you calling me a liar?"

"No. Of course not. But . . . I really don't want to homeschool. And I don't remember ever even talking about it."

"Just because you don't remember it," she said, "doesn't mean it didn't happen."

We were both quiet. She watched me carefully, and I was struck by the horrible truth of what she was saying.

"But . . ." I said.

"I've already been through this with you, but I'll explain again if you honestly don't remember. John and I talked it over and decided that you would thrive with this home-study program. It'll suit your self-discipline so well. I can provide whatever support you need, and John, too, when he has time—he's obviously brilliant."

"But why can I not go to normal school?"

"I don't know how much you know about Agatha's past," she said. "But the truth is . . . since she had her troubles, I don't like the idea of setting you loose among people we know nothing about. Wild people."

I knew very little about Agatha's mysterious "school troubles." But that was irrelevant. Agatha and I were totally different people. She may have fallen in with bad kids, but that didn't mean I would.

"You learn things about people as you get to know them," I said through my teeth. "That's . . ." I was going to say, *That's how making friends works.* But I managed to stop myself, because it seemed disrespectful. "I don't want to go out to parties. I just want to be near kids my own age."

"But you have Agatha," Laura said, surprised. "She's your age."

We stared at each other. It was as if we were speaking different languages.

"I never got in trouble at school," I said. "Not even detention."

"That doesn't surprise me at all," she said, putting her hand on my shoulder. I suppressed the urge to duck away. "I don't mean to imply that we have any doubts about you, Margot. It's just that it's such a big world, and you're very vulnerable. We've grown quite fond of you and we want to make sure you're protected."

Protected from what, exactly? Whatever their phantom fears were, wasn't it equally valid to worry about spending the rest of my childhood deprived of proper socialization? They couldn't cut me off from *everything.* What would two years of isolation do to me?

"Could we talk about this more before making a final decision?" I asked.

She gave me a pleasant smile. "No."

There was a beat of silence, and then next to me, Agatha tipped over her water glass.

I MADE A show of lazing around the library until they left for their appointment, and then I jumped up and ran upstairs. Using Agatha's technique, I hip-checked the door to the green wing. And then I went into the hall and I . . . stood there.

I wanted answers. I wanted to know who Lily was and why Laura never mentioned her. I wanted to know why I'd been beckoned here—even if it was only my subconscious sending for me. What did my subconscious think was so great about the green wing?

It spread before me, silent and dusty, and I walked toward the room I'd been in twice before.

Just as I came to the doorway, the door shuddered slightly.

I stopped. Looking at it, my whole body began to buzz with apprehension. Almost like the room was putting out an electrical current—one that I wanted nothing to do with. But I forced myself forward any-way. It must have been the wind. Old houses were drafty.

I crossed the threshold and stopped.

On the surface, there was nothing spectacular about this room. It was just a bedroom. In the light of day, I could see that it looked rather lived-in—the furniture was all slightly shabby, and the bedspread had the limp, pilled look of having been laundered regularly. It was a perfectly fine room, if a little less fancy than I'd come to expect from Copeland Hall.

But still . . . there was something about it that made me feel almost ill. A bad vibe, you could say.

I stepped into the attached bathroom and turned on the light. I was surprised to see that this bathroom, like the one Agatha used, had been modified to accommodate a person with disabilities. What had once been a bathtub had been replaced by a shower. The shower curtain was pushed off to the side—thin ivory rubber, like something you'd find in a cheap motel room.

The whole thing looked and felt weirdly clinical. Someone had obviously spent a good deal of time in here, but it wasn't personalized at all.

My nerves were vibrating, wanting to cut and run, but I forced myself to be rational. I looked around, and my eyes settled on the tall wooden wardrobe cabinet in the corner of the room. I walked over and tried to open it, but it was locked. So I gave the handles a sharp yank, and to my shock the doors swung open.

It was mostly empty—the bar held an assortment of hangers in various sizes and colors, and on the shelf there was a single pair of bedroom slippers and a folded hand towel. Leaning against the back wall, facing away, was a large picture frame.

Under that was a small drawer. I pulled it out and found a black, fabric-covered box, the size you'd use when giving someone a fancy shirt as a present.

I sat down and put the box on the floor in front of me.

And, well aware that I shouldn't, I removed the lid.

It was full of papers—stuff like medical forms and school letters.

And each one had the same name listed:

LILY COPELAND

I felt shaky, so I leaned back against the bed. As I did, there was a *thunk* from inside the wardrobe. I looked up to see that the picture frame was now nearly falling out, held up only by an inch or so of overlap with the side of the structure. I hurried over to stabilize it, and then I figured . . . I might as well take a peek, right? When I pulled it out, I saw that it was an oil painting, a portrait of a man and two teenage girls.

The man, who looked vaguely familiar, was handsome and confident looking. His expression was mildly smug. He sat on an antique chair, and next to him, with her hand on his shoulder, was a girl who looked about fourteen years old. On his other side, standing slightly back, was another girl, one who might have been about eleven or twelve.

The two girls weren't identical, but they were clearly sisters. The older one had her hair in well-defined curls that fell just past her shoulders. She wore a white shirt with a small pleated ruffle around the neckline. Her blue eyes shone, and a faint, knowing smile played on her lips.

Lily?

The other girl was more serious. Her hair was in a pair of severe braids, her brown eyes steady and almost dull. The painter had depicted her looking at her father, and in her gaze was a sense of admiration—but also a kind of loneliness. The father and his older daughter seemed like a team. But this younger girl was on the outside.

She was unmistakably Laura.

Looking at it, I could actually understand why she would have taken it down. The little girl's hurt shone right through. Her sense of not belonging.

Doubt suddenly washed over me. I shouldn't be here, looking at this evidence of Laura's sadness. She'd hidden this picture for a reason, and here I was, snooping around. It was easy enough to enjoy being nosy when it wasn't *your* secrets being exposed.

I pushed the portrait back into the wardrobe, feeling ashamed of myself.

Then I began to pack up the black box. But just as I was setting the lid in place, I caught sight of a newspaper clipping sticking out from some of the papers. And I couldn't resist.

It was Lily's obituary:

LILY ANNE COPELAND, age 17, was called to heaven Friday, March 18, after a prolonged illness. She passed from the mortal world as she lived, surrounded by her loving and devoted family at home. Miss Copeland, the heiress apparent to the extensive Copeland properties and fortune, was a vivacious girl, well liked in the community and known among friends at Copeland School as an A student with a love of reading and cats. Preceded in death by her mother, Beverly (Turner) Copeland, she is survived by her father, James Barrett Copeland III, her younger sister and faithful companion, Laura, and her aunt, Rosetta Copeland Gilbert. Services will be held privately, for family only. Flowers may be sent to Copeland Hall.

A prolonged illness? Like Agatha's?

No wonder Laura was so frozen, so rigid and emotionally warped. Her older sister had died as a teenager and now her daughter was seriously ill. Who wouldn't be messed up by that kind of awful coincidence?

I read it over a couple of times and then neatly replaced it in the box, which I put away in the wardrobe. On trying to close it, I discovered (to my dismay) that I had broken the latch. I could close the door, but it didn't click tidily into place.

My only comfort was that no one ever seemed to spend any time here, and maybe Laura would never get around to noticing.

As I turned to leave, behind me I heard a slow *creeeeak*.

The wardrobe door had opened.

I stepped back, shut it, and started toward the door to the hall.

Creeeeeeeeeeak.

How aggravating. And even more so because it was my fault.

I went back and spent a minute inspecting the damage I'd done. It was much worse than I'd thought: the latch on the right-side door hung pathetically by one screw on a splinter of wood that had cracked away from the body of the door.

Oh, great.

I reached up to try to hold the wood in place, but it wouldn't stay long enough for me to close the door.

So I looked around helplessly for something I could use to put it back into place.

I walked over to the small desk. Maybe there was tape or glue in the drawers? I searched through them, but all I found were some desiccated rubber erasers and the caps to three pens. I reached my hand back into the drawer—and something touched my fingers.

My first thought was *spider!* but when I crouched down to peer inside, I could see that it wasn't a spider. I reached in and moved my hand around, jogging the underside of the drawer above it.

Something hit the bottom of the drawer with a muffled *whomp.* I reached in and grabbed it. It was a journal, a thin book with a lavender-and-pink swirled design on it. In the corner was a small monogram: LAC.

Lily Anne Copeland. This was her journal.

Suddenly I looked around again. Was this really Lily's bedroom? It didn't look like the kind of bedroom a teen girl would live in, in a house this grand. Agatha's room was about fifty times more posh. And Lily had been the heir, like Agatha now was—or was supposed to be. Didn't she rate a nicer space?

Then I looked again at the bed. I lifted the skirt higher, revealing a white metal frame underneath. The whole thing was on wheels—a hospital bed.

I swallowed hard.

So this wasn't actually Lily's bedroom—it was the sickroom.

Which meant she'd probably died in here.

The feeling that came over me was hard to describe—a sense of being in a place where I wasn't wanted and didn't belong. A feeling of being too hot and too cold at the same time.

I backed toward the main door as if turning around would give a pack of zombies a chance to come for me. I closed the door behind me and headed for the double doors leading out of the green wing.

As I retreated to the safety of the normal hallway, I realized I was still holding the journal. I barely had time to stash it in my bottom drawer before Laura and Agatha came home, earlier than expected. Laura called me downstairs and asked me to fix lunch, which I did, and then Agatha and I ate in mutual silence.

The eerie sensation that had come over me in that room stuck to my skin like tar.

CHAPTER
~24~

"YOU'RE SO QUIET today," Laura said, shoving the pointed end of her trowel into the roots of the bushy green plant. She used the other hand to gather the stems together and pull, until the mass of lavender came out of the ground. As she crushed the leaves in her glove, their scent filled the air.

Like screams, I thought.

She handed the plant to me and I tossed it onto the growing pile. We were thinning out the herb garden, which had become an overgrown jungle.

"Lavender," Laura said, "is wonderful for bees. And the oil is lovely. So relaxing."

She yanked another handful out of the ground.

"So . . . why are we getting rid of it?" I asked.

"No matter how nice something is, you can't let it run roughshod. The other herbs suffer when we let the showy ones take over." She indicated a small spray of tattered yellowish fan-shaped leaves on limp-looking stems. "Do you see how the cilantro has been stunted?"

"Too much shade?" I asked.

"Overshadowed," she said. "And crowded out."

"I know about Lily," I said.

I hadn't meant to say it. It just came out.

Laura froze.

"She was your sister, right?" I asked. "And she died? Is that why you told me you're an only child?"

No answer. Sensing I was in very dangerous territory, I began to flail for something appropriate to say. "I'm really sorry for your loss. I know exactly how it feels to lose a sister."

Then I waited—for the explosion, the tears, the anger, the stony, disapproving silence.

But she looked at me. "Thank you, Margot," she said. "As ever, your empathy and kindness are appreciated."

Well, that seemed a bit of an overstatement, but who was I to say?

She finished rinsing the trowel and then carefully dried it with the rough cotton towel that hung on a hook nearby. After replacing it in its position on the pegboard, she turned to me.

"May I ask," she said, "*how* you came to learn about my sister?"

I had given this some thought. There were two options that would be based in truth—that I had happened across the grave, or that I had discovered her sickroom and broken into the cabinet to snoop through her stuff.

I may not be a master strategist, but I knew enough to know that neither of these was the ideal option. I briefly considered lying, and then I decided to tell her a variation on the truth.

"The family portrait," I said. "Of her and you and your dad. I found it."

"You did?" Laura blinked. "Goodness, where is it? I haven't seen it in years."

"In the green wing," I said. Technically true, right?

She hadn't been expecting this. "How did you get into the green wing? Isn't it locked?"

"I . . . bumped into the doors," I said. "And they opened, so I went in. And then . . ."

"And then you happened across the portrait?"

"Yes," I said.

Oh, no, she was going to ask where. Should I tell her? Would she hate me?

But she didn't. "And I suppose you found the small plaque," she said, "with our names on it?"

"Yes," I lied. Yes, of course, because how else would I have learned Lily's name? Certainly not by rooting through her medical records.

Her eyes bored into me. I waited for her to ask for more details, but she didn't.

"That's good," she said, looking away as if it was no big deal. "I thought we'd lost it."

"I'm sorry if I wasn't supposed to go in there."

She waved the apology off. "That doesn't matter. It's just a hallway. I have it locked to keep Agatha from wandering around and getting lost."

I nodded, relieved.

Her eyes searched the distance absently. Then she sighed. "I could have told you about Lily before. But I didn't want you to think I would leverage my personal tragedy to try to force a connection with you."

That made sense.

"The sad truth is . . . I don't think about her very often anymore. Life has a way of carrying on. With the children, and the business of running the house, I've just managed to stay busy." Her cheeks softened as her eyes relaxed. "Is that terrible?"

"No," I said. "You just do what you have to do to get by. I mean . . . maybe you're not thinking about it on purpose. And that's okay."

"She was my big sister. I looked up to her. She was the heiress, the one who was supposed to take over the estate. And then . . . she got sick, and I had to step up. Our mother died when we were young, you know.

So here I am, fifteen years old, and one day my sister simply . . . collapses."

"That must have been terrible," I said.

"Oh, yes. It was. She . . . lingered for a few months, but was never her real self again. There was nothing anyone could do to help her. It was awful."

Watching someone deteriorate before your eyes, being powerless to save them? I wondered briefly if that would be worse than losing a person suddenly, out of nowhere, the way I had. *At least she had a chance to say goodbye,* I thought.

"Do you want to know something?" Laura said quietly. "I've never told anyone this. But maybe the reason I don't talk about Lily is because we didn't get along." She turned to me, anxious. "I know I'm not the easiest person to live with, but Lily . . . she was something else. She was a liar."

I held my breath.

"Pathological," Laura said. "And she disliked me immensely. She was vicious. But what had I ever done to her, besides try to be supportive?"

"So, did you get to be better friends when she was sick?" The obituary had said Laura was her constant companion—but I couldn't admit to having read the obituary.

"Not exactly friends," she replied. "I nursed her the whole time she was sick. I was there by her side.

It was thankless, and it made her hate me even more."

"That's terrible," I said. "Really. I'm sorry."

"Life is terrible sometimes," Laura said, shrugging her thin, tense shoulders. "That's just the way it goes."

"Yeah."

"Who knows what Lily would have grown into? She fell in with some very questionable friends." Laura clucked her tongue. "Who knows what she might have done to Copeland Hall if she had lived."

I felt stunned and slightly horrified. It almost sounded as if Laura was *glad* her sister had died. That didn't make sense at all. But it did make me wonder if this was how she had developed her fear of Agatha falling in with bad kids.

I didn't ask for clarity. We'd almost reached the house, and I knew that we weren't going to be continuing this talk. As if it was a dirty thing that belonged out in the wild and shouldn't be brought inside.

I WENT UP to the nursery, looking forward to scrubbing away not only the sweat and dirt but also the feeling our conversation had left with me.

"Ags—" I cut myself off when I walked into the nursery. Her chair at the desk was empty. I walked back out and checked the hall bathroom, and then I went back and looked into my bathroom and my bedroom. Finding both of those deserted, I went out and stood in the hall helplessly.

I was about to go downstairs when, across the hall, Agatha's old bedroom door opened. Agatha herself came out, with something tucked under her arm.

She shoved the object at me, and I heard a *clunk*.

It was a shoebox, and the photo on the front was of a pair of royal-blue high heels.

"Okay . . . thank you," I said. "But I don't really *need* blue shoes. Should we put them back?"

She pushed it at me again, clearly wanting me to take them. It seemed morbid, like something a dying person would do. I'd spent enough time that day talking and thinking about dying people, so I stopped protesting. I went into my bedroom and set the shoebox on the floor by the dresser. I'd just return it later.

Agatha followed me in and sat down on the bed, without being invited.

"Are you okay?" I asked. She didn't answer, but she seemed fine, so I let it go.

Laura's gentle knock came from the door, and she peeked into the room. "Have you seen—oh, there she is."

"Yeah, I guess she wanted to hang out in here."

"How lovely," Laura said. "Come, Agatha. Don't bother Margot. She's busy."

I wasn't. Not at all. But oh well.

THE SOUNDS THAT woke me were low and constant—a steady stream of mumbles and unhappy whimpers. At first, I thought it was me. Then I realized it was coming from the other room.

I ran into the nursery. Agatha was thrashing in her bed like a madwoman, and the cries that escaped her were primal, animalistic.

"Agatha!" I cried. I tried to touch her shoulder, but she jerked away. I got a glimpse of her face—she was crying, raking her fingers down her cheeks. She'd already left two long scrapes on the right side. "Stop! Please, stop!"

I knew I should go get Laura, but I didn't want to leave Agatha alone when she was having some kind of fit. Then she grabbed her hair in her fists and pulled so hard I expected it to come out of her scalp in great chunks.

I kept repeating her name: "Agatha, Agatha, Agatha—" And finally, my voice seeped into her head and she looked at me, scooting all the way back across the bed as if I was going to hurt her somehow.

But she was calmer now—still freaked out, tears still rolling down her cheeks, wide-eyed and terrified—but calmer.

"It's me," I said softly. "It's me, Margot. I'm not going to hurt you. I'm here. I'm here."

In spite of the horror of this outburst, something inside me was amazed and hopeful. There was an awakeness about her I'd never seen before.

"Do you know me?" I asked.

She gave me a quick little nod. And then it was like she couldn't stop nodding.

"Right," I said. "I'm Margot. I'm here, Ags. I'll help you. You're so upset. What's wrong?"

She opened her mouth to speak. *"Kah!"* she spat. *"K—gah. Gah."*

I watched, holding my breath. She seemed to be completely breaking down.

"G—go!" she finally said. "Go!"

I froze.

"Go?" I repeated. Was that what she'd been trying to say all this time?

She waved her arm at me. *"Go,"* she said. She was almost pleading.

"I'll go," I said. "I'll go right now and get your mom."

Then she let out a bloodcurdling shriek.

"No, no, no!" she yelled. She began thrashing again. "No!"

"Okay!" I said. "I won't! I'll stay. I'll stay. Agatha, what's wrong? What's happening?"

She was talking. She was communicating. Was it possible that this fit overtaking her was like a fever breaking—that point where your body throws everything it has into overcoming your illness?

What if she was better after this?

"Ags, it's okay," I said. "I'm here. Do you want some water?"

She pressed back against the wall and stared at me. Finally, she nodded.

I passed her the water cup from her nightstand, and she drank it down, then passed it back. Her arm shook.

Laura should be here; she should see this for herself. How would I describe it to her? Or what if it was some kind of serious mental break? What if Agatha was worse after this?

"You're safe," I said, holding my hands up like she was robbing me. "You're safe. Do you understand me?"

She whimpered and shrank back.

"Agatha, it's me," I said. "It's Margot."

I stepped closer, and she leaned farther away.

"Go," she said.

"Okay," I said. I was getting exhausted. "I'll go." I started to turn away.

"Margot!" she yelped.

I gasped and turned around.

"Margot," she said again, like she was practicing. Then she looked at me and shook her head. Her eyes were clearer now, but no less frightened. "Go. Go."

"You can speak," I said, stepping closer. "You can speak, do you hear yourself?"

"I . . ." she said. She seemed to lose track of what she was saying, and she shook her head furiously. "I—"

I stepped closer.

"I'm not—"

There were frantic footsteps in the hall outside, and Agatha's eyes widened.

"You're not what?" I whispered.

Her mouth moved, she shook her head. She couldn't find the word.

But I had a guess.

"Sick?" I asked.

She drew in a sharp breath. Her eyes gleamed.

"You're not sick?"

But Laura came storming into the room. "Margot, what's going on? Agatha!"

At the sight of her mother, Agatha began to thrash and howl again.

"Margot, help me!" Laura said. "Help me! Grab her legs!"

"She was talking," I protested. "She was making sense!"

"She's going to hurt herself. Or us. Grab her legs and sit on them!"

Everything happened so fast I didn't have a chance to refuse. Laura basically tackled Agatha, and I reached out and grabbed her legs, then put my body weight on them. I felt terrible—she was struggling underneath us.

Laura pulled the cap off a tiny syringe and shoved it into Agatha's arm. Laura was strong—she held Agatha in place until the medicine started to take effect, and I felt her legs go limp underneath me.

With an undignified grunt, Laura climbed off the bed. Agatha fell to the side and landed awkwardly on the pillow, too weak to catch herself.

I stepped forward to try to make her more comfortable, but Laura waved me back.

"What happened?" she asked.

"I heard her—she woke me up—I came out and she was kind of freaking out. But she was trying to talk—"

Laura roughly rearranged Agatha on the bed and then began searching the bedding, lifting the pillow, running her hand under the blankets. Then she got down on her knees and searched the floor. With a little sniff of triumph, she grabbed something and shoved it into her pocket.

"Is she okay?" I asked.

"She's all right. I've sedated her. She'll feel better in the morning."

"What did you find on the floor?"

"Her medicine," she said. "She used to spit it out—I guess she's back to her old tricks."

With the efficiency of a nurse, she moved Agatha back into place on the bed. Agatha's eyes were struggling to stay open, and a line of drool had escaped the corner of her mouth.

"Back to bed, please, Margot," Laura said with a sigh. "I'm terribly sorry that she disturbed you."

"It's okay," I said. "But I think maybe she was going to say something important."

Suddenly, the air in the room seemed to still. Laura turned to me, too calm, and said sweetly, "What do you think she was going to say?"

"Well—she said my name," I said. "I think."

"You think," she said.

"It was kind of garbled," I lied. "I mean, like, you know when babies start to talk and they—"

She nodded impatiently. "You're such a dear for having that kind of hope. But Agatha simply isn't in a place where she can speak. Even your name, and we know how much she values you."

I nodded. "I guess . . . I guess I was wrong."

"To bed," Laura said lightly.

I nodded and went back into my bedroom. I felt a fresh wave of fear as I climbed under the covers and switched off the light.

I waited until I heard the nursery door close, and then I went back out, tiptoeing to Agatha's bedside.

The sticky drool was still on her chin. I wiped it away with my sleeve and then looked down at her. Her eyes were slits—but she was still awake.

"You're not sick?" I whispered.

I felt something on my arm—and I realized she had wrapped her hand around my wrist.

"I'll see you tomorrow," I said. "Good night."

Her eyes shut.

I was back in my own bed, feeling wired, when suddenly my door opened.

Laura stood against the dark.

"That was such an adventure," she said quietly. "I thought you might like some tea to help you calm down."

She set the teacup down on my nightstand.

"Thank you," I said.

"Do you want me to sit with you?"

"No," I said. "I'm good. Thanks, though."

"All right. Just checking."

She backed out of the room and closed the door.

I stared down at the tea, then picked it up and took a sip.

I'm not sick.

Of course, she could have just been saying that, but . . .

If she needed that medicine, shouldn't Laura have given her more?

As I thought about this, I sipped my tea. And I began to feel relaxed.

Then I had a thought. I set the teacup down and crossed the room to my dresser, where I opened the bottom drawer and took out Lily's journal. I hadn't had a chance to read it yet.

I carried it back to my bed and turned on the flashlight on my phone, then aimed it at the notebook. I was beginning to have trouble keeping my eyes open—my head felt heavy and wobbly.

I set the book down and aimed the light at it. Then I opened it to the first page:

My name is Lily Copeland.
I'm being locked in a room in my house.
They keep giving me medicine.
But I'M NOT SICK.

CHAPTER
~25~

I WOKE UP groggy. My phone was pressed up against my arm, which was numb, and there was something hard under my shoulder blade.

As I sat up and saw the journal, the previous night came flooding back—Agatha had said my name. She had told me to go. She had told me she wasn't sick.

And Lily hadn't been sick, either.

My head felt fuzzy and slow. I looked down at my teacup, then picked it up and sniffed. The smell made me draw back—it was sharp, cloying, and it made me feel a little dizzy.

I needed to read more of the journal. Was this true? Any of it? Was Agatha really not sick? I'd seen last night that she was capable of speaking, of understanding and making sense.

And Lily . . . if she wasn't sick, what had killed her? Or . . . who?

THERE WAS A light rap on my door, and I just managed to put the notebook under my pillow before Laura opened it.

"Hello, sleepyhead!" she said cheerfully. "It's almost ten thirty."

"Oh," I said, sitting up. "Wow."

"Agatha's downstairs . . . would you like to get up and around and then cut some flowers for the breakfast room?"

"Sure," I said. Anything to have a little time to myself.

I pulled on some clothes, purposefully choosing a bulky cardigan so I could hide the journal. Then I tucked it into the back of my waistband and headed downstairs. I had my phone in my back jeans pocket.

"Would you like a doughnut?" Laura called from the breakfast room.

"No, thanks," I replied. "I'll go get the flowers."

I grabbed the shears and the special flower-gathering bucket (it's a country estate thing, you wouldn't understand) and went outside. I hurried to the garden, aware of my wooziness and trying to make sure I didn't trip. I did sort of wobble into the bushes at one point, but I righted myself.

In the garden, I hurried around until I had a respectable assortment, and then I sat down on a bench hidden from view of the house. I pulled Lily's journal out and opened it to a random page.

There were lines and lines, written in Lily's slightly bubbly, childish handwriting:

The proof of virtue is the ability to obey in the face of inner resistance.

A demand for obedience performed against the will is the ultimate test of rectitude. A child is led to righteousness by the lantern of his parents' steadfastness and must by firm hands be molded into a creature of exemplary humility and worth. Abandoned to the darkness of parental deficiency, the child's quality of character will assuredly be as weak as a lily grown in shade.

I could barely breathe. This was the exact text in Agatha's notebook.

I remembered what Barrett had said: That they'd had to copy passages from Loretta's book as a punishment. But why was Lily being punished? She was sick.

No, she wasn't.

I flipped back to the prior entries. The last page before those, the final real entry, was written in small purple print:

> Laura came in and told me Missy got hit by a car and died.
>
> She's lying. She killed her. I know she did. She won't let me see the body. They buried her already. In the garden. Laura says Dad doesn't even want me to look at the grave but I told her I just wanted to see it. And she told me "curiosity killed the cat." She's evil. She's vile.
>
> The cat first. Me next. Everything she gives me is poison.
>
> I hate her I hate her I hate her.

The next page had only one line:

I'M NOT SICK.

I dropped the journal as if it was on fire.

My body felt chilled by fear and nerves and a general sort of exhaustion. I thought of the cat collar I'd found—*Missy*. Had Laura killed her sister's cat?

Had Laura killed her own sister?

I stared at the page until the letters and words blended together and didn't make sense anymore:

IM NOT SICK

I had to leave this place.

But how? If I left now, could I make it off the property before Laura noticed? If I took the journal, that might be enough evidence. Apparently Lily had hidden it so well that Laura never found it. I was the only person who knew what Laura had done.

I slid the journal back into my waistband, but the cover, weakened with age, came partway off and the first page tore. I felt a great ball of emotion rising up inside me, and it took all my self-control to slow down, take a breath, and try again.

If this was true, Laura was a murderer.

"Margot?" Laura's voice came from behind me, as deadly calm as the glassy surface of a lake. "You look upset. Is something wrong?"

I turned and looked at her in horror.

"Why don't you and I go for a little walk?"

I licked my lips. I didn't know what to say.

"I think I know what's happening," she said. "I'll try to explain. Does that sound all right?"

I nodded numbly, and she beckoned me to follow her. We walked through the garden.

"Last night's little disturbance was very hard for you," she said. "Am I right?"

I hesitated, then nodded again. Did she not know I had the journal?

"You must trust that I know what's best for Agatha," she said. "It's wonderful that you care so deeply for her. And hope so deeply. But I've nursed her for nearly a year."

We came to the Adam and Eve gate, and Laura removed the key chain from her pocket and unlocked it, then gestured for me to go in.

"I also nursed my sister," she said. "I was very young—only fifteen when she first fell ill—and my father put the responsibility on me. When she died, I think he blamed me. And of course I blamed myself."

Which would be natural, if you murdered her.

"You know that Lily was the eldest daughter," she said. "And the heir, as tradition dictated. But she had this idea, during her junior year of high school. She decided that instead of taking over the household, she was going to go to Europe and 'find herself,' whatever that means." Laura sighed. "I don't know why people these days are so obsessed with finding themselves, although, of course, that's not a *crime*, if one has nothing better to do. But when my father suggested she stay here and spend a year working, earning money to pay for this extravagant vacation, she acted like he was asking her to put her own eye out."

She told the story methodically, calmly, not at all sounding like a person who had poisoned her own sister.

"She was so upset that she made herself sick. The emotion seemed to bring out the worst in her. Some . . . darkness. She got mean. She threatened to kill me, to kill our father. Her behavior turned erratic, and I began locking my door at night. Then, one day, she collapsed at school and had to be rushed to the emergency room. The doctors said there was something wrong with her brain."

"Like Agatha's?" I heard a note of probing defiance in my voice.

"Very like Agatha's," she said. If she was annoyed by my tone, she didn't show it. "In fact, what I haven't told you is that Agatha's condition is not the result of a bacterial infection. It's hereditary. She has what Lily had." Then she took a deep, shaky breath. "I pray every night that treatment has advanced enough to save her from the fate that my sister met."

We were following the path past all the grave sites.

"There have been advances, though, right?"

"Yes, but I'll never stop being afraid," Laura said. "And that's why Agatha can't be allowed to 'wake up,' as she did last night. I think sometimes the greatest tragedy of the disease isn't that it killed Lily—it's that it made her believe we were conspiring against her. She and Tom Albright were in love, you know. They were planning to be married after they graduated from high school. It was such a big deal, because to marry an Albright would have been unheard-of only a generation before mine. But Dad was convinced that it was a good match. Tom's loyalty was absolute. He would have brought that into the family and done whatever he could to continue the legacy. It doesn't do to stand on tradition for its own sake, Margot."

Sure, sure, great advice. I'll remember that the next time I know someone who's about to sully the family name by marrying a mere business manager.

"Did Lily have a cat?" I asked. "I—I found something in the garden."

"Oh, the cat," Laura said ruefully. "That cat. A feral stray that Lily had basically kidnapped from a barn near our school. She clawed and bit and would leap out of the shadows, so I was afraid to walk across the room. She'd latch on to your ankle—" She laughed a little at the memory. "It was like living with a monster. I *detested* that cat."

"What happened to it?"

She shot me a sideways glance, as if trying to gauge whether to say it. "Lily drowned it."

I felt my shoulders tense up.

"She did it during one of her episodes," Laura said. "Afterward, when she was passed out, I buried the cat in the garden, thinking we could have a memorial of some kind. But what did we get instead? Defiled soil, as far as I can tell. I don't really believe in those things, but—like I said, nothing grows by the gate."

"Poor cat," I whispered.

"Poor cat," she agreed with a sigh. "And poor Lily. She was convinced that *I* killed it."

We had reached Lily's grave. It lay bare—no vibrant carpet of flowers. There was one small shoot beginning to reach out of the dirt near the foot of the grave, but Laura reached down and plucked it.

"Weeds," she said with distaste. "I'm sorry if I seemed harsh last night. It wasn't easy for me to decide to share this with you. If you were to hear my sister's account, I'm a monster. And perhaps Agatha feels the same way. But I don't think I'm a monster. Do you?"

"No," I said. I mean, maybe.

She seemed pleased. She patted me on the back. "Good girl. Now let's go have some lunch."

We continued along the path, farther than I'd ever had reason to go, and we came across a large pond, which looked cold and black under the dappled shade.

Yeah, no thanks. I wasn't a fan of dark water.

"Isn't this a sweet place?" Laura asked. "When I was a kid, there were always ducks here."

"That's cute," I said.

"They were filthy," she added.

As we were turning to leave, I felt a strange sensation in my back pocket—something incredibly familiar, but also something I'd nearly forgotten about.

Laura locked the gate, and just as we reached the entrance to the garden, I paused and looked over my shoulder. "Oh, I need to clean the shears I was using earlier. They're in the shed, but they're not dry."

To Laura, leaving a piece of gardening equipment sitting out uncleaned was basically like stealing a loaf of bread from a widow. A moral failing.

"I'd better go take care of it," I said.

"Yes," she said. "I'll see you at lunch."

I turned and walked away and felt her watching every step I took.

In the shed, I wiped down the shears and hung them on their little peg, in case Laura had followed me. Then I went around the side of the small building and pulled my phone from my pocket.

I gasped—there were new-message notifications. I scrolled through them and found mostly spam, with a few medical billing notices, but that didn't matter—

What mattered was that there was a cell signal at the far side of the graveyard.

I felt a surge of power. This was big. It was *huge*.

I could call for a cab. I could call anybody. I could call Barrett.

And Laura didn't even know.

I FINISHED ARRANGING the flowers just as Laura walked out of the kitchen with two bowls of spinach salad topped with grilled chicken. She set them on the table.

I glanced at the hall. "Should I get Agatha?"

"No, dear. Not today." And then she gestured for me to sit down. "She's taking a little nap."

A nap? At lunchtime?

"Don't look so concerned," Laura said, a gentle smile on her lips. "She's fine. I'm working with Dr. Reed to make sure we don't end up with a repeat of last night."

"Dr. Reed said she needs to sleep all day?"

She set down her fork, hitting her plate with a loud click. "I'm sorry, the subject is closed."

"Okay, sorry," I said.

The rest of our meal was awkward. I felt like I'd taken an ax and wedged it directly between us, and Laura didn't seem willing to move past it. She wasn't angry, I don't think, but she didn't speak to me, either.

Bad orphan, Margot. Very bad orphan.

LAURA ASKED ME to stay out of the nursery so Agatha would be undisturbed.

But then Agatha skipped dinner, too. Laura claimed she'd woken for a while and eaten a big meal to make up for missing lunch, but I hadn't seen any evidence of this and wondered if it was true.

After dinner, I did the dishes, and then I went upstairs to shower and get ready for bed. When I went into the nursery, Agatha was already in bed, asleep, with Laura standing over her.

Laura turned to me, raised her finger to her lips, and whispered, "Shhhh. She's worn out, sweet girl."

"She's been asleep for most of the day," I replied, keeping my voice low. "How can she be worn out?"

"I spoke to Dr. Reed, and we've adjusted her medications a bit," Laura said. "So I think it will be smoother sailing from now on."

"New medication? Does the doctor think she's getting worse?"

"No, no," Laura said. "She's doing fine."

LAURA BROUGHT MY tea and handed it over. "Careful, it's very hot. The new electric kettle is a bust, I'm afraid. I should go back to using Grandmother's old one."

I took a sip and did indeed burn my taste buds right off.

"I'll just wait," I said, setting it aside.

"Probably a good idea," Laura said, a bit sarcastically.

She was treating me a little differently now. Maybe it was because Barrett and John were both gone and I was the only human contact she had (not counting Agatha, of course). Or maybe it was because we'd talked about Lily, and sharing her pain had made her feel closer to me.

Whichever it was, I didn't like it.

With cold, calculating Laura, you always knew where you stood.

With this Laura, I kept overstepping in small ways that irritated her.

I couldn't stop thinking over our conversation about Lily. If she'd been telling the truth—and she could have been—that just made the journal one more sign of Lily's messed-up mind. It would be easy to see how a paranoid person with a lot of time on her hands could produce page after page of deranged ranting.

On the other hand, a normal person being held prisoner and being overmedicated would probably produce strikingly similar rants.

So which was it? I knew Laura's side of the story. I knew Lily's side of the story.

But what bothered me the most was Agatha's side of the story.

I'm not sick.

I believed her.

And that meant that when she said *go*, I should believe that, too. I should leave this place, even if it meant going to the state institution.

The only thing that was holding me back now was Agatha—even before this new regime of powerful medication, I had hated to think of her here, all alone. We were, in our own way, friends. I cared about Agatha. I wanted to protect her. And how could I do that if I abandoned her?

Easy, really. All I had to do was tell Barrett what I knew. He would look out for his sister, right?

But would he do it, even if it meant, say, calling the police on his mom?

It seemed absurd. Laura wouldn't hurt Agatha. That was ridiculous. Everything she did was to keep Agatha safe and cared for. She'd taken care of her every day for nearly a year.

But what if Laura was the *reason* Agatha needed caring for?

I fell asleep miserably mulling it over.

A STRANGE NOISE woke me, and I jumped out of bed, on high alert. The previous night's episode had me ready for another chance to communicate with Agatha, whenever it might come. So I raced out to the nursery.

Agatha was awake. But this was different. She was convulsing. Her legs were jerking, her arms twitching.

I ran to her bedside.

She looked up at me through bright eyes. A strangled humming sound emerged from her, and that's when I realized that she was choking.

I grabbed her by the shoulders and turned her to her side. Immediately, the noises she was making changed—they became more intense, more desperate.

I shoved my arms under her armpits and hoisted her up, then dragged her off the bed, staggering under her weight, and leaned us both forward.

She vomited a spray of thick gray-brown liquid all over the floor.

Then she took a deep, long gurgling breath. The effort sounded painful, but she took in enough air to take another breath, and another, and then finally she was breathing normally—with a bit of a rasp, but getting enough air at least.

Still supporting her, I collapsed back onto the bed and laid her out on the mattress. She was limp, but breathing.

Agatha gave a shuddering sigh, and suddenly a whisper of air escaped her lips.

"What?" I asked, leaning over her. "What did you say?"

Her eyes struggled to stay open, then quickly lost their focus and rolled back in her head. She dropped out of consciousness without even a hint of struggle.

I looked at the floor. Gross. and it wasn't my job to clean it . . . but I didn't feel like involving Laura.

Was I scared of her? Maybe.

I spent a half hour cleaning up, then maneuvered Agatha back under the covers, gently wiping her unresponsive face before I finally switched off the light. I was beyond exhausted, myself, and as I dumped the dirty towels in the bathroom hamper—I'd worry about explaining that another time—fatigue washed over me. I washed my hands and splashed water on my face and wondered how I would make it back to bed before collapsing. But as I lay restlessly under the covers, I couldn't stop thinking of how Agatha had looked, struggling for air.

I carried my pillow and Blue Bunny back out to the nursery. I peeled back the covers on the bed opposite Agatha's and climbed under. If I pulled my pillow back a little, I could rest my head but still see the rise and fall of Agatha's chest as she breathed. When I closed my eyes, I could hear her soft snoring.

Go.

Yes. It was time to go.

CHAPTER
~26~

THE NEXT MORNING, I felt strangely out of sync. Whether it was my own fear or Laura's suspicion, something hung in the air between us.

I awoke to her small sniff of surprise when she came into the nursery to find me sleeping across from Agatha.

"Good morning, Margot . . . ?" she said. It was a question.

"Oh, hi." My mouth was cottony. I sat up and rubbed my eyes. "Agatha had kind of a rough night, so I thought I should stay close."

Oh, crap. I hadn't meant to tell the truth. Laura raised her eyebrows. "What kind of a rough night?"

"Uh . . . I think there's a chance that maybe whatever the new medication dose is . . ." I felt like I might burst into flames under the intensity of Laura's gaze. "Maybe it's too high?"

She was politely interested. The way a cat shows polite interest in a mouse. "And what makes you say that?"

The obvious thing would be to explain the throwing up. But something nagged at me, and I dodged. "Just . . . bad dreams, maybe?"

"Ah," she said. "Did you come and look for me?"

"No," I said. "I'm sorry. Should I have?"

"Not necessarily," she said, with a kind smile. "It seems you handled it wisely. You did what you thought was best."

Then she looked down at Agatha, still asleep, and set her hand on Agatha's motionless arm.

"Why don't you get started with your day?" she asked me. "I'll take over."

"Okay," I said. "Do you want me to make oatmeal?"

"I've eaten already," she said. "Just make something for yourself. I'll be down later."

So I got dressed and made myself a bowl of oatmeal, expecting Laura and Agatha to come down any minute. I settled on a chair in the library and read about women's fashions from the Renaissance to the Second World War, which was when the book was written. I skipped around, looking at illustrations, and reading captions praising the "stunning advances of the modern age."

When I looked at the clock, I was shocked to see

that two hours had passed—and there was still no sign of Laura or Agatha. I went back up the stairs just as Laura was emerging from the nursery. Her expression struggled to be tranquil, but she was clearly stressed.

"Why don't we let Agatha sleep a little longer?" There was a crispness to her voice. "I think it would be best if she's not disturbed."

"Do you need help with her?" I asked.

Her pleasant smile was made unpleasant by the fact that she refused to make eye contact with me. "No, thank you," she said. "In fact . . . I wasn't sure when to bring this up, but I've been feeling lately like we're asking too much of you. You work so hard, and then on nights like last night, you're forced to get up out of bed and deal with bad dreams."

"I don't mind." The top of my head prickled. "Really, it's okay. I like being there for her."

"I know," Laura said. "But I don't want you to feel that you have to be there twenty-four hours a day."

"I'm her companion, though," I said. "Isn't that what I'm supposed to do?"

"I don't know that it's the best thing . . . for either of you right now. My great-grandmother had very interesting things to say about special friendships among young women. She felt the attention of a proper young lady should be focused on the home in general, rather than on one particular person."

"I'm not *focused* on her," I said. "I mean—I'm just trying to be there for her."

"Yes," she said offhandedly. "You certainly are."

"I'm going to run up and brush my teeth," I said.

"I'm sorry," Laura said. "Was I not clear? I'd rather Agatha's rest not be interrupted."

It took me a moment to realize that this meant I couldn't even go into my own bedroom.

"Perhaps you can spend a little time in the garden," she suggested. "Get some fresh air, and then you and I can have a nice lunch before Mr. Albright brings the weekly papers."

"Okay," I said. "Do you want me to make something?"

"Oh no," she said, heading for the stairway. "You enjoy your free time while it lasts."

I nodded and headed for the garden, where I wandered for a miserably hot half hour. I had my phone, but not the key to the graveyard, so I couldn't reach the signal.

Back inside the house, I popped my head into Laura's morning room, and she glanced up. "Yes?"

"Is it okay if I go shower?"

She took off her pearly-pink reading glasses and held them in the air. "Why wouldn't it be?"

"Earlier, you said you didn't want Agatha interrupted."

"That won't be a problem," she said, waving me

off. She put her reading glasses on in a gesture that dismissed me handily.

I hurried up the stairs and into the nursery, expecting to see Agatha asleep in her bed.

But she wasn't there.

The bed was empty, the mattress stripped of its bedding.

I looked around in a panic. Where was she? Where did she go?

I was on my way out to the hallway to search for her when I happened to notice the door to Agatha's old room. It was closed, as usual, but there was something different: a new lock. Someone had added a shining metal dead bolt to it. The kind you needed a key for, only there was no key in sight.

Just like the one on Lily's door.

"Don't be alarmed," Laura said, gliding up toward me like a wraith. "That isn't to keep us out—it's to keep Agatha in."

From her pocket, she pulled a small key, and turned it in the lock.

"Weren't you going to take a shower?" she asked. "Don't let me keep you."

Then she opened the door only as much as she needed to slide through. I craned my neck to see past her, and two images burned into my brain: First, that the bedroom had been cleaned. Second, that Agatha lay unconscious in the bed, looking small and utterly defenseless.

AFTER MY SHOWER, I set the table, and Laura brought out two bowls of soup. I didn't have much of an appetite, but the food smelled good, and I could feel her eyes on me. The thought of a discussion about whether I was eating enough—and why not, and what else might be wrong—was too much. So I swallowed bite after bite, trying to look as if I was enjoying it enough to make Laura happy.

But soon, if everything went according to plan, I wouldn't have to worry about making Laura happy.

"I hope you're not worried about Agatha," she said.

I almost didn't hear her, but at the last second I realized she'd been talking to me. "Oh, I guess I might be," I said. "A little."

She gave me a strange, unhappy smile. "I'd like to remind you," she said, "that I'm her mother. And I realize that you've built an identity for yourself around the idea of being her companion, but—"

She stopped suddenly. Perhaps the stunned look on my face clued her in to how terrible she sounded.

"Actually," I said. "That's kind of something I wanted to talk to you about."

She waited, spoon midway between her bowl and mouth.

"I've decided to go."

"Go ahead," she said. "If you're not hungry—"

"No," I said. "I mean go away from here. Go somewhere else. Which probably means the state institution, but . . ."

She stared at me blankly for a moment. "Margot, I'm surprised. I thought you liked it here."

"I do," I said. "But . . . I think it's best if I leave."

"Best for *you*?" she asked. "Certainly it isn't the best thing for our family. It's a bit selfish, if you think about how it might affect *us*, don't you think?"

Yes, because everything revolves around the Sutton family. "I'm sorry," I said. "This is how I feel."

Besides . . . hadn't she just said I was too attached to Agatha? Did she mean *she* depended on me, somehow? I had a hard time believing that.

I seemed to be having a hard time believing a lot of what Laura said lately, didn't I?

She sighed. "Well, then. What's your plan?"

I felt a little shaky. "I was actually wondering if I should just leave today. When Mr. Albright comes."

That legitimately shocked her. She blinked and pressed a hand to her chest. "I don't think that's a good idea," she said. "There's not nearly enough time to get things situated today."

"That's okay," I said. "He can just drop me off. I think they have to take me."

She watched me carefully. I expected some kind of argument. Maybe more pointed accusations of selfishness.

But then she shrugged. "Okay," she said. "If that's how you feel . . ."

"Thank you," I said.

She leaned forward. "How *are* you feeling? You look a bit flushed."

"I feel fine," I said.

"Hmm," she said dubiously. "You don't look fine."

"I am," I said. "I promise you."

Laura watched me steadily. "Go up to your room and get in bed. You're not yourself, Margot."

What? "I don't need to get in bed. It's lunchtime, and I feel fine."

"You're unwell," Laura said. "This tantrum confirms it."

"I'm *not* sick," I said.

And then I thought, *Uh-oh.*

The only thought in my head in the next moment was: *GO.*

Go, go, go. If it meant running ten miles down a country highway and hitching a ride with the first tractor-trailer that rumbled by, fine.

I got up and headed for the front door. I had to get outside.

Suddenly I felt freezing and hot at the same time. The air in the house was suffocating. The ceiling seemed to rotate above me. I raced for the front door, pushing on the handles, but they were stuck in place.

I turned the lock, but still the door wouldn't open. I started to panic. I needed to be alone, like an injured animal.

"Margot," Laura said, in a singsong voice. She had followed me from the hall and stood several feet away. "As I suspected, you're very unwell. To bed with you."

I shook my head. I wasn't going to bed. I wanted out of the house. My head seemed to be wearing a massive, tight helmet. My whole skull hurt.

She stepped closer. "You shouldn't be here."

And then I remembered the voice that had answered me, that first day: *You're right.*

I'd known since my first day here that this was a bad idea.

This was a bad place. What was the word Laura had used? *Defiled.*

There seemed to be strong hands pushing relentlessly in on my temples. The pain was almost unbearable.

And still Laura kept approaching. "Let me help you," she said softly.

No. I tried the door once more. Why was it locked?

"You're being silly, Margot," she said, in a hard voice with a painted-on coating of fake patience. "Let's go upstairs."

I felt a sudden, oily pressure inside my neck, just behind my ears, and a sick sour bubbling filled my stomach.

"Leave me alone," I warbled pathetically. My shoulders sagged. My sweaty hand slipped off the doorknob.

"Margot," Laura said. "Turn around *this minute*."

So I did.

And then I threw up all over her.

CHAPTER
~27~

I HUNCHED OVER the toilet in the bathroom, having spent the past hour regurgitating everything I'd ever eaten in my life. My throat and nostrils burned, and dark, merciless pain throbbed behind my eyeballs. My stomach felt like a knotted rope, and all the muscles in my body were tender and tired.

A fresh convulsion struck, and I bent over and retched.

"Are you feeling any—" Laura came into the room and stopped short when she saw me. "Oh. I guess not."

I didn't answer. I was too busy dying.

She smoothed my hair down, then stood back until I was finished.

Laura was a highly useful person to have around if you were sick. After my explosive vomiting display in the foyer, which may have ruined a priceless antique

Persian rug as well as Laura's blouse and skirt, we settled into a wordless truce.

She'd helped me up to my room—a painfully slow process that involved her carrying a trash can and me retching every time I tilted my head a millimeter to the right or left. Once there, she helped me change into a pair of pajamas, which meant she saw me naked, but I didn't care. My old high school's marching band could have watched me change, and I wouldn't have cared. Caring took energy. All my energy was being forcibly expelled from my body.

Then she'd rolled up my sleeves, put a soft headband in my hair to keep it away from my gross mouth, and set up the bathroom with everything a person needs to comfortably die of barfing: A thick towel for me to kneel on in front of the toilet. A box of tissues. And, in a gesture that struck me as almost a joke, a cup of water—as if I was ever going to ingest anything again.

At some point she'd managed to clean herself up, too, and now there was no indication that she'd ever been in any state other than her usual hard-won perfection.

Now she leaned over and wiped my forehead and the back of my neck with a cold, wet washcloth, which felt like a light shining down from heaven.

"Would you like to get in bed?" she asked.

Would you like to train for a marathon? Would you like to multiply two eight-digit numbers in your head?

I tried to shrug, but it threw off my equilibrium and made me heave again.

"No," I croaked.

I could feel her watching me. Then she left.

My misery was so great that it overshadowed the emotional storm I'd been caught in downstairs. There comes a point where your body just takes over and your brain shuts down. Any attempt to think made me feel weak and desperately tired.

Still, left alone in the bathroom, I felt a wash of sadness. I'd been abandoned.

Then the door opened again, and Laura came in carrying a pillow and a stack of blankets.

"Here you go," she said gently, arranging a make-shift bed on the floor. "Maybe you can get comfortable."

With her help, I scooched onto the bed and then verrrrrry slowly lay down. The softness of the pillow and the coolness of the fabric made me want to weep.

Laura sat down on the tile next to me, and using only her fingertips, she softly combed through my sweaty hair while I tried feverishly to form words of apology for my earlier rudeness.

"Shhh, poor Margot," she whispered. "Poor, sick Margot."

It felt heavenly.

"By the way," she whispered, "I'm so sorry, but when I was washing your clothes, I accidentally put your phone through the wash cycle. It's ruined, but we'll get you a new one."

I reared back slightly at this very unwelcome news, but even that made me feel ten times worse. So I went back to meek acceptance. There would be time for protest later.

I DREAMED THE room was filled with thousands of tiny creatures. They covered the floor and walls and dropped from the ceiling. They crawled up my legs and over my arms and through my hair. I tried to see what they were, but they were too small and moved too fast. All I knew was that they were everywhere, that they wanted to block out the light and air and smother me in darkness—and I was powerless to stop them.

I was too weak to scream out loud.

But in my dream, I screamed for hours. For days.

It didn't help.

I WOKE IN bed. My head was luminously pain-free. My body was weak, but the fact that my insides weren't actively trying to escape through my throat was like angelic wings lovingly caressing me.

I felt weightless, amazing. It was a new world, one where nothing could touch or hurt me ever again.

It was nighttime—I could see stars through the small window, and fingers of wispy white clouds.

I sat up. My head bobbled and my muscles might as well have been full of air. My vision was bleary and every bit of light was vaguely outlined by a shimmering halo.

But I still felt great. *Wow, I feel great,* I thought. *I feel so great.*

My feet touched the floor, and I noted the smooth coolness of the floorboards. I propelled myself to a standing position and almost tumbled forward. I paused, trying to gauge how much effort it really took to change positions. And then I slowly made my way out into the nursery.

I stopped by the bathroom to pee and found a bottle of energy drink waiting for me by the sink, the cap loosened for my weak fingers. I took a few tentative sips and let the salty wetness soak my tongue. Then I set it down—no point tempting fate, although I felt so much better that I couldn't even imagine throwing up—and went back out to the main room.

Every movement seemed to have a little wispy tail that I couldn't control. If I moved my hand, it kept moving for a moment after I tried to stop it. If I turned my head, my shoulders wanted to turn, too.

I looked around, at Agatha's empty bed, at the way the moonlight fell on the toy box and the shelves with their furry stuffed animals, at the idyllic pattern on the wallpaper. I felt almost as if the room had me under some kind of spell, and I'd been transported a hundred years into the past.

Why did I feel so weird?

I felt like I'd been drugged.

It came to me matter-of-factly, and then once the thought was in my head, I couldn't shake it out. Why would Laura drug me?

Why had she possibly drugged Lily? *To make her sick.* I shook my head—I mean, *To make her healthy again.*

Like Agatha, right?

I tried to picture myself living here a hundred years ago, impossibly rich and surrounded by luxury. The servants' hall would have been packed with maids and butlers eager to fulfill my every whim, and my closet would have held a rainbow of fine gowns and priceless jewelry.

I wandered to my closet. *Fancy,* I thought. *I'm fancy.*

But none of my clothes were remotely fancy enough. Sweaters. Jeans. Bah.

Then I caught sight of Agatha's shoebox. The one with the Polaroid picture of a pair of blue stilettos.

Fancy.

I pulled the box over to the bed and sat down next to it, misjudging the height of the mattress and free-falling the last couple of inches.

"Whoops," I whispered, and a giggle bubbled out of me.

I tried to be careful as I lifted the lid off the shoebox . . .

And then I deflated.

There were no shoes in this box.

Stupid box. All it held was a . . . I reached down and grabbed the small black rectangle.

A phone?

A new-looking smartphone. It had a charging cable wrapped around it, and slid between the cable and the phone's screen was a handwritten note.

I unfolded it.

Please call me if you need anything, I programmed a bunch of numbers into the phone already (mine, B's, Sofie's). I am SO WORRIED about you. I'll try to visit over spring break or summer. Get well SOON PLEASE! I miss you so much!

XOXO Kiley

Well, this was weird. Was this one of the friends who had supposedly abandoned Agatha? If this note was real, then that wasn't true at all.

But . . . why would Kiley have sent Agatha a phone? Surely she would have had her own. And why would Agatha have hidden it for so long, then brought it to me? That made me remember the tiny bag of items I'd found for her in Lily's room. The key, the weird vial . . .

I stared at the wall. There was an answer here somewhere. But my brain wasn't capable of staying on one subject long enough to parse out this riddle. Images and thoughts and memories slid together like the mixed-up colors of a preschooler's painting.

Quickly, I tucked the phone into the back pocket of my pajama pants and shoved the shoebox under the bed. The second I did so, I went from feeling relaxed and dreamy to feeling scared. I shouldn't have a phone. Laura wouldn't like it. Not one little bit.

If she wanted you to have a phone, she wouldn't have destroyed your old one.

Right . . . Laura was mad at me. Laura hated me.

Remembering that wrecked my sunny, contented mindset.

I looked around at the small, enclosed walls of my bedroom, and then wandered out to the nursery. I felt so alone without Agatha here. And I was worried about her.

I went as far as the hall, where the light from the window illuminated the wallpaper and made me think of skeletons reaching their skinny bones out of their graves.

This house was the worst. Honestly. Who could live here?

I should leave, I thought.

And then, after swaying precariously at the top of the stairs, I thought:

I can leave. I could leave now—go outside and sneak into the graveyard and call someone on my fancy new phone. I could call Barrett. He'd help me. Or Kiley. She seemed nice.

It didn't matter who I called—the important thing was to leave.

This decision gave my thoughts a sudden clarity. My body still felt dreamy and drifty, but my mind felt briskly efficient.

I can't let Laura know I'm leaving, I thought. I was going to have to sneak past her bedroom, which shouldn't be a big deal.

Laura and John's bedroom, which I'd never been inside of, was at the very far end of the downstairs hallway, past their offices and at least one more parlor. Their room had a large set of wooden double doors that were never open.

But tonight they were.

I crept closer and saw a gap of about three inches.

Peeking inside, I could make out blue light on one of the walls.

I knocked.

"Laura?" I called.

No answer. She was out somewhere, roaming around.

I knocked again. And then, when there was no reply, I gently pushed the door open and slipped inside.

The bedroom was as grand as you could have hoped in a house like this, with a massive four-poster bed canopied in a heavy silver-blue fabric dominating the room's center. Off to the side were wooden armoires in a long row, and another door leading to a darkened space—a closet or a bathroom.

But what really got my attention was the laptop. It sat open on a desk, the screen a bright rectangle of light.

I walked closer, keeping an ear open and an eye on the door in case I needed to jump away. I was well aware that just being in here was disastrous, but if I was near the door, I could at least claim that I'd only stuck my head in to look for her. Sitting at the computer, surfing the internet? Not so convincing.

If you'd asked me, I would have said I was detoxed from screens. That my time at Copeland Hall had broken through the addiction to the images and content that used to enthrall me. But that clearly wasn't the case, because I was drawn to the glowing rectangle like a zombie to a nice fresh bowl of brains.

I walked over to it and leaned down to see the image. I was dying to know what kind of internet content Laura found suitable and interesting.

But this was just a static image, in strange gray tones.

Then something about it struck me as familiar—the shapes of the objects. Their relationship to each other.

A bed. Another bed. Two doors. A desk, two windows.

This was the nursery. But . . . I didn't remember seeing a camera in there. If I had, I would have been weirded out and spent every day feeling self-conscious about being watched.

I noticed multiple tabs at the top of the screen and clicked through them one at a time: The hallway. Agatha's old bedroom, from a strange, high angle—with Agatha in the bed, asleep.

Barrett's bedroom. The foyer. The library.

And then, the very last feed—a camera placed high in the corner of my tiny bedroom.

I stood back, watching the live feed with a mix of horror and disbelief. With a growing sense of mortification, I wondered if I had ever changed clothes in that room. Had Laura seen that? Had John?

Oh, God, and had Barrett and I ever kissed in any of those rooms?

Yes, yes, of course we had.

I felt danger mounting with every second I remained at the computer. I knew she wouldn't be pleased to come in and find me there. But there were more answers I needed.

On the sidebar, under the link to the security feeds, was a folder labeled SELECTS. I opened it and found a list of subfolders—divided by room. I opened NANNY'S ROOM and was greeted by a list of long, convoluted file names. I clicked one, and it opened.

I shivered. The image showed Barrett and me, standing close. I knew we were about to kiss. The volume was down, but I could hear tinny versions of our voices.

She could *hear* us, too?

I told myself to calm down. If I asked Laura about this, she could give me a reasonable explanation, right? She had a reasonable explanation for everything. She could explain why the cat had died and why Lily wrote such angry things and why Agatha had to be sedated and . . . I lost my train of thought and looked at the computer again. I was vaguely aware that I had overstayed my welcome.

I fast-forwarded through a few more selects from my bedroom.

And then I found something that made me gasp.

It was me—getting out of bed in the middle of the night. Opening the nightstand drawer and pulling something out. And then writing the word *GO* on the wall, in black letters . . .

My mascara. I'd used my mascara. But somehow I had no memory of doing it. I *couldn't* have done it—I would never write on the walls—except I *had*. Every time it happened had been captured in its own little video clip. Laura, I realized, must have fast-forwarded through these feeds every day.

With a sick, heavy feeling in my stomach, I closed the folder and made sure the screen was set back to the correct camera feed. Then I went to the door, peeked into the hall, and upon seeing that the coast was clear, I padded silently back to the foyer.

I was beyond exhausted. My body felt like it was made of paper, ready to be blown over at any second. I looked forward to my own bed the way a kid looks forward to birthday cake. But when I entered the nursery, I paused in the doorway and looked around.

My eyes took in the room compared to the view on the security camera, and I looked up at the shelf on the wall.

It was full of stuffed animals. I'd heard of nanny-cams—decorative stuffed animals that were actually cameras, used by parents to keep an eye on their babysitters.

I pressed up against the wall and shimmied around to just under the shelf. There was a toy chest nearby, and I dragged it over. Then I climbed up on it and reached across the shelf.

One by one, I knocked over each of the stuffed animals.

. . . The way Agatha had knocked over Blue Bunny.

The third one in the row, a floppy-eared puppy in a little tuxedo jacket, made a clicking sound as it fell. Keeping its belly aimed down, I pulled it toward myself. Along its back was a strip of Velcro, which I pulled apart. And inside, where in a sweet children's story you would find a little heart, was the spidery mechanism of a surveillance camera. Its lens was one of the black buttons on the puppy's jacket.

I closed up his back again.

Had Agatha known about the cameras?

Was that why she hated my bunny? In her confused state, she had associated him with the stuffed animals that kept silent watch over her every move. The ones that her mother used to observe and control her.

I climbed down from the toy chest and went back around the walls to my own room.

I lay down on the bed, feeling like the pillow and mattress were rising up around me, holding my body in place in a soft, heavenly mold.

No, no. I couldn't sleep. I had to leave. I *would* leave, right now. I'd get up and walk out the door and never come back.

For a brief moment, I opened my eyes, but the strength it took to keep them open was beyond me.

CHAPTER
~28~

"MARGOT?" LAURA'S VOICE rang out from the other side of the bathroom door. "How are you today?"

I coughed a few times, then forced myself to stop. My throat was raw from all the coughing and throwing up I'd been doing.

It was day four of my illness, which seemed to be some kind of stomach flu. Even Laura, with her time-tested nursing skills, seemed a little squicked out by my never-ending ability to produce vomit.

"Okay," I said. My voice was on the verge of giving out. I opened the bathroom door and Laura came in with a clean set of towels and washcloths.

She sighed when she saw me. "Goodness, you've been through it, haven't you?"

I nodded. I wasn't above a pity party. Lay it on me. If the devil himself wanted to give me sympathy, the door was open.

"Better than yesterday?" she asked. "You want to try breakfast?"

"No," I said. "Just something to drink, please."

"Got it," she said. "Already on your nightstand."

I'd been surviving on orange-flavored energy drinks, although I'd skipped the last couple because I was starting to feel like I was made from sugar. So I stuck with water and dry toast, eaten in narrow strips, one every fifteen minutes.

"Is John coming home today?" I asked.

Laura put her hands on her hips. Her voice was affectionate and exasperated. "It's so sweet, how you look forward to his return. But the case he's working on requires his presence in the city. He won't be home for quite a while. It's just us girls for now."

It was the same answer she'd given me every day. I didn't know why it seemed important for John to come back, but it did.

"If you're feeling better, there's something I'd like to show you," she said.

I FOLLOWED HER down the hallway and through the doors to the green wing. Laura opened the double doors with a key.

A shadow of worry passed over my heart.

Calm down, it's just a hallway. I'd been here before. So when she held the door open, I went in.

"I mentioned to you once that I have a hobby . . ." I followed her to the first door on the right—the sickroom. "Do you like the scented soaps and lotions that I've given you?"

"Yes," I said. "They're very nice." Now my heart was thud-thudding. My spidey sense tingled. What was happening?

She pulled a small bottle from her pocket. "Oh, try this, it's lovely."

What? I took a small sniff, and the spicy aroma of cinnamon hit my nose.

"I've been thinking about my autumn scents a little early," she said. "My mother and grandmother always did spiced apples and cranberry, but that seems so old-fashioned, doesn't it? Every candle store in the country does spiced apples and cranberry."

I shrugged a little. I was out of my league. I didn't spend a lot of time in candle stores, and I didn't want to offend her with any clueless takes on season-appropriate smells . . . *What is going ON?* I wondered.

"So what I'm thinking is cinnamon, vanilla, and . . . you'll never guess. Smell this."

She held up another tiny bottle. I sniffed it.

Our eyes met. She was bursting with anticipation. "Cloves," she said, making the word into two syllables: Cllll-*oves*!

"Wow," I said.

"Right? Oh, it's such fun. I was really looking forward to doing all of this with Agatha."

"Okay, cool," I said lamely. "I wonder if I should get back to my room."

"Probably so," she said, frowning. "You do need your rest, don't you? Here, one more." She held up a new bottle. "This one is subtle. Don't be shy."

I put my nose directly above it and gave it a big sniff. The scent was slightly sharp and unpleasant—not what I would have called subtle.

She took the bottle away and slipped it into her pocket. "Did you know I went to college?"

"I think . . . you said once . . ." I stopped talking. My mouth felt awkward and I suddenly couldn't think of the words I wanted to say.

Laura turned slowly and watched me.

"Laura, I feel sick." My voice rose. "I'm going to throw up."

"Here," she said, helping me over to the bed. "Sit right here."

She helped me onto the bed, which (I noticed for the first time) had already been turned down.

Laura tucked me in tightly. "Yes, I went to college," she said. "I studied pharmacy."

"What's going on?" I whispered.

"Just lie back," she said softly. "Lie back until you feel better."

I jerked away. I didn't want her touching me. I didn't want to be there. I felt awful, inhuman. Weak and growing weaker by the moment.

"I'm fine," I said again, trying to sit up. "Let me go, I'm fine. I'm leaving."

I meant it, too. I would have left if it meant crawling down the driveway on my hands and knees, but Laura didn't give me the chance. She easily pushed me back against the bed.

"Margot," she said. "You're very unwell. I've brought you to this room because you're sick. I can help you, but you have to be a good girl. I'm going to give you some medicine now, and we'll talk more in the morning when you're feeling more like yourself."

"No," I whispered, looking away.

She took hold of my chin and turned it back. "Come on," she urged. "Look at me."

I opened my eyes, but I couldn't focus on her face. She seemed to be getting closer and farther, closer and farther . . .

Then she pulled my jaw open and, using some

kind of plastic device, shot something into the back of my throat. I began to cough and almost spat it out, but she held my lips shut.

"Swallow," she said firmly. "Swallow and I'll let go."

I had no choice.

"I have a question for you," she said. "When you get to the institution, what will you tell them about us?"

She stared down at me.

"Will you tell them I give Agatha too much medicine?"

I goggled at her helplessly.

Her eyes narrowed. "You come into my home. You lie, and steal, and sneak around. You poison my daughter's mind against me. You make my son forget his duty to his family and entice him to put his hands all over your filthy body." She was looking at me with hard, glinting eyes. "You make up theories about terrible crimes that you think I've committed. You snoop through the house and stick your nose in my family's own personal business. Our history. Our secrets."

I stared up at her in horror.

"And then you decide one day, after upending our family's peace and happiness, that you're just going to saunter out the door? No. No. That's not how it works, Margot."

"I'm sorry," I whispered.

"Yes," she said, standing back. "Good. You should be. We'll talk about it tomorrow."

"Please—"

"There is nothing you can ask for that you will get tonight," she said. "You've crossed a line. And you've hurt my feelings. Now, sit back and relax."

I shook my head.

"You don't trust me?" she asked. "You think I'm just a clueless housewife? You think I don't know what I'm doing? Is that what you'll tell them? That I give my children too much medicine?"

"No, I won't," I said. "I promise."

She stared at me. "You will, because you're a child, and you have no idea how important any of this really is. Families like mine built this country, and if anyone is going to keep it moving forward with dignity and honor, it will be us."

Honor?

"What are you going to do to me?" The loudest I could manage was a whisper. I felt so weak. Exhausted.

"I'm going to do for you exactly what I would do for my own family," she said crisply. "Take excellent care of you and make sure you get all the medicine you need to be a good girl."

Then, unceremoniously, she walked out. I heard the *click* of the lock.

After she left, my head lolled to the side, and I looked around the room. I was far too tired to get up and look for an escape route. Now suddenly I noticed that the windows had bars, and the door was reinforced with metal panels.

No food. No water.

She'd been planning this. I'd been sick for days—probably her fault, now that I thought about it—and now I was too weak to fight back.

I HUDDLED ON the bed, staring outside through the barred windows. I was still dizzy and a little light-headed, both of which got worse when I started to seriously contemplate what was happening. I'd woken from an unpleasantly deep sleep—I didn't want nightmares, but some level of awareness was kind of reassuring.

Otherwise it felt too much like death.

Gradually, my adrenaline-fueled energy burst wore away, and my eyelids grew heavy. Even after a full night's worth, I welcomed sleep—I was exhausted and my mind was so strung out.

But I'd forgotten about the nightmares.

It didn't take long to remember—to be slipping into unconsciousness and suddenly sense something waiting for me, just on the other side of the knife-edge drop-off into sleep. This day, it was something dark and wet and horrible; it smelled of death and mud and burnt rubber.

Once I realized it was there, I tried to backtrack, to claw my way out of sleep. But it was too late. It had sensed me and sent tendrils of leathery black vines to wrap around my ankles and hold me in place. I felt it coming nearer, a lumbering mass of shadow without details.

It knocked me over and then hovered in the air above my body, savoring my fear, tasting my tears.

I expected it to have teeth, or claws, or scaly skin. But it was worse than that—it was all gray flesh and endless pockets of darkness, and instead of attacking me, it began to slowly lower itself over me, until I could feel its cold, moist flesh pressing down all over my body. Until its face covered my mouth and nose.

In the dream, I tried to scream. But when I opened my mouth, a hundred tiny black tendrils appeared and filled my throat, silencing me.

In real life, that wasn't an issue. I woke to the sound of myself screaming, and once I had started, I couldn't stop. I could sense the beast there, stalking me, in this dark and sterile and unfamiliar room.

I screamed and screamed. And then I realized that no one could hear me.

CHAPTER

~29~

WHEN I WOKE, my eyes fixed on the window, where I could see the rolling green hills through the metal bars, and for a moment I thought, *What a pretty view*.

Then I stumbled into the awareness of what was actually happening, and I jumped off the bed as if someone else was in the room with me.

It was real. I was locked in—and that realization brought the sinking despair of powerlessness and hopelessness. Say Laura wanted me dead—all she really had to do was just not come back, right? Sure, I had a little bit of water. But eventually you die, even with water.

I paced around in circles for a while before deciding to try to preserve my energy, in case I got the chance to fight back.

The one bright spot was that, while I was completely tired and my throat was desperately sore, the rest of my body felt almost normal. I was hungry and thirsty, but I didn't feel the nausea or dizziness that had been hanging over me for four days.

This seemed to indicate, obviously, that Laura had drugged me. And with the recurrence of my nightmares came the realization that she had been drugging my nighttime tea all along. Now that I knew for sure what it felt like to wake up with chemicals pulsing through your body, I recognized it—that sleepy-strange dizziness, the unfocused confusion.

Her system was bound to fail sometime. All she'd been trying to do was get me to behave, and look where that had gotten us. I'd been miserably pondering the idea that I might have been okay at Copeland Hall if I had just minded my own business and been a better orphan. But there was no such thing as being a good-enough orphan for Laura. Not even her own daughter could meet her impossible standards. Not even her own sister.

The day wore on, and I did what I could to fight off the hunger and a bleached kind of boredom that left the stage wide open for every worst-case scenario to run on infinite repeat in my head. I was coping all right, I told myself. Could be worse. Could be worse.

At one point, I found Kiley's phone unexpectedly tucked into my pocket, and while there was no signal,

I had to maintain hope that I might eventually get to one. But when I switched it on, I found it only half charged, so I quickly shut it off again and hid it in the desk drawer.

Laura left me alone until the sun began to slide down toward the hills, at which point she knocked lightly and came in, pausing by the door. "Just so you know," she said, "every entrance and exit in the house is locked. You might find a way out . . . but you might not. So if you hurt me in any way, you're endangering Agatha, who's currently very well secured behind a door only I can open. Understood?"

I nodded.

She sighed. "I am so hurt and offended, Margot, that I didn't sleep well last night, and it's your fault. It's hard to believe that while I was making plans for our family that included you in a position of honor, you were undermining us."

I opened my mouth to speak, but she held up her hand. "I think it's time that you worked on your manners. I've brought a book with me—a very significant book to my family. And one of the first lessons is that children should be *seen* and not *heard*."

She handed me a small blue book with a fabric cover. The author was Loretta Seaver Copeland, and the book's title was:

Philosophical Foundations for Personal Morality:

The Rights and Responsibilities of the Privileged Class

"You should read it," she said. "Or perhaps you have already, as I found it hidden in your bedroom drawer. I think you'll learn quite a bit from it. It will probably do you good."

Oh, perfect. The book about how all teenage girls were basically evil. Of course Laura would see this as required reading. I set the book down next to me on the bed and suddenly realized that if she had searched my room, she would have found my other secrets: the key, the origami money, Lily's journal.

This was bad. So bad.

She turned to leave.

"Laura—"

"I think you'd better go back to calling me Mrs. Sutton," she said. "That type of familiarity doesn't suit me when it comes from someone *outside* my family circle."

She turned to leave again.

"*Mrs. Sutton,*" I said. The words were like shards of glass on my tongue. "Would it be possible to get some food, please?"

She looked at me appraisingly, but there was a hint of approval that I assumed was directed at my manners. "Page two hundred and fourteen," she said.

"Second paragraph. Copy it twelve times. I'll be back shortly, and if you're finished, I'll leave you something to eat. If not, you can try again tomorrow."

Tomorrow?

She handed me a small notebook and a child's pen. It was fat, round, plastic.

Before I even flipped to the page, I knew what the text would be:

The proof of virtue is the ability to obey in the face of inner resistance. A demand for obedience performed against the will is the ultimate test of rectitude. A child is led to righteousness by the lantern of his parents' steadfastness and must by firm hands be molded into a creature of exemplary humility and worth. Abandoned to the darkness of parental deficiency, the child's quality of character will assuredly be as weak as a lily grown in shade.

I did my best to copy it, but I grew tired and my hand began to cramp. Still, I managed all twelve times before Laura came back. She carried a tray that held two plastic bottles of juice and a covered plate of food that smelled amazing.

She set it on the foot of the bed and held her hand out for the notebook. Then she proceeded to peruse my work.

"Your penmanship is unacceptable," she said.

Then, before I figured out what was happening, she had set the juice bottles on the bed but taken the tray of food. The door locked with a *click*.

I sat in disbelieving silence.

No food?

But how long had it been since I'd had a real meal—one I hadn't thrown up?

I grabbed the first juice bottle and chugged it, although sadly I didn't appreciate the taste because my mind was stuck worrying about food. I craved the second bottle, too, but made myself save it. I might need those calories.

I sat feeling helpless, then reached for the notebook and pen and wrote the paragraph twelve more times, forming the letters as slowly and neatly as I could.

Sometime later—it was dark outside—she came back.

"I fixed my work."

I was so hungry that my stomach had begun to growl every minute or so, with a sound like a lion yawning.

She looked it over and held out a granola bar.

"Thank you," I said, tucking it into the waistband of my pants. "Thank you. I'm very hungry."

She smiled. "Well, I can help you with that. I've brought your medicine."

"What does it do?" I asked.

"It's *medicine*," she said, like I was an idiot. "It helps you."

"With what?" I asked.

"Various things," she said. "I pride myself on seeing very clearly in what ways I can personally help a person—a child, I should say—advance in his or her moral journey. Look at what I've done for Agatha. I've saved her from her own destructive instincts. I've made her safe. And I can do the same for you."

She said all this in a reverent, almost prayerful voice.

"Please," I said. "I just want to go. If you let me go, I won't say anything."

She looked me up and down. "No medicine tonight, then?" she said, and swooped out of the room.

The door had locked before I realized that she had taken my other juice bottle. The one I had saved so carefully.

Out of everything that had gone wrong, that was the thing that broke me. I collapsed to the floor, sobbing.

That night, the nightmares were the worst I'd ever had. I was chased down by horrific, distorted versions of my family. I awoke throwing up every last crumb of the granola bar.

I HAD NO energy to do anything but lie on the bed. My lips were cracked and bleeding. My legs and arms buzzed but felt weak—too weak to help me escape. So this was what she was going to do? Starve me to death?

She came in the door, and I didn't even turn my head to look at her.

"Margot," she said. "I've brought you something."

Food? Maybe it was food. I tracked her movements with my eyes. She came closer and set down a covered plate. Next to the plate was a bottle of water.

"I want you to take this," she said. "It will help you feel better."

Maybe if I behaved, she would bring me food. When she held a pill out to me, I took it and put it in my mouth while she uncapped the water. I took a swig and swallowed.

Laura looked on with an expression of joyless gratification. There was no real emotion inside her, I realized. Just performing motherhood, performing happiness, performing sadness. Maybe the anger was real, but maybe it wasn't. Maybe she was the kind of evil that feels nothing, not even the pleasure of tormenting.

"Do you see?" she asked. "I'm a good mother. A good mother."

I couldn't have begun to comment.

"Page ninety-six," she said, handing over the blue book. "Third sentence. Fifty copies, please."

Then she left.

I looked at the plate and died a little bit inside.

On it sat a single dry slice of toast.

Still, I tore it to pieces and shoved it in my mouth.

Then I flipped the book open and grabbed my pen.

Page 96, third sentence:

There is no luckier fate for a child than to be trained up by parents who have the strength of will to remain firm in the face of childish weakness.

Lucky, I thought. *Yeah, okay.*

I was asleep by the seventh repetition of the sentence.

Instead of a simple bad dream, I woke up to see a tall, thin demon staring down at me. She had long fingers with pointed talons, and her skin was blue-gray and covered in scars—jagged hash marks. Remembrances of the lives she'd taken.

She was Death. And she was here for me. I wanted to move, but I couldn't force a single muscle to obey me. So I lay in stark terror, unable even to scream, while she dug her talons into my back and neck and limbs.

Finally, I woke up. On the bed next to me was another pill—this one yellow, round, medium-sized; and half a bottle of water.

Laura had been in here while I was asleep.

Shaking with hunger, I took the pill and drank the water.

Before long, the shaking had been replaced by a feeling of being utterly warm and secure. I was so relaxed that when Mrs. Sutton came in, I smiled at her. She smiled back at me and forced another pill down my throat.

"Good girl," she said indulgently, ruffling my hair like I was a dog.

I WAS AWAKE . . . I guess.

I tried to close my eyes, but doing that actually took more effort than looking. I didn't look at any-thing—well, nothing that would have appealed to the old me. But the new me was calmer, easier to please. New me found a small dark spot on a ceiling tile and kept a very close eye on it.

Laura came in. She shone a light into my eyes and spoke to me, but her words were muffled, like my ears were full of cotton.

She helped me sit up in the bed, and sitting was easy. Anything was easy when you were just doing that one thing. It was when you tried to change what you were doing, or combine it with something else—thinking, for instance—that it got hard.

"I think we have the dosage just right," she said. Then she began to feed me tiny bites of food. Which was fine. I may have been hungry at some point, but now I didn't care. I drank some water. At her urging, I got up and used the toilet. Then I got back into bed. "This is lovely, Margot. Don't you feel peaceful? It's going to be so easy for you to be a good girl now. You'll see."

Yes, easy. It was so easy.

"Here you go," she said, sliding a pill onto my tongue and chasing it with some water. "Sleep well."

No dreams that night. Only darkness.

CHAPTER
～30～

SHE CAME BACK later, humming cheerfully, and slipped another pill into my mouth. Then she fed me small bites of plain chicken and helped me use the toilet.

"Oof." She stood back and sighed. "*You* need a shower. Can't you smell yourself?"

A short time later, she told me to get up off the bed. The lack of politeness didn't bother me—it was much easier to understand direct orders. With her hand on my arm, we shuffled down the hall to the main upstairs hallway. We went into the larger bathroom, and I sat down on the chair in the shower while she washed my hair and sprayed my body down.

Just like she did with Agatha. I was just like Agatha now.

It wasn't that I didn't know what was happening . . .

It was that I didn't care.

Afterward, she took me back to the sickroom and put a pair of pajamas on me.

"Tomorrow," she said, "we'll get you dressed in the morning—the way I do with Agatha."

Okay, I tried to say, but my mouth wouldn't cooperate.

"It will be a lot of work, caring for both of you at once," she said. "But you know me, I like to stay busy."

All I could do was stare, and that fact seemed to please her.

"Hang on," she said. "Wait right here. I'll be back with a pair of socks."

I was alone. The door was open. Could I run? Yes. But where would I go?

Somewhere else. Anywhere else, obviously. But . . . nah.

I SAW MOTION out of the corner of my eye. But it wasn't enough to make me turn my head and look.

Then a new face appeared in front of me.

A new-old face, that is.

Agatha? Yes. Agatha.

Her hands touched my cheeks, my hair, as her eyes searched my expression.

It's okay, I wanted to tell her. *It's okay.*

I wondered what she had wanted to tell me all those times. Now I knew what it was like to be her.

If you wanted something badly enough, you could push through this fog. But it was the wanting I just couldn't wrap my head around.

Her hands gripped mine, and I felt her slip something smooth and cool into my palm.

Suddenly, there was a commotion at the door.

"What are you doing in here? Bad girl!" Laura yanked Agatha out by the arm. "Bad, bad."

I saw Agatha wince under her mother's severe touch, and something inside me stirred.

"Back to your room," Laura was saying, and she dragged her roughly away.

When Laura returned, she was carrying a short stack of clothes for me to put on. After that, she seemed distracted. She ordered me to lie down and then closed the door to the room.

I closed my eyes and tightened my fist around the object Agatha had given me. This would be a good time to rest.

Except there was an image I couldn't get out of my head. It was Laura grabbing Agatha, shaking her.

Agatha closing her eyes and pulling back slightly, like a young child afraid of being hit.

I cared a little about that. Just a little. But enough, it turned out, for me to make the halting walk over to the desk and put Kiley's phone in my pocket.

Then I lay down and fell asleep.

Caring was so exhausting.

A LITTLE WHILE later, Laura came in with another pill. She watched me swallow it, then patted my pillow and told me to lie down, that she'd be back in a while.

I lay back obediently. But then I felt something in my hand. Something small and smooth. I'd been holding it the whole time, and Laura hadn't noticed.

It was a tiny container of colorless liquid, and the scent was lemony, but less "mmm, lemons in bloom" and more "lemon-fresh bathroom scent."

I stared at it.

Agatha had risked getting herself in trouble to give it to me.

I uncapped it and drank the contents.

You only live once.

A FEW MINUTES later, I felt a spasm in my stomach. I'd been lying still, staring at the ceiling, drifting in and out of consciousness. Then all of a sudden my throat convulsed, and I was choking—gasping for air. I flipped onto my side, lifted the pillow, and vomited on the bed. Then I put the pillow back and lay down again, dizzy and confused.

My head wasn't clear by any means, but there was an awareness there that hadn't been present before.

I could land on a thought and follow it to its logical conclusion: Agatha had wanted me to throw up. And now I felt better. Agatha was helping me. She wanted to save me from her mother.

How nice, I thought. *How lovely.*

And then I fell asleep.

I woke when the sky was pink and raw—though I had no idea if it was dawn or dusk, and I could feel a difference in my body. Now with the most recent dose of tranquilizers purged from my system, the desire for survival was creeping back in. I really did kind of want to save myself . . . if it wasn't too much trouble.

I mean, maybe it wouldn't work. But it was worth trying.

I climbed out of bed. My muscles were tight and sore, my head thick and aching.

I could move, though. And that was something.

I checked to make sure my phone was in my back pocket. Then I walked to the door. It was locked, but when I hip-checked it, it popped open. So Laura had only locked the bottom knob, which meant she didn't consider me a flight risk anymore.

The hall was quiet, but I didn't dare go down through the foyer.

I'll be back for you, Ags, I thought. *I won't leave you here.*

The back stairs were locked now.

But just outside those doors was a rusted metal hatch, built into the wall.

I remembered Barrett saying that there were little elevators for the servants to use for trays and luggage.

I pried open the hatch. It was a small box, and once I climbed inside, I would be in complete darkness. There were also a couple of very ominous-looking signs warning against putting any body parts inside of it.

But it was my only option.

Trying not to think about the story Barrett had told me—was it some poor housemaid losing a hand?—I crammed myself inside. It was open on one side, and there were metal cables—presumably attached to pullies. I grabbed one and pulled, and with a collection of squeaks and squawks, the box began to move. I lowered myself slowly and stopped when I heard the shelf beneath me hit something with a *clunk*.

There was another hatch here—I pushed it open and looked out.

I was in a small vestibule, one I'd seen a few times before. It was located directly next to the back service door.

The heavy hatch door closed with a resounding *clang*.

As the sound echoed through the house, I knew the time for slow, silent movements was over.

I hurried for the kitchen door but lost my balance and fell, then struggled back to my feet. It was like trying to run through water—the willingness was there, the movements seemed like they should be so easy—but my legs couldn't obey.

At this rate Laura would catch me without even trying.

But I still went. I moved as fast as I could toward the garden. The sky was growing brighter as the sun began to rise. When I threw a searching glance up over my shoulder, I happened to catch Laura's shocked face at the upstairs window. Then she disappeared.

I felt as hopeless as a snail running from a hawk . . . but I kept going.

I turned into the garden.

What I saw stunned me—

In every planter bed, like splashes of blood on the other plants, were red lilies. Everywhere.

I headed for the graveyard.

As I ran, I pulled Kiley's phone out of my pocket and held it up. No bars. No bars. No bars.

I came to the Adam and Eve gate and realized suddenly that I had left my key behind. I was filled with despair—to make it this far and then fail?

But the door swung open in front of me.

I rushed through. My ankle tweaked and I had to limp along the path, holding the phone up to keep an eye on the screen.

Finally, fifty feet in, a single bar appeared in the upper corner of the screen. It wavered, went away, and then came back when I kept going. Another fifty feet, and a second bar appeared.

Holding my breath, I pressed the phone icon and dialed 9-1-1.

It was ringing. Then, suddenly, the service dropped out, and the call was lost.

I dialed again, moving farther back. There was motion through the trees, and I saw Laura rushing along the narrow walk. She scanned the area, saw me, and began to run straight toward me.

As she approached, I slipped the phone into my pocket. Without looking, I reached down and tapped the screen. I'd been on the contacts page. Maybe I'd managed to call an actual person.

It was my only hope.

Then I ran until I was backed into a corner, with no way out, and she came loping out of the thick tree cover. She stood like a hound treeing a raccoon. Behind me and to the right was a wall. And to my left was the dark, lazy pond, its surface broken by groupings of lily pads.

"Come on, Margot," she said. "Be reasonable. Come back inside."

"No!" I said. "If I come back, you're going to keep me drugged twenty-four hours a day."

"That's ridiculous," she said. "What on earth would make you think that? The pills I give you are medicinal. They're to treat your illness, Margot. Your brain problems."

"I don't have brain problems. You poisoned me," I said. "You're poisoning Agatha. And you killed your own sister—"

I was saying these things as loudly and clearly as I could, hoping that if some random person was listening, they would be alarmed enough to send the police.

Of course, they'd also have to know who and where I was.

Oh, great. I'm going to die.

"Stay back," I called. "Stay back or I'll scream."

She shrugged. "No one can hear you scream out here. But you're being silly. No one is trying to hurt you. You know, I've always thought that you were such a nice girl. Cooperative. Thoughtful. Why would you start behaving this way after everything our family has done for you?"

"Because you're sick," I said.

Her face darkened. "That's uncalled-for."

I had no chances left. And my hope was flagging.

As Laura approached, cutting through the flowers like an ice-breaking ship crushing everything in its path, I felt my courage begin to drain away.

"We can do this the easy way," she said, "or the hard way."

I stared at her. I was still so tired. Still felt so fuzzy.

"Be a good girl. Come back inside, and we'll start over. No hard feelings. Now that I know you have a rebellious streak, I can help you with that." She stared at me. "I can help you be a better person. Raise you properly."

There was no hope left.

"I've told you before, Margot," she said. "I'm really quite fond of you. So come back. Don't fight. If you try to fight, I'm going to have to come to the conclusion that you might be more trouble than you're worth."

I shook my head.

"Your parents did a terrible job," she said. "Teaching you how to be a respectful child."

That ignited a little flame of anger in me. The will to fight, which had been gone, flared back.

But I still wasn't strong enough. Laura came over and pushed me back against the wall. I cast a desperate glance down toward the phone, and she noticed.

She reached into my pocket, pulled out the phone, said into the mouthpiece, "I'm sorry, this was a prank call," and then tossed it into the pond.

I could feel my strength flagging. My legs were on the verge of collapsing out from under me.

Her expression had changed. Until now, I'd actually believed that she wanted, in some twisted way, to "help" me.

"I'm *terribly* disappointed." She stepped closer. "We have one rule, Margot—what is it?"

My voice shook. "Be respectful."

"Yes. And as it turns out, you can't even follow one simple rule. You had your chance to be good, but you chose degeneracy instead. I'm terribly sorry. I don't think I can help you. You're too far gone." Then, to my horror, she raised a small syringe and plunged it into my upper arm.

All of my sharpness, my bravery, my plans . . . they

began to melt away as I felt the medication spread through my body like tingling heat.

My legs went numb, my arms weak.

She leaned closer. "I want you to know that Agatha's going to pay for helping you. She's going to be punished. Now you have to die with that on your conscience. You've caused a lot of suffering that could have been avoided."

"Leave her alone," I whispered.

She stared me down, her eyes as sharp as jagged steel. *"A child is led to righteousness by the lantern of his parents' steadfastness and must* by firm hands *be molded.* Firm hands. When Agatha is capable of behaving herself in a way that befits her birthright, then she can be 'left alone.' Until then, I will personally direct her behavior in order to minimize the damage to herself and to our family."

"You're going to kill her," I said. "She almost choked the other night."

"If she has the will to live," Laura said icily, "she'll live."

I stared at her in horror. What kind of mother was this? Whatever kindness or gentleness may have existed in Laura had been hardened by time into the beastly woman she was now. More worried about her family's past and reputation than their well-being.

I stared into her eyes and imagined that I could see

her soul, a putrid, rotting swamp of anger and pride. But everything was starting to get glowy and soft.

"Come, Margot," she said sweetly. "Let's take a walk."

I hesitated too long, and she gave me a push that made me stumble on the uneven ground. We walked along the thin strip of wet dirt bordering the pond. If I slowed, she pulled my arm, and my body moved again as if I was remote-controlled.

The sun wasn't quite up yet. The early-morning air was soft and dim. Laura had taken the time to put on a preppy rust-colored jacket, but I had nothing on over my pajama top, and I began to shiver. The shivering grew stronger and stronger, until my teeth chattered.

"Common side effect," Laura said. "You're going to get pretty itchy, too. I don't use it for Agatha—can't have her scratching her skin to bits. But you can go ahead and scratch. It doesn't matter now."

Soon my arms and legs and the sides of my ribs felt like they were on fire, and I tried to scratch them but found that my fingers were getting clumsy and my head was starting to swim.

"Here's the part you probably can't understand," she said. "I don't blame *you*, Margot. I blame the world. We live in a world where nothing is sacred. Children don't honor their elders. Families don't honor their ancestors, their traditions. Everything is cheap now. Everything is worthless."

I swayed, and she put an arm around my waist and began to walk, leading me farther along the edge of the water.

"Agatha is a lot like you, actually. I think she's had quite a setback, influenced by you and your poor behavior. I'd hoped I could begin her recovery by Christmas, but now it seems like it'll have to be next summer. Or longer. So you see what you've done to her—after claiming to be her friend."

The inky blackness of the pond water seemed to be listening . . . waiting.

"Agatha has been a worry to me since she was seven," she said. "But girls always are, I suppose. *I* should have been a boy. When I was born, my father wouldn't speak to my mother for a month. I don't blame him. This isn't the natural role for a woman. We're too soft, too tenderhearted."

I made a sound.

"That's impolite," she snapped. "If I'm *not* those things, it's because I never had the luxury to be. It's because everything always rested on me. And no matter what I did, it was never good enough. My father was hard on me—he was never hard on Lily; he loved her. She had an independent spirit, he said. She never cared about saying the right thing or believing the right thing—she insisted on having her own way. I wasn't like her. I cared too much about things he didn't value. But he should have. Behavior, history, dignity. That is the framework on which everything else is built."

Even in my state of confusion, I thought: She's wrong. Those things aren't any kind of framework. They're window dressing, at best. My mother never cared about that kind of thing, and she was twenty times the mother (and human) that Laura could have ever hoped to be.

We came to a small footbridge that passed over a place where the pond narrowed slightly. Laura braced me more carefully there, watching out for my footing on the rough boards.

"I tried to give you a chance. You could have had a place here, if you had behaved. If you had known your place." She looked right into my eyes. "Goodbye."

And then she shoved me backward off the bridge.

I plunged into the cold, dark water, and I'm not going to lie—

Some part of me thought . . .

Ahh, at last.

CHAPTER
~31~

I DIDN'T SINK right away, but I was too weak and dizzy to swim, so I started to slip under the surface of the water. My legs kicked for the bottom, but it was nowhere to be found. They kept kicking and kicking uselessly as I slid down into the darkness.

The impact of hitting the water had shocked my mind out of its fog.

There is, of course, an instinct that takes over when you're fighting for survival. But what people who haven't been through it don't realize is that sometimes there's also the opposite instinct—the instinct to let go. To accept the fate dealt to you.

I'd messed it up before, but here was my second chance. I could get it right this time.

With the water pressing cold against my skin, there was clarity. I saw flashes and visions of the accident in my brain. Things I'd never remembered before. I saw

Siena's head slam against the window and come away bleeding. I saw the airbag trap Dad against his seat, misshapen by the water into a mask that stuck to his face. Dina was to my left—I felt her hand grasp for me and then fall away, and I knew without looking that something was terribly wrong.

And then it was just me and Mom.

She had somehow managed to turn on the light inside the car. I could see her fighting with her seat belt, which reminded me to unclasp mine. She'd also triggered the sunroof, which was now half-open, giving us our only chance of escape but also allowing water to rush into the car. My seat belt was undone. Easy peasy.

I waited for her, expecting her to float free and come with me to the surface.

But she didn't. She couldn't. Her belt was stuck; the latch was damaged.

She looked at me and pointed up, out the sunroof.

I was stunned, paralyzed.

"*Go*," she said, in the half moment before the water flooded us.

I shook my head.

She reached up and grabbed my wrist.

GO, she mouthed. *GO!*

She shoved me toward the sunroof, and at the last second, she pulled my face down to hers and kissed my forehead. Then she held me up and I saw her mouth move in the shape of the word:

GO.

So I did. I went. I lived. Because it was what my mom wanted.

And maybe because it was what some impossibly small part of me wanted, too. I mean, sure, it wasn't the obvious choice. A clueless decision, in fact, made without any thought of the aftermath. Not a thought about how much surviving would suck, how much misery and complication waited for me once I broke through the surface of the water.

When it counted, I made a split-second deal with whatever force propels us all into and out of existence, and that deal was: *Let me live.*

But why?

I don't know.

I'll figure it out later.

But let me live, and I promise I won't stop looking until I find something to live for.

CHAPTER
~32~

NOW I FELT it again, like a warm glimmer of flame inside my cold, numb, painful body.

Let me live.

But why?

Because.

Why, Margot, why? There must be a reason. You've had time. If you haven't found something by now, why bother fighting? Why bother with the pain and loneliness? Why not just give up?

Because . . .

Because I have a friend who needs my help.

And the forces of the universe shrugged their shoulders and said, *Hey, why not?*

The smallest bit of strength came back to my legs, and I kicked and kicked until I reached the surface and took a breath.

That bought me enough time to reorient myself, to

start half swimming, half flailing toward the edge of the pond. I knew Laura was out there, but I didn't worry about it. Worrying about Laura wasn't part of the deal.

Just stay alive.

Agatha needs my help.

My lungs were on fire. I felt as if I were carrying a hundred-pound weight. But I fought and fought and didn't stop. Ten feet out, I began to slide back out of consciousness, but I felt something—as plain as day, I felt something shove me toward the surface.

I was so shocked that I woke up, and then seconds later, I felt something I'd felt before—a loose layer of mud under my hand. Mud under the toe of my bare foot, squelchy and horrible but also wonderful, because it meant I was alive to feel it.

I did it. I lived again.

Then a pair of mushroom-brown slacks and feet in preppy rain boots were in front of me.

One of the boots stepped down on the fingers of my left hand.

"You've got grit, I'll give you that," Laura said grudgingly. "But it's not enough. I want you to close your eyes and sleep, Margot. Just let go. You've worked so hard."

And then I felt a hand on the back of my head, pressing my face into the mud, where the water was about two inches deep.

I tried to struggle, tried to turn my head, but it was as if none of my muscles were hooked up to my brain.

Cold, dirty water seeped into my nose, filled my mouth. My ears were still above the water, so I could hear Laura's breath, fast and heavy. And her voice, smug. Assured of victory.

"You're no stronger than the cat was," Laura said lightly.

Ah, but this wasn't fair.

Mom, I can't breathe.

Margot, someone whispered.

So close. Closer than Laura.

I knew that voice.

Margot, fight.

What a ridiculous suggestion. I couldn't possibly. There were enough drugs coursing through my body to take down a full-grown giraffe.

Fight, the voice said.

Mom?

I surged up out of the mud, knocking Laura off balance, and came out of the water coughing and choking, spitting up cold mud. There were bits of dead grass and algae between my teeth.

"Mom?" I called into the night as Laura sat up.

"Lie down," Laura said sharply.

I felt something surge through my body—adrenaline, rage, and a sense of righteousness.

"Don't touch me!" I shouted. I got to my feet, feeling like a swamp beast.

Laura was unimpressed. She came closer. She reached down to grab me by the hair—

I shoved her so hard she went flying and landed in the dark water.

I began to back away.

Laura struggled to her feet and started toward me again.

I shoved her a second time—and as I did, I noticed something. In the front pocket of her jacket was a second small syringe.

How many doses did she think it was going to take to get rid of me? I was almost flattered.

She came close enough for me to grab it, and then I pushed her away. As she flailed, I pulled the cap off the syringe, and when she came at me once more, I plunged it into the spot where her neck met her shoulders.

She gasped and grabbed for her neck as if she'd been stung.

"You've been giving me this stuff for a long time," I said. "Maybe I built up a tolerance."

I saw her eyes make a panicked sweep of our surroundings—the first sign that she was losing her balance.

"*You* probably don't have a tolerance, though," I said, stepping toward her.

"Stay away from me," she hissed.

My body might as well have been made from wood, but I kept moving. "You're a coward," I said. "You can't make people do what you want, so you just try to shut them up."

"Stop!" she said. "What are you doing?"

She seemed to think I was going to kill her—which I wasn't. In fact, if she'd fallen into the water I would have dragged her out.

But I did plan to knock her down hard enough so she wouldn't get back up.

I moved slowly, steadily, in her direction, and she continued to scrabble away from me, rendered silent by her fear and the sedative coursing through her veins.

Finally we reached the corner that held Lily's grave.

Laura knew where we were. She glanced over her shoulder and made a strangled screaming noise.

The grave was covered in a thick, lush blanket of lilies, their faces wide open.

I didn't even have to lay a finger on her. I walked close enough for her to panic and fall backward into the flowers, which seemed to part and then close around her. Her cries were awful because they were the guilty, terrified cries of a person being dragged to hell.

Like in my dream . . .

I stopped short, and suddenly I realized who the lurching figure in my dream had been—it was *me*.

Oh, that's funny, I thought. All I'd been afraid of was myself.

And then I turned and walked away, confident that Laura wouldn't be standing up anytime soon.

I made it as far as the Adam and Eve gate.

Up ahead, I saw a pair of uniformed police officers moving quickly through the garden.

I paused for a moment, then crumpled to the ground like a rag doll. I found myself staring at a flower I'd seen before—the tiny blossoms so cheerful and sweet. They seemed to be watching me like a thousand curious, tiny creatures.

I saw the officers approach and the surprise in their eyes, and then behind them I saw a weak, staggering figure, teetering in her long nightgown.

"Hey, Ags," I tried to say.

And then I passed out.

I AWOKE BRIEFLY as they were loading me into the ambulance. The paramedics said some comforting things that I couldn't remember even moments after they were spoken. Through the open doors I could see Agatha watching me, wrapped in a blanket. She seemed worried.

Beyond her were about eight police cars.

And past them, at the entrance to the garden, I could have sworn I saw my mother.

She looked at me. Her eyes were shining with love and pride and sorrow.

And then she disappeared.

EPILOGUE
~SIX MONTHS LATER~

"TONIGHT," AGATHA SAID, "you, me, Barrett, some rando Barrett knows—Pauline's Pizza?"

I looked up from my biology textbook.

"Say yes," Agatha said. "Please? Barrett misses you."

She slipped off her Camden blazer and hung it on the hook on her side of the closet door, then slid onto the bed next to me and grabbed Blue Bunny (who had magnanimously forgiven her for the earlier mistreatment). She held him in front of my book.

"Barrett keeps whining about you and it's driving Agatha craaaazy," she said, in a very poor impersonation of what Blue Bunny's actual voice would sound like. "You should just do her a favor and go."

I shut the book and flipped onto my back. "I have a bio test to study for."

"That's in three days."

"I'm too tired to go out."

"No, you're not. I'll buy you a coffee."

I tried again. "It's freezing and I'm tired of Pauline's. We just went there last week."

"I have nineteen coats, and no one is ever *tired* of pizza. Stop making excuses."

There was a knock at the door, and Kiley Chambers popped her head in. "Helloooo, cupcakes," she said. "Margot, can I borrow your Spanish notes? I was at a yearbook meeting, so I missed class."

"Sure," I said. "Hand me my backpack."

Kiley shouldered Agatha off the bed and sat down next to me. She set a magazine on the pillow and picked my backpack up, handing it to me. While I dug through it for my Spanish binder, Agatha continued to wheedle.

"Just not today, all right?" I said.

"Then when?"

"When she's ready," Kiley said. "God, leave her alone."

Kiley had become extra-protective of me. I've heard of some cultures where, if someone saves your life, you're their servant. Kiley had inverted that. I think she took seriously the idea that it had been *her* number I called that night, *her* quick thinking and calling the police that had saved my life (and probably Agatha's, too), and that made her feel like she was my bodyguard.

Agatha sat on the edge of the bed and picked up the magazine. "He's just in such a weird mood since we saw Mom last week. It's making me sad."

"Even if he's sad, it's not Margot's job to make him feel better." Kiley made a face. "How's your mom?"

"Same." Agatha shrugged and her voice became clipped, as it always did when Laura came up. "Won't talk. Just sits there. Mad at us for selling the house, I guess."

In her ranting when the police found her, Laura had inadvertently confessed to murdering Lily. Whoops. Now she was locked away, pretty much for life.

At the state institution, of all places.

We could have been roommates, I thought, when the court's decision came through.

"Well, *sorry,*" Kiley said, "but that's what you get when you try to murder children. You get your fancy old house sold."

"Stop, Ky," Agatha said quietly. And Kiley, who was actually an excellent friend, stopped. She picked up her magazine, and I glanced at it.

"Hey, can I see that?" I pulled it out of her hands and turned it over. The ad on the back cover was a picture of a model holding up a new phone to take a selfie.

It was Tam.

"I know this girl," I said. "I met her at the group home."

"She *loves* that phone," Kiley said.

"She's pretty," Agatha said.

Yeah, she was. I stared at it for a few more seconds.

"Keep it, if you want," Kiley said with a shrug. "I don't care."

"Thanks," I said, tucking it onto my shelf.

After Kiley left, I turned to Agatha. "I'll see him," I said. "Soon. But not yet, okay?"

Agatha frowned. "Okay."

"Soon," I said.

She sat down next to me and sighed. "No, no, take your time. He can wait."

"But will he?" It was a little troubling. Because the fact was, I did like Barrett. Very much. And I missed him a lot. Sometimes all I wanted in the world was to sit and talk and . . . I don't know, kiss a little (okay, a lot).

But I couldn't stop myself from thinking that the time wasn't right yet. There were still too many things I had to figure out.

It was one thing to be best friends with Agatha— that had fallen into place as if we'd been made for each other. But taking things to the next level with Barrett? No matter how much I wanted to spend time with him, it was . . . complicated.

"He *will* wait," she said firmly. "He told me *specifically* to tell you to take your time."

I flopped back on my pillow and hugged Blue

Bunny. How much time would it take? How long until I walked through the day feeling like a halfway normal person again, and not That Orphan Who Almost Got Murdered by That Homicidal Rich Lady?

"I don't know," I said to the ceiling. "There's a lot to figure out. And it's so hard."

"You don't have to figure it out right now," she said, lying next to me so that our shoulders touched. Her voice was wistful, sad. "We don't have to figure anything out."

She intertwined our fingers so we were holding hands. We did this a lot. Sometimes I felt more like we were sisters than just friends. I felt like something connected us under our skin, inside our brains.

Like maybe Laura's cruelty had taught us how to see the parts of ourselves—and of each other—that no one else could see. And we might always be hurting, we might always be damaged, but we were more than that, too. We were the parts of us who had saved ourselves. Who'd had enough. Who'd chosen to live.

I knew it was as hard for Agatha as it was for me. I knew she had nightmares, too.

But when I woke up in a panic, she was there to remind me I was safe. And I did the same for her.

Agatha took a deep, searching breath. Her hand squeezed mine, and I could tell we had come to that quiet part of the day when the hurt was closest to the surface. But we had each other. We weren't alone.

And that made all the difference.

"Aren't we lucky, Margot?" she asked quietly. "Do you ever think about it—how lucky we are?"